Broken Alpha

Everleigh Fox

Copyright ©2025 by Everleigh Fox

Broken Alpha

All rights reserved.

No part of this book may be reproduced in any form or by any electronic or mechanical means, including information storage and retrieval systems, without written permission from the author, except for the use of brief quotations in a book review.

Without limiting the author's and publisher's exclusive rights, any unauthorized use of this publication to train generative artificial intelligence (AI) technologies is expressly prohibited. No generative artificial intelligence (AI) was used in writing this book. This book was professionally edited by Danielle Polisseni of D.P. Editing, a live editor. The otter image was created by David Guynn.

This book has only been authorized to be published in full on Amazon in paperback and Kindle by Everleigh Fox. Should this be found in its entirety on any other site in any other form, it is a pirated copy and against the author's wishes.

This is a work of fiction. Names, characters, places, and incidents either are the product of the author's imagination or are used fictitiously. Any resemblances to actual events, locales, events, businesses, or person, living or dead, is entirely coincidental.

To my friend, *H*, who inspired this story.
Sorry I said you looked like an Omega.

TRIGGER WARNINGS

- Family Manipulation
- Feelings of Inadequacy
- Panic Attacks
- Somnophilia
- Derogatory Comments *
- Miscommunication
- 3rd Act Relationship Strain

TRIGGER WARNINGS

- Nonconsensual Marking

- Talks of Abortion

- Unwanted Pregnancy

- Assault Toward A Pregnant Person *

- Talks of Miscarriage

- Blood

- Near Loss of Partner and Child

- The Word 'Cock' is mentioned 127 times ;)

* Not Between MCs

Contents

1. Luke — 1
2. Aidyn — 8
3. Luke — 15
4. Aidyn — 23
5. Luke — 32
6. Luke — 45
7. Aidyn — 49
8. Aidyn — 57
9. Luke — 64
10. Aidyn — 65
11. Luke — 77
12. Luke — 86
13. Luke — 97
14. Aidyn — 107
15. Luke — 123

16. Aidyn	132
17. Aidyn	139
18. Aidyn	145
19. Aidyn	152
20. Luke	160
21. Luke	168
22. Aidyn	173
23. Aidyn	180
24. Aidyn	188
25. Luke	192
26. Luke	200
27. Luke	209
28. Aidyn	212
29. Aidyn	222
30. Aidyn	230
31. Luke	248
Acknowledgements	254

Luke

A ccording to society's standards, I'm broken.

The lineage of my family has been drilled into my head since I was four, with strong emphasis on the fact that we were Alphas of title and legacy. We could trace our line to the first colonists who landed in Plymouth, breeding little Alphas into the New World to fight for American independence and participate in every war since. From the age of nine, my future had been planned for me as a member of 'The Great Ellis Family'.

However, what is expected of me and my reality are two separate things. Every child takes a designation test once they enter puberty. With my classmates, I took the same blood test as everyone else, and, as expected, an Alpha symbol was handed to me on a piece of paper with my results. The first case of the 'unexpected' came with the dominant symbol beside my designation. Dominant Alphas are rare worldwide, with only about one in fifteen thousand of the Alpha population being dominant.

What makes dominants so different from their normal counterparts is that our pheromones are more potent and our knots are slightly more prominent. We can be a tad bit more aggressive and assertive. We also have better control over our pheromone levels and how much we expose ourselves to others, and we're less likely to become more animalistic during a rut, keeping a clear head as if we were the leader of the pack. However, our sense of smell is more substantial as well, and therefore we're more susceptible to the scent of an Omega. Technically, a dominant outranks the others, but that mentality slowly dies with each new generation of pups, regardless of designation.

Being a dominant was something that my parents could brag about, something that raised our social status among their elite circle of friends. So, if I'm so 'unique,' how am I broken?

Two reasons. The first is that I have never scented an Omega. Pheromones are how we recognize each other and help us find mates. Betas don't have a natural scent, often using an artificial blend because they want to fit in. They don't like that they're 'normal' in a unique world. I had thought my first partner was a Beta until he went into heat three years into our relationship. That's also when I learned about my second issue.

In order for a male Alpha to produce offspring, they develop a knot at the base of their cocks, ready to lock themselves to their Omega and breed the newest family line. Knots rarely reveal themselves during masturbation, so I never suspected I couldn't produce one until my partner. As teens, we learn through sex education that knots are just a normal response to sex, a much needed element in reproduction, and to take care of our distressed Omegas. I had a boyfriend in college, Anthony, but I wasn't interested in pups at that stage in our relationship. After his suppressant failed, he went into heat and needed a knot to soothe the ache inside him. But a knot never formed, and we broke up after his difficult heat, with him stating that he couldn't trust me to provide for his needs.

I should've been devastated; I loved him, but at the same time, I didn't feel anything about our breakup. Regardless, I became desperate to know if the issue was as simple as we weren't well matched or if the problem was me. I began sleeping around, partnering with Omegas, even Betas, and a random Alpha—all in the hope that something within me would correct itself. Naturally, the issue was me.

Despite excessive tests, the final outcome was that I was not a properly functioning Alpha. In the social circles established by my family, Omegas they deemed worthy of carrying on the Ellis line were practically thrown at me in hopes that I would bond with them and produce more little Alphas. Every single one of them were lovely people, but I could not scent them. My college buddies would talk endlessly about how their mates smelled. Gardens in full bloom, a coffee shop, spiced apples, frosted vanilla. I was making myself sick, straining to catch even the smallest whiff of an Omega scent. And nothing.

I used to dream of holding my Omega close, nose buried in their hair or neck as we snuggled close in the early hours of a Sunday morning, trapped in blankets, our legs tangled together. We'd enjoy each other's company, our pheromones mingling in the room, refusing to get up and greet the day. Refusing to let the real world into our bubble. But it was clear this was only a dream and would never be a reality for me. I'm broken and therefore not worthy of any Omega, regardless of their status.

I have kept this secret from my family so they only view my refusal to find an Omega as nothing more than rebellion and plain stubbornness. In college, I changed my major, wanting to pursue a degree in Designation Science, and my family told me that was not an acceptable field for someone of our status. I was throwing my life away; no worthy Omega would lower themselves to marry a dominant with such a commoner profession. They refused to cover the rest of my schooling, but luckily I had seen this coming and had already invested in small properties at the advice of a financial planner who got me into contact with a real estate agent who happened to be his Omega. Through them, the properties were a huge success and allowed me to live comfortably now.

Sighing, I put my phone in my pocket, ignoring the text from my mother asking if I was bringing anyone to my father's birthday celebration at the end of the month—even though she knew very well I wasn't seeing anyone per our last conversation a month ago. Standing up, I stretched before grabbing the filing box by my office door and exiting the room, heading for my classroom on the upper floor. A couple of students had arrived early, glancing up from their phones and pausing their conversation as I entered. Greeting them kindly, I set my box on the small desk beside my podium before picking up the whiteboard marker from its tray and wrote my last name on the whiteboard.

My ABO Psych and Biology – ABOPB, as some of the staff and students call it – was a general stop for most students who aspire to be a therapist or a doctor, and I was rather good at figuring out which students would be which. Those studying to be doctors had an annoying habit of trying to prove they knew everything, which they normally didn't, and could be arrogant with their answers and how they addressed the class. I surmised they had a need to prove they were something—something special like the rest of us—because most of the world's doctors were Betas. Most suffered from horrible 'middle child' syndrome, complete with an entitlement complex.

The students studying to be therapists tended to be Omegas, given their nurturing nature and overwhelming need to comfort. They dominated in that field and were the students who took the most notes but didn't participate in the majority of the discussions; it was easier for them to watch it all unfold and form their own opinions before supplying their input.

There were many, mainly traditionalists, that believed that Omegas wasted their money by getting a higher education. Heats often made it difficult to hold down employment, and prolonged use of suppressants could be damaging to an Omega's health. That being said, there were several laws in the works that, if passed, would legally give Omegas 'heat time' and protect them from the unemployment line. This wasn't to say I didn't have Alphas in my class; in fact, they outnumbered the Omegas who took my course. They were loud and opinionated, children from wealthy standing and influential parentage. They were probably never told the word "no" in all their lives, and they enjoyed lording their statuses over the Betas in the class, knowing full well that it was their parents who would be employing Betas to ensure their hospitals ran smoothly.

Placing my phone on the podium and checking the time, I cleared my throat, eyeing the now mostly filled seats.

"Good afternoon, class," I began, forcing a fake smile and stepping before the podium beside my tiny desk. "Welcome to Alpha, Beta, Omega Psychology and Biology. Normally, class starts at 1 pm, but since it appears most of you are here already, I will start about ten minutes early and get you guys out of here earlier, too, since this is just introductions."

This generally earns me a few cheers of excitement, as the first day back is exhausting for most students. The fake smile remained in place while I moved toward the first person in the row of tables in front of me, holding up a piece of paper in my hand.

"Every day you come to class, you will be required to put your name on a sheet of paper at the front of the class. Attendance is 5% of your grade in this class, so make sure you sign the paper before or after class. For today, though, please pass the paper down the row, and I'll collect it after class. Purchasing the textbook is a must for my class; you can't wing it on lecture notes alone. I hear the textbook is cheaper if you buy it digitally on Amazon. I don't care which version you get as long as you get it by next week."

I moved back to the front of the class, popping off the lid of the file box and grabbing a stack of papers. Counting the number of students in each row, I handed each student a stack of paper, instructing them to pass the handouts backward.

"Quizzes are 5% of your overall score, with participation in class discussions equating to 10%. Class papers are 20%, the midterm is 25%, and the final exam is 35%. I know we have a lot of shy students, and you may not feel comfortable participating in debates and discussions; I get it. You can make up the percentage from class discussions by doing well on your homework and tests and still pass the class with an A. Since today is orientation, I know you've heard the same university policy from each of your teachers, but in case you haven't, I have to mention it as a precaution.

"This university is open to all designations. However, Omegas are required to take their suppressant every day before setting foot on campus. Much like the real world beyond these halls, we don't make allowances for bonded Omegas. If you're not on them already, talk with your Alphas and find the best method for you and your pack. This class has an online variant in spring, which may be better suited for you if that is the route you wish to take. If you're not a bonded Omega, you're required by federal law to be on them, so I guess this doesn't apply to you."

If I were honest, I hate the discussion of suppressants. They have been around for decades, effectively suppressing the heats of Omegas, acting as a form of birth control. However, they have had to constantly evolve as Omegas became more and more immune to the formulas used to craft them. I also struggled with the idea that the university and the country could dictate what an Omega put in their bodies, even if it didn't affect me as a broken.

Clapping my hands and rubbing them together, I put the false smile back on my face. However, before I could continue, the scent of a thriving forest exploded in the room, followed by a loud bang at the front of the room as a late student entered my classroom.

His cheeks flushed pink as all eyes focused on him. His blond hair stuck to his face as he panted, his round glasses sliding down his nose from sweat.

It was clear that he had run through the halls not to miss the class, his backpack slightly open in front of his body as he held it by the strap. He wore jeans and a white tee shirt beneath a plaid overshirt. The white tee shirt clung to his chest as he dipped his head in embarrassment. Muttering an apology, he walked past me to the empty seat on the right-hand side of the classroom toward the back.

Every classroom was equipped with neutralizers, but they were powerless to stop the onslaught of earth and pine. Under the enticing scent was something chemical, almost like rot. Something foreign and sour, sterile like a hospital. As the student took his seat, I couldn't stop staring, my brain finally piecing together what was happening. At thirty-one, I was smelling my first Omega, and my cock was painfully hard behind the podium.

Aidyn

"Well, your results are in the realm of what is normal for you, but you said you're getting dizzy spells?"

I looked at Doctor Easton, who sat across from me while I sat on crinkly paper on an uncomfortable blue medical exam table. I had been feeling nauseous and dizzy for about a month as I adjusted to yet another round of new suppressants. I thought I could struggle through the side effects until I passed out in the bathroom a few days ago, bruising my hip.

"Yes. And my meals threaten to come back up in the evenings," I reiterated.

"My concern is that you might have too many suppressants in your system, and they're causing a reaction. Since you started seeing me six months ago, you've been on five suppressants. One made you borderline narcoleptic, and another raised your blood pressure and made you erratic. I honestly don't really want to put you on another set without flushing the previous ones out of your system first. We could try taking you off them temporarily with a medical note and let them work their way out of your system naturally."

"No!" I almost shouted before blushing at being so loud. "I have two semesters left before my degree, and the university has a strict suppressant policy. Even with a medical note, I could not attend classes; not all of them are available online. I can't skip this semester."

Doctor Easton sighed but nodded, squinting at the computer screen before him. He silently tapped away at the keyboard while I glanced around the small office. Everything about the Omega clinic was sterile, with its white tile flooring and white walls with random paintings hung up to make the rooms look less depressing. It didn't help.

Diagrams of Omega anatomy hung on the office door. Pamphlets on suppressants, finding a pack, and how to defend yourself against an unwanted Alpha sat on the counter by the door. In a world where most gave in to their basic animalistic urges, defending oneself from a rutting Alpha was paramount. While Betas and Alphas participated in normal physical education activities in school, such as basketball and soccer, Omegas were taught proactive self-defense. We were also taught situational self-defense, such as escaping from a trapped and enclosed room, being cornered in a dark alley, and fleeing from a kidnapper. It had been drilled into our brains to look around ourselves to find the nearest exit in case we needed to escape and locate at least five things we could use as a weapon in self defence. Even at five-foot-seven and one hundred and thirty pounds, I could easily toss someone over my shoulder that was twice my size and build. I knew how to get out of handcuffs made of metal, rope, zip ties, and cable. I could even squeeze myself through the smallest gaps and outrun most Alphas like a cat.

I hated that I had to live my life like this. I hated that despite my forced training, I still let my guard down in high school, during my senior year at a graduation party. I hadn't wanted to go, but the friends I hung out with at the time forced me to attend. If I hadn't gone, however, I never would've met my best friend, Erik. I hadn't known it at the time, but the people I had called friends had set me up as bait for the head of the football team, a large Alpha twice my size, filling his head with lies that I had a crush on him, calling him my mate. The jock had zero interest in me, only seeing me as an easy target, that I would give in to whatever he wanted on account of my "crush." He hadn't anticipated me kneeing him in the balls as he cornered me leaving the bathroom, trying to drown me in his pheromones that smelled like someone had set a skunk on fire, before I ran into the living room, looking for the front door, knocking the drink out of Eric's hand. One look at my face told him all he needed to know, putting himself between me and the jock without a second thought as the Alpha came barreling into the living room, anger evident on his face. Erik later explained that he did kickboxing as a hobby and that was the only reason he had been able to knock the Alpha out so quickly, breaking his nose. After that, I didn't attend any more parties, and Erik continued to hang around me until I got used to him being there. I lived vicariously through him as he regaled me with his wild nights and crazy antics at the parties he continued to attend.

"I'm honestly at a loss here," Doctor Easton said, pulling me from my thoughts. "The best solution I can think of is we flush the current suppressants out of your system with a saline flush, and it's like starting from scratch. Suppressants are normally in your system for about thirty to sixty days, so you have too many that are counteracting against each other, and that could be why you fainted. If I give you something now, it's like slapping a Band-Aid over it without treating the cause. But we don't know what the cause is. It could be the current suppressant or the cocktail that's running through you.

"However, doing the flush would put you into a heat; the best time for that would be over a school holiday. If that is the route you want to go, we certainly can revisit that before your winter break. In the meantime, let's switch you to the injection form of your current suppressant. Hopefully injecting it directly into your system will help. I can try to give you something for the nausea. However, it hasn't worked in the past, but it might at least help you keep your meals down."

I nodded, instructing him to put in the order for the suppressant injections and hopped off the table before checking my watch. SHIT! If I didn't leave now, I would be late for the first class of the semester. As things stood now, I would still have to run. A sense of urgency consumed me as I relayed the pharmacy information to the staff for the prescription. I practically bolted out the door, tossing my backpack over my left shoulder. Luckily, the Omega Clinic was only about three blocks from the university, but I would still have to run if I wanted to make it on time. Dashing across the road to the quad, I narrowly avoided one vehicle whose driver was more focused on arguing with their passenger than the scrawny guy who dashed out in front of them. Finally reaching the classroom door, I threw it open with more force than intended and entered the room.

Instantly, hundreds of eyes were on me as I caught my breath, slipping my backpack off my shoulder. Unsure of how it came partially unzipped, I hugged it tightly to my chest and made my way to an open seat in the back, mumbling an apology to the teacher as I walked by. Taking my seat, I could still feel the eyes of my fellow students upon me. Technically, I was on time with a minute to spare, but the teacher had apparently chosen to start a little early, something I made a mental note of for the future.

Once seated, I could get a good look at the teacher, who stood at the front of the classroom behind a wooden podium. He stood at a height of above six feet, with broad shoulders and a wide, firm chest that filled out his business shirt rather well. His dark brown hair was combed back, but it looked like it was done with his fingers and not a comb. A close, tight beard decorated his lower face. He had piercing blue eyes that followed me to my seat, lingering on me before turning to the rest of the classroom, but a strange expression remained transfixed on his face, brows furrowing. With his gaze no longer on me, I lifted my head to watch him, my Omega uncharacteristically taking notice. It didn't matter that the Alpha before me was my teacher, my Omega clearly liked what he saw. I shook my head, forcing myself to pull out my notebook and pen to distract myself.

Trying not to focus on our teacher, I glanced around at the other students, finding Erik staring at me, waving at me before flipping me off because it took me so long to notice him. I chuckled and waved back, noticing that the teacher watched the motion and flicked his gaze toward Erik, his frown deepening.

"Alright, I think that concludes our first class," the teacher said, not stepping away from the podium. "If you haven't signed the roster sheet, please ensure you do so, and I'll see you all on Tuesday. Don't party too hard; it's just the first week!"

A small chuckle broke out among the other students while the shuffling of chairs and backpacks became deafening. I watched as the teacher glanced at me again before disappearing out the classroom door. Worried that I made a horrible first impression on the teacher, I didn't notice Erik come up behind me before he clapped me hard on the back, making me jump.

"Almost didn't make it, huh?" he chuckled, his gray eyes focused on me.

"The damn doctor's visit ran longer than it should've," I replied, ensuring my notebook was zipped up in my backpack this time. Thank God my laptop hadn't fallen out while I ran here.

"What did they say?" Erik's tone shifted from joking to concern, his voice lowering to not include those around us in our conversation. Erik was up to date on my medical mishaps and happened to be at the apartment we shared when I passed out.

"Unless I want to take time off school, they are switching my suppressant to one I inject directly into my side."

"I can help with that!"

"Yeah, no," I said with a smile on my lips. Erik has had a crush on me since shortly after we met, yet he knew I wasn't interested. Part of it was because he was a Beta, but not *because* he was a Beta. My body craved an Alpha, just the nature of being an Omega, and to date him would be setting him up for pain. Long-term suppressant use could result in an Omega getting very sick, infertility, immunity, and sometimes death. I had been on the mixture of suppressants for a year, and in another year, I will need to go off them for two heat cycles in order to avoid the prolonged effects.

A year ago, I had gone into heat, and Erik had to help me. It wasn't fun for either of us, as he had to use a knotted cock sheath to give me any relief, and even then, it wasn't enough. I don't know how much pleasure he got from the experience, but it was miserable for my Omega. It knew it was a falsehood and wanted none of it. I had come out of my heat to find Erik covered in scratches, bites, and bruises and looking exhausted. I could never put him in that position again, which would mean that I couldn't be faithful to him in our relationship, needing an Alpha to get through my cycles. I promised I would never use him like that again, despite the feeling I got that Erik would be over the moon if I needed him again.

The second reason is I just wasn't interested in him romantically.

"You'll try to inject me with something else, and I'm simply not interested."

"Yea, yea," Erik grumbled. "You know, I hope you never meet your Alpha; then you'll have no choice but to accept me."

"Uh-huh," I responded, rolling my eyes. "Whatever you say. So, what is your impression of the teacher? Does he seem like he's going to be a hardass or..?"

"He's liked around campus. His grading seems pretty straightforward, nothing too crazy or hard. I'll give you my notes so that you have them later. Should be a decent class, nothing too complicated."

I could only grunt in acknowledgment as we headed to the cafeteria for lunch. I couldn't get the way the teacher looked at me out of my head. The way his blue eyes stared at me. I thought I could detect the slight scent of honey and citrus coming from him, but with the suppressants, I couldn't tell if that was his pheromones or a cologne he wore. It wasn't uncommon for Alphas to wear cologne in a professional environment; something about masking their original scent despite the fact that every class was equipped with de-scenters.

It confused my Omega, and he didn't like it. He wanted to find its source and roll around in the scent, marking my body with it. I suppressed a whimper by shaking my head and picking up a tray from the stack at the buffet. I've been around Alphas my whole life, and not once had my Omega responded the way it did for Mr. Ellis. That needed to be checked and corrected immediately. Packed up, stuffed into a box, locked, and shoved under the bed until graduation. No distractions, no relationships, and definitely not with a hot, attractive teacher.

Luke

I glared at my erection as I sat in my office. It was quite the feat to get to my office before anyone saw the tent in my jeans, and I will admit that I ignored the call of my name at least twice on my dash for cover. But *please* explain to me why I still had a hard-on that refused to go away!?! I didn't want to take care of it manually at work, that's just not appropriate and vastly unprofessional. I tried everything I could think of to get it down, from drinking cold water to walking around, jogging in place, and thinking of my 7th-grade science teacher — that woman was horrifying, by the way— and trying to see how many Pokémon I could name from memory. Nothing!

Sighing, I got up and locked my office door. Sitting back at my desk, I took the landline off the receiver and set my phone to 'do not disturb.'

Filled with disdain and disbelief that I was actually fucking doing this, I finally released my cock from my jeans. Stroking the shaft from base to tip, watching my hand and foreskin swallow the head of my cock, the movement alone gave me cause to moan; the sudden pleasure and relief were pure bliss. I pulled up a frequented porn site on my phone, checking multiple times that the volume was turned off before queuing up a video that I knew had gotten me off before. It was filmed from the camera's perspective, looking down as the blonde twink in the video stroked the cock of the man before him. He knelt before the bigger man, settling between his thighs, and the Alpha's cock looking huge in the small hands of the blond. But I struggled to focus on the couple, my brain drifting to the Omega in my class. I could imagine him vividly, sitting on his knees under my desk, his delicate mouth wrapped around my cock as he reached between his legs to eagerly stroke himself, maybe his fingers sliding further down to explore his dampening hole.

Choosing to abandon the video and let my fantasies take over, I used my free hand to reach below my shaft, cupping my balls and squeezing them lightly before tugging them gently downwards, pulling them away from my body. In my fantasy, the Omega would lean down upon command to lick them, maybe even take each ball into his mouth, and the idea had my head tilted back and suppressed a moan. My upper teeth bit into my bottom lip as my hips began to thrust forward, fucking my fist as if it were his mouth. I imagined him struggling to take my Alpha cock down his tiny throat, eyes watering at the corners, but he wouldn't complain, my hands sliding through his soft hair to guide him. The pressure began to build at the base of my spine, my balls tightening in response, and I sat straight in my chair and looked around me. Cursing at myself for not having a box of tissues, I settled on the microfiber cloth I generally kept nearby for cleaning my computer monitor. I chose to replace my palm with the cloth, using it to rub along my shaft as I imagined the Omega stroking himself in time with my movements, eager for me. Briefly, I wondered if he would swallow before the pleasure blinded me, erupting from my shaft and ending in the cloth.

Post-nut clarity can be a bitch, and I groaned in frustration and disgust as I stuffed myself back into my pants and tossed the cleaning cloth into my laptop case to wash when I got home. The emotions that consumed me were so foreign that I couldn't organize them properly. Anger, regret, shame. Those I understood. It was the confusion and desire for that Omega that I couldn't understand. How incredibly unsatisfied I was; it wasn't enough, but it had to be.

First thing first, he wasn't mine. He was real, not a fantasy, and in no way, shape, or form mine. He would come to my classroom twice a week for an hour and a half for a lesson and then leave. Sure, he was the first Omega I felt an unbridled desire for. The first that I could scent, the first my Alpha acknowledged, and I had zero answers as to why. He was a stranger, yet the pull was distracting. But...not mine.

Secondly, and most importantly, he was my fucking student! I'll be honest: I never read the handbook on student/teacher relationships because I didn't think it would ever apply to me. It was such a common trope that everyone knew it happened; it was so cliché for it not to, but surely the university had a policy against it, right? I should probably look into that. Not that things would play out that way, of course. Not at all.

Reaching for my phone, I pressed the contact for Ryan Easton. The Eastons were good family friends, with Ryan and I having gone to high school and college together. The Ellis family has used Easton Medical for a few generations, and I'm pretty convinced we have our own filing cabinet with all our medical histories in it somewhere. When he wasn't working at the family practice part-time, he was generally picking up a few hours at the local Omega clinic run by this university. Being a Beta made it easy for him to treat both designations, and he enjoyed the work.

"Evans!" Ryan's voice boomed over the line, almost making me jump.

"What the fuck Reynolds, you sitting on your phone?" I asked, rolling my eyes at the nickname and using his.

"Kinda. I was looking at *Knotters*. What's up?"

"Do you have time to squeeze me in for a few blood tests?"

"Always. Everything okay?"

"We'll see," I replied, grabbing my laptop case and leaving my office.

"Well," Ryan said, biting into the sandwich I'd brought him as he reviewed my test results.

"Everything seems pretty normal. Your blood pressure is a little high, but nothing to be concerned about. So what got you in such a state that you needed immediate results? Afraid you picked up something?"

"No, nothing like that," I shook my head, arms crossed over my chest. If everything was normal, then what the fuck was going on with me? Why am I suddenly so aware of a certain Omega? "I met someone."

"Really?!" Ryan looked at me excitedly. "If you tell me you met them on *Knotters*, I'm going to be pissed. I've been on there for months; all I've gotten were hookups. Which is great, don't get me wrong, but I would love something a little longer than a night."

"Well, yeah. *Knotters* may be advertised as a dating app, but everyone knows it's for discreet hookups. And when have you ever complained about meaningless sex?"

"Since I needed a date for my brother's pack initiation. You're coming, right?"

"Probably. But you know how I hate those things." Pack initiations were marriages, just under a different name. Instead of marrying one person, you're marrying everyone within that pack. Adam Easton found himself a pack while he was backpacking through the national forests in Canada for a nature photography job he managed to pick up directly out of high school. Adam was roughly four years younger than us, and he already found himself in a pack with a female Omega; him being a Beta didn't seem to bother anyone in the pack. However, the fact that Adam was younger and the first of the Easton sons to get hitched meant that Ryan was probably getting pressured by his parents to settle down.

"Yea, yea, lone wolf. Though, apparently, not so alone anymore." Ryan gave a sly grin. "But why would meeting someone cause this reaction?"

I studied Ryan for a moment. Being the family doctor, he knew about my medical history and my condition, but it certainly didn't make it any easier to talk with him.

"He's an Omega."

"And?"

"I can scent that he's an Omega," I sighed, avoiding eye contact.

"I'm sorry, what?!" Ryan exploded, almost dropping the sandwich in his hand. "You picked up his scent? I thought that was impossible for you!"

"Why do you think I'm here, having you run so many tests I already knew would return normal? I was hoping something would pop up and I could have answers! My Alpha responded so urgently to him that I had to take care of things in my office!"

"Wait...so you met him at school? Did you knot?"

I knew the question wasn't meant to be rude, but I couldn't help but bristle at it. That's a private thing between me and my Omega, not something I should discuss with my best friend, even if he were a doctor.

"Yes, I met him at the school. And no, I did not. One doesn't normally knot when it's handled solo."

"While that is true, you're not normal, no offense. Generally, when a young Alpha masturbates for the first time, a knot can form, so I was curious about your first solo session since your discovery, from a medical standpoint, obviously. So what now?"

"No fucking clue. Don't mention a thing to my parents. I would prefer it if none of this made it into my file, but how else will you explain the blood work?"

"Easy. You came in for a routine check-up. Your last one was two years ago, and I've been nagging you to come in. So, what are you going to do about the Omega? I take it you're not dating."

"No, we're not." I sighed, pinching the bridge of my nose. Lord knows I wish we were. I would give anything to leave this office and wrap my arms around my Omega. Just having him by my side would be nice. Maybe a late lunch before we headed back home and —

"Well then," Ryan said, cutting me off, amused, looking at the bulge that seemed to be forming in my pants.

"Oh, for fuck's sake!" I blushed, crossing my legs and putting my jacket over my lap to hide it from his view. "Is this going to be a thing now? Am I a teenager all over again, getting turned on at the slightest thought? I wasn't even thinking of anything sexual! How am I supposed to hide this while I teach? It's a little hard to give a lecture with a fucking hard-on!"

"I mean, you could just fuck the Omega."

"Not an option," I growled.

"Get a cock cage?" Ryan teased, his eyes glinting. "Male chastity is all the rage these days."

I raised an eyebrow at him. That wasn't a bad idea. It would prevent me from getting too hard, and surely discrete ones exist. I could wear it when I leave for the day and take it off when I get home. It would only be worn a few hours a day and twice weekly since my class met on Tuesdays and

Thursdays. Though to get used to it, I should probably wear it around the house like a pair of new shoes.

"Jesus, I was joking!"

"And yet," I grinned broadly.

If you had told me I would one day be measuring the circumference and diameter of my cock for a fucking chastity device, I would've laughed at you. Yet here I was, sitting at my home computer, my dick in one hand and a tape measure in the other. It was suggested to measure at least three times to get a proper measurement and to do it while the body is warm. After taking a shower, I gathered my measurements and ordered a cage that had nothing to do with fancy designs but everything to do with discretion and functionality for what I needed. I needed it to arrive by Tuesday, so I paid out the ass for rush delivery for it to arrive by Sunday afternoon. That didn't give me much time before it got used on Tuesday, but I figured it was enough. The class was only an hour and a half long; I should be okay, even if I might be uncomfortable.

The cage arrived on time without incident, in the advertised discreet packaging. Figuring out what part goes where was a little cumbersome, but I got everything in the proper place. I tried my hardest to warm up the metal before feeding my softened dick through the chamber, and I swear

I felt my balls try to absorb themselves into my body as the cold metal touched me, making it a little difficult to get everything fitted in place.

Once I had done so, there was a noticeable weight on the lower half of my body, but not enough that it could be distracting and uncomfortable. To familiarize myself with the device and being in captivity, I wore the cage most of Monday evening when I got home, and by bedtime, I didn't notice it anymore except for a slight ache in my balls, which I could easily live with.

As Tuesday morning arrived, I slipped the cage in place as if it was a part of my standard routine, leaving the key on top of the dresser. I reached for the gray slacks that I had to dig out from the back of my closet yesterday with a look of hatred and disgust. After trying on an assortment of pants, I learned that jeans showed the cage a little too easily for my comfort, drawing attention to the fact that I was in chastity for my own good. Slacks that had pleats in the front and didn't hug my waist proved to provide the best cage discretion. I used to pride myself on being business casual in jeans and a smart shirt, refusing to conform to the older professors with their slacks and sweater vest travesties. Yet here I was, dressing just like them to hide my desire for an Omega I shouldn't...or couldn't have.

The weather was transitioning from summer to fall, but it couldn't decide how the day would go. I also didn't have control over the temperature in my classroom. Aidyn Keller was one of maybe three Omegas in my class, and Alphas tended to run hot. Because of this, most classrooms had air conditioning pumped into them, lowering the temperature even in the dead of winter. Finally deciding on a thin quarter-sleeved sweater, I pulled it over my head and took a deep breath before grabbing my coffee travel mug and my laptop bag and leaving my condo.

Aidyn

I woke with one of the most horrendous headaches of my life. It felt like someone was squeezing my skull, expecting it to pop. Sitting up in bed, my body felt warm with zero traces of fever, yet my head was swimming so much that I had to place my head on my knees or I was going to throw up. God, I felt like death.

I was certain that this was the result of the new suppressants, and tears of frustration pricked at my eyes. I was *so* exhausted. Tired of being a dominant Omega, tired of the endless cocktail of medications and nothing working like it was supposed to. Dr. Easton's words came back to me about the risk of organ failure, and I wondered if maybe I should find a deserted island somewhere and live off coconuts and bananas. Away from society so I didn't have to take any more of these fucking chemicals.

A sense of urgency consumed me as bile rose up my throat, and I bolted from the bed. Flinging my bedroom door open, I pushed Erik out of the way as he opened the bathroom door before emptying my stomach into the toilet. I dry-heaved into the bowl, my back and ribs protesting the lack of substance my stomach could provide. With a groan, I sat on the floor, resting my head on the wall, my hair sticking to my forehead. I should cut it.

"You okay?" Erik asked, kneeling beside me. I opened my eyes to see his face full of concern and confusion.

"I will be. I need to adjust."

"The suppressants?"

I could only nod slightly, but the motion made me want to vomit again. Erik got up, and I heard him moving around in the kitchen, setting the teakettle on the stove. This isn't the first time I've reacted badly to my suppressants, and I have found that a combination of green tea, ginger tea, and peppermint tea helped with the nausea and headaches they caused. Erik knew this and the protocol for getting things started for me. He was probably already setting the water to boil, pulling out a travel mug and some honey, and draping the tea bags in the mug for me.

Forcing myself off the floor, I started the shower before stepping under the lukewarm water. I already felt overheated but couldn't stand cold showers. Using the wall to brace myself against as another wave of light-headedness washed over me, I took advantage of the cool tile and leaned my head to rest against the coolness until the tile warmed beneath my skin. It took every ounce of my energy to rush through the mundane tasks of washing myself, having to pause every once in a while as nausea tried to get me to empty my stomach once more. I don't know where I pulled the energy to shower completely, but by the time I exited the bathroom, I contemplated crawling back into bed to sleep.

I found a short-sleeve shirt that was long enough to cover my ass and a pair of fitted grey jeans in my pile of clean clothes, pulling them on slowly.

The season was changing into the cooler months of the year, but adjusting to suppressants always made regulating my body's temperature difficult, so wearing warm clothing was next to impossible for me. There had been times when I was sweating in a room where others were shivering.

Grabbing the suppressant shot from my nightstand, I measured out the dosage from the vial I received from the pharmacist. Pinching the flesh next to my belly button, I pushed the needle into my stomach, hissing softly as I pressed down on the syringe plunger. Fuck, I hated this type of suppressant. Taking a pill instead of injecting myself daily was so much easier. I tossed the needle and syringe into the special garbage can beside my bed that I had picked up at the pharmacy before lowering my shirt just as Erik knocked on my door.

"Maybe you should stay home," Erik said, handing me the travel mug. "You look paler than a vampire."

"And yet, I can't miss a day." I sipped and winced at the hot liquid as it burned my tongue.

Erik knew better than to argue with me, so he nodded, and together, we took the city bus to the university. Normally the bus didn't bother me, but today it was overcrowded and hot. Every time the bus jerked, someone bumped into me, their touch like an unwanted heat pad against my sensitive skin. The second a seat near the window opened up, I pushed my way toward it, desperate for fresh air that the open window provided, even if it was just a crack. The passengers behind me grumbled in annoyance, complaining that it was too cold to have the window open, but I ignored them. Resting my head against the thick tempered glass, I closed my eyes, letting the breeze ruffle through my hair.

When the bus pulled up to the university, the majority of the passengers got off, and it was relatively easy to move with the flow of exiting passengers. I was slightly upset that it wasn't raining since that would make the cool temperature drop even further, but the cloud cover that had rolled in while we were on the bus provided a promise that there was still a chance.

We made our way across campus in silence, Erik picking up on the fact that I was conserving what little energy I still had. The pounding headache in my head had gone away, but I still felt hot and sluggish, my stomach still uneasy. I had random bouts of lightheadedness that I needed to stop for as my vision swam and clouded. The most recent attack happened outside the classroom door, and we paused for it to pass.

The classroom was empty upon our arrival, and I groaned at the wave of heat that greeted us. It was as if someone left the furnace on overnight and didn't open any windows. We sat toward the back of the room, and I opened the window behind us to let in some of the breeze, hoping it would prevent me from overheating during the lecture. If this was going to be a constant issue, I would need a mini fan to help keep me regulated, but I would have to get one that I could plug into my laptop via a USB drive if I were going to have the ability to use it in class. Every month, my parents sent me an allowance that I'm supposed to use for rent, food, and schooling, but, to me, this didn't qualify under any of those categories. To purchase an item outside of what was discussed, I would have to be able to justify the expenditure, even if I had a little money left over each month.

"Just do it," Erik said, taking my phone from my hand, where I was looking at mini fans when I voiced the idea to him. "If you overheat in class and get sent home, you're not participating. It's a health concern."

He selected the cheapest fan to plug into my laptop, pressed the 'one-click' option that automatically purchased the item for me, and returned my phone. It'll be here tomorrow. I took out my laptop, turning it on, before taking another packet of anti-nausea medication from my backpack and downing the last of my tea while the classroom filled up around us. The medication only took away the most severe feelings of nausea, and I needed the assistance in order to sit in a classroom that was way too warm for an hour and a half. Every once in a while, I could feel the breeze coming in through the window, and I would close my eyes to enjoy the pleasure of it before it disappeared again.

As Mr. Ellis entered the classroom, my body stiffened instantly as the Alpha glanced around the classroom, his eyes landing on me. He watched me briefly, frowning slightly, which deepened when he saw Erik beside me. When his gaze moved from me, my Omega panicked slightly, wanting the Alpha to return his attention back toward us, and I could feel a strange sound crawl up my throat. Before it reached an audible octave, I stifled it with a cough, clearing my throat. What was going on with me? Was I so upset his gaze left mine that I almost called out to him in a room full of people? I had to force myself to open the document I used for class notes, pulling myself out of whatever fantasy it tried to manifest. I don't know what's going on, but I need to get it under control.

"Today begins our first lecture," Mr. Ellis began. "To understand ABO psychology and biology, we need to start with the history of ABO and the theory of evolution. Humans have long been described as adaptive creatures, something we can easily see as we move through the early stages of humanity from Homo erectus to Homo neanderthalensis to Homo sapiens. We adapted to the world, creating hunting and gathering tools to meet our survival needs. There was once a theory that male body temperatures were hotter than their female counterparts because the males hunted, and the females stayed in the cave to prepare food, baskets, and tools and took care of the offspring.

"The adaptation of survival is clear today and can be found in the Inuit people with high-fat diets to accommodate living in the Arctic. In the high-altitude Tibetan Plateau, mutations have been observed that help the oxygen concentration in their blood. The Sea Nomads of Sama-Bajau have evolved to be able to dive underwater for long periods due to the evolution of their spleens.

"Out of the need for survival, we assume this is where the first Omega appeared on humanity's radar. The first documentation of Omega-like behaviors appeared in scriptures dating to the Bubonic plague, otherwise known as the Black Plague. Roughly 60% of Europe's population was wiped out, but it is to be believed that that percentage could be higher. Scientists theorize that the first Omegas evolved to help repopulate. The first documentation of Alpha behaviors doesn't show up for at least another two years. Despite this, what we know now about Alpha and Omega reproduction leads us to believe that the first Alphas probably showed up simultaneously as their Omega counterparts.

"Imagine the poor bastard who had no idea why he suddenly had a knot and had to go to a Tudor-era doctor only for them to apply leeches to his penis to get the swelling to go down," Mr. Ellis continues, creating a small wave of chuckles that bounced around the classroom. He turned and added more information to the whiteboard.

"Over time, Alphas and Omegas have been hunted, exploited, experimented on, politicized, and fetishized, Omegas even more so. In this class, we will discuss the biology of the Alpha and the Omega, how genetics can play a part, the psychology of both designations, and how their designation can impact one's thought process and development. Such as, are the behavioral patterns of both designations based on nature or nurture?"

Mr. Ellis continued through his lecture, and I tapped away at my keyboard, keeping up with him with little difficulty. Toward the end of the class, I noticed a faint scent of citrus and honey, something I had smelled last week when I entered his classroom. It was an Alpha scent, and I thought it odd that in a classroom full of Alphas, this one scent was the one that stood out to me, especially with neutralizers installed. It cut through the artificially created scent that Erik wore, and it scratched at the back of my mind, distracting enough that I zoned out until I heard an Alpha speak up.

"Well, Alphas are the superior designation. Equating us to animals and animal urges does seem a bit much, don't you think?"

"What makes you think you're the superior designation?" I spoke up before I could stop myself. Erik froze beside me, his eyes darting between me and the Alpha, who turned to look at me, an Omega who had the audacity to question him. I just smiled at him.

"Alphas are more dominant in presence, stronger, and have better control over our traits. Studies have shown that even the rare dominant Alphas can control their pheromones, often appearing weaker than they actually are to fit in better with society. Omegas can't control themselves around us Alphas; they act like animals in heat, focusing solely on breeding, yet we can function just fine. Omegas need us to function."

I didn't mean to laugh at the guy, but his ideals were so stupid. We couldn't function without him? "I'm sitting in this classroom right now, with zero desire to breed with you."

The angry growl that escaped the Alpha did little to stop me. He wasn't my Alpha, and I didn't have to listen to him. The fact that he growled at me to back down and submit to him only pissed me off more, making me want to resist. "That's because you're on suppressants."

"Or you just don't do it for me." I smiled at him, catching a glance at Mr. Ellis. The look on his face was not a kind one. His hands clutched the podium and were white at the knuckles. But he wasn't staring at me. His sharp gaze was fixated on the Alpha, who argued with me, looking at him as if he wanted to tear out his throat. "If that is how you define 'superiority,' I'm concerned for you, and it's a good thing you're in this class. Maybe you'll figure out how your brain works."

"Aidyn!" Erik hissed at me, grabbing my wrist. I pulled it out of his grasp and smiled at him before turning back to the Alpha.

"There is no superior designation; it's just an ideal that Mommy and Daddy told you growing up to make you feel special. We don't actually need your knots; we have toys for that now. Even I used a Beta during my last heat; he only needed a toy to satisfy me. If anything, you're just sperm donors."

"How dare you," the Alpha growled again, standing up and looking as if he was about to hop over the row of desks to strangle me, an acrid scent pouring from him as he flexed his pheromones, trying to force me into submission.

"Enough," Mr. Ellis snapped.

There was an edge to his voice, a low, deep, threatening growl that had my body responding by producing slick, dampening the seat of my boxers. Fear cut through the arousal as I glanced around, praying that no one else could tell I was responding to the man at the front of the classroom in such a way. It wasn't quite an Alpha's bark, but it was close enough that I stopped breathing, my heart pounding in my ears. The scent of burnt cloves cut through the air, and my Omega stirred once more, reacting in a way I was not at all happy with. It was like he wanted to submit and grovel out an apology to make the Alpha happy again. To purr at his feet, rubbing my cheek against him, scenting him to calm him down. To remove the anger that marred his handsome face as he looked between the Alpha and me.

"Class is dismissed; you two stay after class."

"Now you've done it," Erik hissed at me, and I could only shrug. "Are you going to be okay with going home alone?"

I nodded. He had another class after this one, and if I needed to, I'd hang in the library waiting for him. The class emptied quietly, the other students trying their hardest not to look at their teacher or the two students in trouble. Mr. Ellis' classroom was on the second floor of the building, and we awkwardly walked down the stairs in silence to one of the left side wings that housed the teacher's offices.

"Mr. Keller, please stay in the hallway while I talk with Mr. Forester. Do not move."

It felt like he wanted to lecture us separately like petulant children, and I hated that. Sure, we did behave like children, but we were adults, and standing in the hallway was torture, waiting for my turn. I picked up a little of what Mr. Ellis was saying, but he didn't shout at the Alpha, which made it seem almost worse than if he did. The door opened, and the Alpha stepped into the hallway. He sneered at me before he walked by, saying nothing as I stepped into the office, closing the door behind me.

Entering the office, I realized then that the scent of citrus and honey was the scent coming from Mr. Ellis—his office smelling strongly of him—hinting that he spent a lot of time here. It was laced with the burning scent of cloves, his anger evident on his face as he leaned against his desk. I couldn't suppress the whimper that escaped from my throat as it surrounded us, my body heating up with what felt like the worst fever I'd ever had, sending shivers coursing through my system. Mr. Ellis's expression changed instantly as he moved away from his desk toward me.

"Aidyn?" he asked in concern.

Luke

Aidyn felt hot to the touch when I grabbed him as he fell. I cradled him in my arms and lowered us to the floor by the door to my office, his forest scent consuming my senses, almost as if I were back hiking through the woods of the Pacific Northwest. It surrounded me and clung to my body like the fingers that Aidyn used to grip my arms tightly.

"Where is your suppressant?" I asked him; my voice panicked as my Alpha began to take charge.

Fuck, I wanted him. His scent was sweet, while also damp, the scent of rain on pine. It was a siren song to my Alpha, stirring within me desires that I knew would be horrible if I acted upon right now. My Alpha disagreed, meeting this Omega's scent with its own, and I knew I was very close to a rut, on the edge of animalistic tendencies that would have me claiming him as if he was mine to do so, yet thankfully I was caged, the key to my freedom safely at home on my dresser. I was painfully aware of the itch in my canines—the sudden urge to bite and claim. I watched his eyes glaze over as his heat began to take control, a soft sound escaping his lips that seemed to have a direct line to my cock. It strained against what I now deemed as the inhumane cage I forced it into, and pain began taking over, cutting into the haze and allowing me to think.

Aidyn pushed his full weight against me, forcing me onto my back. He began to nuzzle his face into my neck, rubbing his cheeks against me like a cat, his glasses bumping against my face, smudging the lenses. Fuck me! I never thought an Omega would scent mark me, and now I had one so blissed out he wasn't even aware of what he was doing or how frustrating this whole situation was. I fought the groan that threatened to escape from my throat. I had a suppressor shot in my desk drawer, as was required by all teachers, but I couldn't get to it with his weight on me. I tried to move backward, to pull my legs out from under Aidyn's weight, but he seemed to apply more pressure, pinning me to the floor, and I growled in frustration. Aidyn flinched at the sound, responding with a soft whimper, determined to fix the frustrated Alpha before him.

I hated the hurt look on his face, and I reached a hand upwards, cupping his cheek, as he tilted his head in, nuzzling into my palm. "Aidyn, I'm trying to help you. To do that, I need you to get off me. The medicine is in my desk. It'll help, trust me."

If he heard me, he made no effort to comply as he repositioned himself, lowering his body and nuzzling the crotch of my slacks, his cheek rubbing over the cage and my cock. A dull thunk sounded where the frame of his glasses tapped the metal. A look of confusion washed over his face as he stared at my groin, and I couldn't help but chuckle at the absurdity of all this. In his hazed state, he didn't understand the hard metal gripping me like a vice, causing me a world of pain, while also preventing him from giving into his instincts.

Relying on my Alpha strength, I pulled free from his grasp. My Alpha growled in anger at being separated from his Omega, a sound that Aidyn responded to with his mewl of annoyance and uncertainty, watching me as I stood up to pull the suppressant pen from my top drawer. Uncapping it, I sat on the floor, pulling Aidyn into my embrace again, nuzzling my nose into his neck, and absorbing the pheromone scent he gave off. A soft vibration started in my chest, my Alpha's purr calming the overheated Omega in my arms. Sadness washed over me. The first time I ever purred for my Omega, and he wouldn't remember a moment of it.

But he was not mine, and I had to stop this. It didn't matter the pull he had on my Alpha. We didn't have any relationship beyond teacher and student; we haven't even spoken to each other. He was not mine, and I had to keep reminding myself of that. Using one hand, I unbuttoned the fly of his jeans, his instinctual need to be knotted making it easier for me to pull them down. His cock stood at attention behind his boxers that had the cutest little T-rexes printed on the fabric. I couldn't help but chuckle at them but groaned as the scent of slick pooled in the fabric, causing it to stick to his skin.

Grabbing the pen, I pushed up the side of his underwear, exposing the side of his thigh, before taking a deep breath. Curling my fist around it, I stabbed the pen's needle into Aidyn's leg, pressing the release trigger at the tip to disperse the suppressor into his bloodstream, my face buried in the crook of his neck.

"I'm so sorry, Little Fawn," I whispered against his throat.

We sat in my office for fifteen minutes while the suppressant reacted to his heat. I don't remember a damn thing I said while holding him against me and murmuring into his hair, rocking back and forth, and releasing a steady stream of pheromones to calm his agitation. His body calmed down, the fever from his heat disappeared from his skin, and he passed out, his head heavy against my chest. Lifting him and cradling him to me protectively, we left my office, dodging very few people on our way to the nurse's office. His limp body was oddly light but a warm comfort to me, and I couldn't take my eyes off his slackened face. He was pale and clammy, his hair sticking to his forehead, and his glasses were on the edge of his nose while his head bumped against my chest as we moved; yet he was the prettiest thing I had ever seen.

Placing him on an empty cot in the nurse's office, I was consumed with the idea that he was better off in a nest of his creation with fluffy cloud-like pillows and fuzzy blankets, not being left on a hard metal cot. My inner Alpha let out a low rumble deep from my chest as I pulled the thin cotton blanket over Aidyn before removing his glasses and setting them on the table next to him. Moving toward the sink, I turned on the cold water and grabbed a few paper towels from the dispenser beside the sink. Dampening the paper towels and squeezing out the excess water, I turned back toward Aidyn. The nurse ignored us while I sat beside him and tried my best to clean the sweat from his face, using the towel to brush his hair back at the roots. Unable to help myself, I leaned forward, a low purr barely audible rolled through my chest as I nuzzled into the side of his neck, breathing in his scent. I couldn't stay with him; the less people who knew about what took place in my office, the better. I couldn't be here for him when I so desperately wanted to; the vision of him waking up confused, maybe stressed and irritated, made me ill. Stepping away made me positively violent, my Alpha screaming at me to return to his side, to pull him tightly against me, and drown him in my scent. Aidyn was coated in our scents when I left him, the nurse didn't ask questions, and I prayed she didn't report me to the board. She probably took it as a distressed Omega, and it was my duty as an Alpha to calm him down. That was the only logic that I was using to calm my anxiety. But at the same time, if it meant staying by his side, being reported wouldn't be the worst thing. Sitting in my car, panting and sweating despite the autumn chill in the air, I tasted blood. Glancing in the rearview mirror, I noticed I had nicked my bottom lip with my canines.

Briefly, I wondered what it would feel like to sink them into his flesh, to be bonded and owned by him. Marking was a serious action. The bonding process was initiated by the Alpha first, lacing their bite with their pheromones and breaking the skin with our canines. To complete a bonding ceremony, the Omega then bites their intended Alpha, sealing the bond. In a perfect world; the bonding process was a hundred percent consensual, however, there have been several cases of Alphas forcing Omegas to complete the ceremony. What should be a joyous occasion turns into an event that leaves them traumatized and miserable. If it was ever found out that an Alpha forced an Omega to bond, the Alpha could face life in prison. However, nothing can be done for the poor Omegas still chained to their situations. Scientists have been working to try and find a solution to reverse the effects to help victims of a forced marking, but as of now, nothing has worked. It was a stronger bond than any marriage, and to be away from your bonded was agonizingly painful.

As I drove further away from the university, I wondered if the pain of being separated from my bonded would feel like this. Uncomfortable, my skin crawling as if I was having a terrible reaction to medication or recovering from a drug habit. I was fidgety and antsy, my nails running up my arm and across my thigh, my thoughts running a mile a minute. My heart thundered in my ears, loud and erratic.

The first thing I did after entering my condo was remove my clothing, stripping naked in the entryway. My clothing felt tight and restrictive, chafing away at my sensitive heated skin. I made my way into the bedroom, grabbing the small silver key from the top of my dresser, and removed my metal prison quickly, my cock hardening the second it was free. I shoved the device into the back of my sock drawer, determined never to see or use it again. It had done its job, preventing me from taking Aidyn in my office, but it also offended me. I realized his scent still held me firmly in its grasp, deep in my senses, and I couldn't bring myself to step into the shower to wash him off, adding to the restlessness I was experiencing. My

Alpha paced in my head, my body tight and stiff. I knew what a rut was; I've studied it and seen videos and examples, but I don't think I've ever personally felt it, and this was hell. Like I was going insane.

To ease my agitation, I dug through my nightstand drawer and pulled out the only masturbatory toy I owned. It was a cheap, non-gender-specific sleeve that hadn't been used much. While I may like men, I didn't give a shit what the toy I thrusted into looked like, and I had little desire to spend an outrageous amount just to have a need met. I grabbed the bottle of lube that also hadn't been used in probably a year, and I lubricated my painfully hard cock and the inside of the toy before sliding the silicon canister over my length. A groan escaped my throat; immense pleasure consumed me when my hips acted on their own, thrusting upward and forward to meet the sensation of the grooves and nodes designed to aid in my pleasure. No longer restrained, my rut consumed my body.

Growling, I thrusted into the toy roughly, my knees bumping into the edge of the bed as I held the device level on the bedspread. My pheromones mixed deliciously with the one that had now imprinted itself upon my senses. Twice, this Omega student called to me. Twice, I could not answer his siren-like call, and my Alpha was agitated, like a tiger pacing its cage. His Omega had wanted me at that moment, and my Alpha was ready to accept, but the position I'd put him in wasn't a good one. I was the only Alpha in his space when he went into heat; for all I knew, it had nothing to do with me specifically and everything to do with biology and instinct. The fact that I could scent him had my brain contorting the situation to suit its own narrative, creating thought processes that I otherwise wouldn't have had. As if trying to justify a situation that was disturbing and unprofessional.

Thank God Forester wasn't in the same room. I could see in his eyes how badly he wanted to punish the only Omega to have probably stood up to him in his entire life and how he tried to force him into submission in my classroom, releasing pheromones as if it was his right to do so. Growling at the thought of another Alpha trying to force *my* Aidyn to submit drove me overboard. Struggling to outlast my current state as my orgasm climbed, kneeling with the device firmly in my hand, I was unaware I had moved onto the bed.

My thoughts were a kaleidoscope of Aidyn—begging for me in my office, of forests, the scent of rain, and the feeling of home. Of an Omega who spoke his mind and of the scent that marked me. The Omega who felt warm in my arms, his needy desire so evident on his face when he looked up at me. I wasn't aware I had brought my forearm up to my mouth until my orgasm ripped through me. I felt the sharp pain of my canines slicing into my forearm, biting myself as my rut rode itself out, blood dripping onto my thigh and onto the comforter. I struggled to gather my bearings, panting as I leaned back on to my heels and looked at the mess on my bed sheets. A mixture of blood and semen that I knew I had to wash immediately, or the blood stains would set in, but my brain was elsewhere, trying to figure out how the hell I was going to survive roughly 15 weeks of this.

Sighing, I began to withdraw from the toy, only to stop when I felt a slight painful tug at the base of my cock. The fuck? I tried again and was immediately met with a sharper pain. Hissing, I looked down and realized, with shock, that the first thing I ever knotted was a cheap silicone toy.

It took forever for the swelling of my knot to subside, even after standing under the spray of the cold shower I forced myself into. I stood under that spray for what felt like hours, contemplating my situation as if it would have given satisfactory answers, and instead all it did was give me a headache. When the toy finally fell to the tile with an odd deep squelch, I groaned at the release of pressure and the embarrassment before washing the offensive silicone and turning the shower off.

Stripping my bedsheets, the sweater I had worn tumbled to the ground, Aidyn's scent still faintly woven into the fabric. Like some sort of creeper, I grabbed a Ziploc bag from the kitchen before folding the sweater and sealing it in plastic, praying that its "unbeatable seal technology" would lock his scent away like a memento. I placed the bag in the bottom of my dresser as my phone chimed with a call from Ryan, asking if I could go out for some drinks tonight. The idea of drinking on a school night didn't really appeal, but the self-love session I had hadn't released any of the tension in my body. The next best thing was alcohol. I agreed to meet him at the bar we frequented often and wasted no time in ordering myself a beer and taking a seat at the bar.

Morgan's was located between our apartments, and we had been coming here since college, often drinking away the stress of finals and the pain of Ryan's many breakups. I swear, he was so bad at relationships that the bartenders started to know our names and orders, which was awkward and made me feel like an alcoholic. The bar was rather cliché in design, with dark fabrics and wooden beams with low lighting and music that was way too loud half the time. Simple and average, which is kind of what I liked about it, plus its location was perfect for Ryan and me.

Taking a swig of my beer, I started doom-scrolling through social media when the chair beside me shifted. Looking up, I expected to see Ryan, but instead, I found a petite man with curly black hair pulled back at the temples, tied into place by a rubber band at the back of his head. He set his motorcycle helmet on the bar counter before he acknowledged the bartender, ordering himself a beer. I stood at around six foot two, where this guy probably didn't come up to my shoulder like Aidyn did.

Everything about him seemed small and delicate, ethereal like an elf. If size played any part in the stereotype, I would bet he was an Omega. But I had met a few short king Alphas that I wouldn't be putting any money on that bet.

"I'm sorry, but that seat is taken," I replied, setting my phone face down on the bar.

The man turned a brilliant set of sapphire blue eyes on me, a corner smile on his lips as he rested his chin in his palm, his elbow on the countertop. "I know. By Ryan Easton, right?'

"Yea, how did you —"

"He told me you'd be here tonight. He told me where I should meet you and that I would find you at the bar, probably already a beer in hand, not paying attention to the world around him."

"Ah, I see what this is. Remind me to kill him later." I drained the rest of my beer and ordered another one.

Ryan had a really fucking nasty habit of trying to set me up with people he thought I'd be interested in. He hadn't done it in a few months, so I figured he'd given up. Apparently he hadn't.

"I'm Sterling," his voice taking on a sultry tone before nodding to the bartender when he brought our drinks.

"I don't care."

"Ryan already told me your name, so there is no need to tell me yours."

"How nice of Ryan to tell you so much about me, yet I know nothing about you." I wasn't trying to be rude; Sterling did nothing wrong, but I was annoyed the more he opened his mouth. Ryan had lied to set me up, and I was going to kill him.

Sterling chuckled, unaffected by my annoyed behavior, and turned more towards me, plucking the bar menu from its stand between us and glancing over it. "Ryan works with my sister at the clinic. I mentioned I had a free night since my buddies canceled on me, and he suggested I come here instead. He said anything I purchase is on him, so why don't we both go nuts?"

While the idea of draining Ryan's wallet on a blind date sounded enticing, doing so with Sterling next to me made it less so. There wasn't anything wrong with Sterling, but he wasn't Aidyn, and I had zero interest in letting Sterling believe that this could be something more. If I was going to have a third beer, I should probably put something into my system, but I couldn't bring myself to. The food here honestly wasn't bad, but it was limited since this was a basic bar. Mainly fried foods and wings that pair nicely with a beer of your choosing. I planned to call Ryan once I left here, intending to rip him a new asshole. When the hostess at the bar took Sterling's order, he ordered a basket of pretzel bites and some onion rings, but I waved her off when she glanced at me.

"Look," I finally said. "I'm sure you're a really nice guy, but I'm simply not interested. Rack up the highest bill you can on Ryan's tab and enjoy your night."

Standing up, I grabbed my jacket from the back of the seat and pulled it on. Turning toward the exit, I felt Sterling reach out to stop me. Fighting not to recoil at his touch, I glanced at him, unable to make out the expression on his face, but his eyes moved to the seat I just vacated.

"What happened to your arm?" he asked, glancing at my injured arm.

"Nothing that won't heal in a few days. Have a good night."

I put cash on the counter for my two beers and left the bar. By the time I had returned to my car, I had tried to contact Ryan twice. When he didn't pick up the first time, I punched in the number again but only received silence. I sighed and put my forehead on the steering wheel. Ryan meant well; I knew he did, but I couldn't date someone I didn't want. What bothered me the most, at that moment, however, was that I couldn't tell what Sterling's designation was. Even with suppressants, Omega's were said to have a chemical scent mixed with hints of their pheromonal scent, yet I could detect nothing from him except leather from his motorcycle gear. So why could I scent only Aidyn Keller? What made him so fucking special that he could consume my very being?

"So you really couldn't tell that he was an Omega, huh?" Ryan asked, stabbing a grape with his fork at breakfast the next day.

"No. And stop setting me up with people. I'm not interested!" I said through gritted teeth, glaring at Ryan as I took a sip of coffee, wincing at the mediocre taste. I woke this morning feeling uneasy and a tad nauseous, despite not getting drunk last night, and just couldn't bring myself to stomach anything other than the liquid of the gods. Even if it was burnt.

"To be honest, I just thought you needed to get laid. Sterling is kind of a slut, his words, not mine. I don't think he actually does relationships, he prefers no-strings-attached sex."

"I'm also not looking to get laid, nor do I need your help to do it!" I growled low under my breath, startling an Omega nearby who glanced our way.

Ryan merely shrugged and took a bite of his toast. I woke this morning still on edge and rather embarrassed with myself and at who I was becoming. I had been unable to sleep and found that pulling my sweater out of its Ziploc helped. I had fallen asleep with it clutched close to my chest, my nose buried in its fabric, the scent of woods a sweet lullaby to my jumbled mind. I was grateful that I hadn't woken up in a rut, but I was still rather embarrassed by how clingy my Alpha was to an Omega he had zero chance with. Maybe Ryan was right, not that I would ever tell him that. Maybe I did need to sleep with someone, but the only thing I could think of at the bar last night was how badly I wished the person beside me was Aidyn.

"So, are you going to tell me what happened to your arm?" Ryan asked, snacking on the last of his bacon.

"Not in the middle of a diner during morning rush hour, no." I grumbled.

"Now I'm even more curious."

Ryan gestured to our waiter, and we paid our bills as we exited the diner. Overnight, clouds and rain brought a chilly edge to the wind and dampness to the earth around us, settling in my bones. I zipped up my leather jacket and waited for Ryan outside, my head tilted to the sky. With a jingle of the diner bell, Ryan came out with a furious expression on his face.

"How the fuck did Sterling manage to spend $156 at a fucking bar that we pay $50 tops?! What the fuck did he order???"

My laughter came deep in my chest and bubbled to the surface while we walked to his car. The diner was less than a block away from the college, so I had just parked my car there and walked over to meet him. It was Wednesday, which meant I only held office hours for a little bit to be available to my students should they need it. It's also the time I take to grade papers, put together lectures, and construct the quizzes and tests for the term. It also meant that I didn't get to see Aidyn today, and it made my Alpha antsy.

"Arm. Do I need to treat it?" Ryan finally asked; this time, his expression was serious.

"It wouldn't hurt for you to look at it, but honestly, it's not anything major." I took a deep breath before avoiding his gaze. "I...I think I went into a rut yesterday."

"You think? Either you did or you didn't, dude. You would know if you did. Wait...is this your first rut?"

"Yes," I growled, feeling heat rise into my face from embarrassment. "It was my first one, and apparently, I bit myself in the process while I knotted a cock sleeve."

Ryan stared at me, mouth open in surprise. His eyes were large as they blinked at me before he erupted into a fit of laughter, leaning against his car to hold himself up. I just glared at him, annoyance evident, until he finally got a hold of himself. His arms were wrapped around his stomach, and he panted as he looked at me before erupting into laughter again.

"Careful you don't impregnate your cock sleeve. Your Omega would be so jealous!" Ryan spat out, tears rolling down his cheeks.

"And we're done here."

I continued to walk past his car and headed in the direction of the college before Ryan stopped me, apologizing despite the large grin still on his face. Pulling the first aid kit out of the back of his car, Ryan inspected the bite marks on my arm. They still looked a little angry and tender to the touch, but the swelling had gone down drastically. He pressed around the corners of the marks to ensure there was no fluid buildup before he cleaned the wounds and applied ointment and a bandage.

"Well, you didn't bond yourself to yourself, so that's good. It would've been the first case ever if that happened, and I could've won some award or medal for making the discovery!" He laughed, closing the first aid kit. "It's not infected, so keep it clean, and it'll heal up in a few days. It's clear that your Alpha instincts kicked in, and you were trying to mark someone. It's like you're experiencing puberty all over again. You sure you couldn't scent Sterling?"

"I'm sure. You know other Alphas and Omegas frequent that bar. I couldn't detect anyone's pheromones, as if I were a Beta. I'm not sure what's going on, if I'm honest. Why can I scent one Omega but not another?"

"I wish I had answers for you. Your case is really unusual, and to experience a first rut and a first knotting this late in life isn't normal."

Luke

Upon entering my classroom Thursday afternoon, I was confused as my eyes drifted from student to student. Aidyn's woodsy scent was present, yet he was not. It was mild, as if watered down and stale, faint with an underlying scent of sandalwood and cinnamon wrapped in it, like a holiday spice. Except something seemed off about the scent as well, and I realized it was artificial, something the neutralizers couldn't filter. They were designed to filter out pheromone scents, not perfumes and cologne, leading me to the conclusion that it belonged to a Beta. Immediately my eyes zeroed in on Erik Harllow. Next to the seat that Aidyn normally occupied was a very exhausted-looking Beta, and I tilted my head in confusion. I watched him open a can of energizer coffee and pour some of it into the large iced coffee cup before he topped it off and took a sip. I couldn't help the thoughts swirling in my head as my Alpha tried to piece together the puzzle before him. Harllow was exhausted. The last time I saw Aidyn, he was experiencing a heat cycle, and Aidyn's comment about using a Beta for his last heat came flooding back to me. The idea of him sleeping with Harllow created a low growl in my chest, my teeth grinding together as I fought to regain control.

During my lecture, I prayed that Aidyn would walk in late like he had the first time I saw him. When he didn't, my Alpha grew agitated, and I could feel him begin to pace in my head like he had the night I left Aidyn in the nurse's office. I began to feel anxious and restless again, which channeled into anger when Harllow fell asleep toward the end of my class. The hustle and bustle of the students around him as they packed up their things to leave startled him awake, and he grumbled to himself while he followed suit. With the classroom mostly empty, the scent of Aidyn was more obvious, and I needed to find out if he was fucking my Omega or not.

"Mr. Harllow, a moment, please."

Harllow looked up before nodding, stuffing his laptop's power cord into his backpack, and making his way toward me. The closer he got, the stronger the woodsy scent was, mixing with the artificial scent of sandalwood and cinnamon. I fought the growl that threatened to escape from my throat; its vibration rattled in my chest, and from the shocked look on Hallows' face, I could tell he heard it.

"Yes, sir?"

"I'm just curious as to why you're sleeping in my classroom. If you're not feeling well, you should've stayed home."

"I'm sorry, sir." Harllow blushed, the red tinge to his face clashing horribly with his auburn hair. "My roommate is sick, and I stayed up most of the night trying to care for him. We share the same class, and I knew he would be furious if I didn't try to take notes."

"Your roommate?" I tilted my head. Maybe they weren't lovers. He just smelled like Aidyn through association.

"Aidyn Keller. He....got sick Tuesday, and I've been trying to care for him."

"By fucking him?" I snap, the words leaving me before I can stop them. *Fuck! Get a hold of yourself, Ellis!*

"Excuse me?" Harllow narrowed his eyes at me, his face void of any expression. His body went rigid, and I knew that was a stance meant to fight off anyone who dared to endanger someone he wanted to protect.

"Mr. Keller went into heat in my office on Tuesday afternoon. You reek of an Omega in heat under that artificial scent you wear. Are you fucking him and claiming that you're caring for him?"

"How I take care of my friend is no concern of yours, *Mister* Ellis."

Venom laced his use of my honorific, reminding me of my place, and I fought every cell in my body not to answer the challenge. I knew I had overstepped. I would be really lucky right now if he didn't march over to the dean and report me. My heart was pounding in my chest, and I knew now was the time to keep my mouth shut before I got myself into more trouble. He hadn't confirmed anything, but he was right. I had no claim to Aidyn. I stared at Harllow for a moment before I grabbed my bag, slung it over my shoulder, and headed toward the classroom door.

"How can you scent him? None of the other Alphas seemed to notice; the government requires neutralizers to filter out pheromones in buildings."

I turned to look at Harllow. He was still angry, fury etched on his face, but curiosity was in his eyes.

"Why sandalwood and cinnamon?"

"Aidyn likes it. Said his ideal Alpha would smell like autumn."

Ah. Now I got it. Harllow was a Beta in love with an Omega who wasn't the least bit interested in him, but he was still willing to try. He changed his scent to something he thought would appeal to the person he loved, and in the end, it did nothing to change his circumstances.

"How is Mr. Keller?"

"Shit. He's in pain, and he won't let me help him. He hasn't had anything to eat or drink since we got home after I picked him up from the nurse's office two days ago. At first, when he was still coherent enough, we tried his emergency suppressants, but they weren't working. If this goes on for another day without relief, I'm going to call the Omega clinic."

"*Don't*," I barked, flinching at the hardness of my tone. Omega clinics were the worst places for Omegas in heat. They could never figure out a reliable method of helping out an Omega who truly needed help. The most common method was putting them in a room with an Alpha with an implant that halted sperm production. The government had deemed this method as medically necessary for Omegas in heat, using Alphas, who have been pre-screened for cleanliness and disease-free, but most Omegas come out of their heat feeling violated. Legal rape for the greater good, in a nutshell. The alternative was being in a medically induced coma until it passes, but this also has its own drawbacks, and Omegas hate this option too; this is why they either find suppressants that work or have a pack. So, where did Aidyn fit in all of this? University policy stated that he had to be on suppressants, and every semester he has to present proof, like other Omegas.

I sat my bag down by the door, zipping off my leather jacket and handing it to Harllow. I also grabbed a business card from my pocket and used a whiteboard marker to write my personal cell number on the back of it. "I was the only Alpha around when he went into heat. I'm the one who took him to the nurse's office, and they wouldn't let me stay with him. See if the jacket helps calm the worst of his symptoms. If he doesn't improve by Saturday morning, call me. But there is no way in fuck he's going to one of those clinics."

Aidyn

I don't remember much of what went on during the past week. Despite being on suppressants, I still went into heat because, naturally, the medication didn't do its fucking job. Vaguely, I remembered an Alpha being nearby and begging for him like a pathetic animal, begging him to knot me and end my suffering. At some point, Erik brought me home and set me up in my room, but by then, the agony of my heat was almost unbearable, and I curled in on myself. He had tried to help me, but I pushed him away, my Omega crying out for the Alpha from earlier, which was probably a fevered illusion. There was a moment when suddenly the pain became tolerable, and I was coherent enough to drink water, but I still couldn't stand Erik anywhere near me. I knew it was hurting him. He had helped me in the past, but I couldn't accept him. *Where was my Alpha?*

Why wasn't he here to take care of me? I need him. Go find him! Erik only met my questions with silence.

When I finally came out of my heat Monday morning, my bedroom smelled of sweat and slick, and my body felt sticky, clammy, and sore. Once I had the strength to pull myself out of bed, I immediately opened the bedroom windows, turned on the air purifiers, and stripped the sheets and blankets off my bed. My body was sluggish and heavy, as if recovering from a horrid flu, and I had to fight through the fog to start the laundry and step into the shower to scrub my body until it was pink under the hot spray. I needed to call Doctor Easton as soon as possible; this never should've happened in the first place, and we needed to figure something out immediately. I cannot go into heat again. God, how would I explain a week's worth of absences?

Upon returning to my room, I noticed a faint scent of citrus and honey, almost like lemon tea. Looking around for my glasses, I found them on the floor by the nightstand. Placing them on my face, I began searching for the source of the scent, finding a crumpled leather jacket on the floor, its owner's scent growing stronger as I picked it up.

"That belongs to Mr. Ellis."

I turned around to see Erik leaning against the bedroom door frame, arms crossed over his chest. He looked exhausted, but his face and body language were emotionless.

"Mr. Ellis'?" But how did it get here, and why? I turned back to the jacket, holding it up and blinking at it as if it held the answers.

I struggled to sort through the fog of my memories. I had gotten into a debate with another Alpha in class and was instructed to go to Mr. Ellis' office, where I assume I went into heat. He must've taken me to the nurse's office, and they called Erik since he was my emergency contact before my parents. I must've gotten his jacket then.

"Did...did he do anything?" I tried to take an assessment of my body, anything that could give an indication of having done anything of a sexual nature. All I could feel was the ache in my muscles from an aggressive heat.

"He fucking better not have, or I will fucking kill him," Eric replied, anger lacing his words. "All he said was that the jacket might help. You were really out of it, Ade. You were refusing substances, and you were running a really high fever. Once I gave you the jacket, you clung to it like a lifeline, and 24 hours later, the worst of your symptoms stopped."

I said nothing as I sat on the edge of my bed, still staring at the jacket. I vaguely remember when my heat became less painful, cuddling against something. Was it this? I knew my Omega liked Mr. Ellis, but liking someone and calling out for them while clinging to an article of their clothing was something else entirely. I knew Erik's gaze was on me, preventing me from giving in to my desire to bury my nose in the fabric. There was a moment in our history, after one too many drinks, when Erik asked what my ideal Alpha scent was. I told him the scent of fall. Pumpkins, cinnamon, sandalwood, oak, nutmeg, and cardamom.

Fall was my favorite season, so I always pictured my Alpha would smell like my version of it. It didn't go unnoticed that a week later Erik started smelling like sandalwood and cinnamon. I had told him a few times that I wasn't interested, though I couldn't tell him that sleeping with him during a heat was a colossal mistake. He still tried in little ways, but he hadn't moved on from the week we shared my heat nearly two years ago, hoping I would come around on my own. I never expected an Alpha that scented like a cozy cup of tea on a cold day would be so... alluring to me.

"How are you feeling?" Erik asked, interrupting the tense silence.

"Like I've been hit by a semi-truck that knocked me into an oncoming train."

"Well, you don't look too bad for surviving two accidents."

I huffed out a laugh and laid down on the bed, my arm over my eyes and the jacket across my lap. Eric sat beside me before lying down too, moving the jacket. My Omega protested at having the pleasant Alpha scent removed, and I fought the urge to snatch it against me. I could feel Erik brush my hair back, a comforting action that normally pleased me, but today, something felt off and different. But I couldn't tell him to stop; I couldn't tell him that something had changed. Mr. Ellis was an Alpha that I couldn't pursue. He was my teacher, for one thing, and relationships were messy and complicated, especially between an Alpha and Omega. But I also knew nothing about him. He could be part of a pack, he could already have an Omega, hell, he could have pups on the way if he didn't have any already, and here I was, trying to figure out if I could make him my Alpha. I sighed and tilted my face, raising my arm a little to look at Erik, his gaze fixated on me. When our eyes met, he smiled softly, leaning forward and kissing my forehead.

"Why don't we order Chinese for dinner later tonight, and I'll give you the notes on Mr. Ellis' lecture? I tried to make excuses to your other teachers about you catching a nasty flu, but I doubt they will let you make up any quizzes, so you'll have to study hard for the tests and focus on the classwork. See if you can borrow notes from anyone else."

"Sounds good, thanks, Erik."

Erik got off the bed and left my room, and almost immediately, I grabbed the jacket, curling into a ball on my side and inhaling the scent, committing it to memory. I couldn't keep this item; I knew that, so the next best thing was to try to drown myself in it before I had to give it back in the morning. I really don't want to give it back.

When I left the house on Tuesday for Mr. Ellis' lecture, I was armed with an appointment booked with Dr. Easton for Friday, a full document of notes from Erik, and Mr. Ellis' jacket in a Starbucks paper bag we had lying around. When we arrived on campus, Erik and I went our separate ways as he left to attend morning classes, and I made my way to Mr. Ellis' office. My body shook from the adrenaline caused by anxiety coursing through my bloodstream. I always shook when I got nervous, and I had to assess my body to ensure it wasn't emanating pheromones. When I was satisfied that everything was good, I sighed deeply before knocking lightly on the door.

"Come in," I heard the gruff voice from beyond the wood, and my Omega reacted instantly, happy at the sound of the Alpha it wanted. I thumped my forehead against the door before turning the handle and stepping into his office.

"Mr. Keller!" The surprise was evident on his face as he saw me. He stood up and moved around his desk, his gaze roaming over my body, and my Omega shuddered at this Alpha's acknowledgment. His gaze lingered on the bag in my hand before it flicked to my face, his blue eyes watching me carefully.

"How are you feeling? Mr. Harllow told me you were ill. You can shut the door if you'd like."

I nodded, closing the door behind me.

"We both know it wasn't a real illness, Mr. Ellis, but I appreciate the deception nonetheless."

"Well. Technically, it was. A heat can present symptoms of an illness with fever and a rise in body temperature."

He continued to watch me when I didn't respond, sitting on the edge of his desk. I felt this mysteriously powerful tug in my body to greet him like an Omega should greet their Alpha. Wrapping my arms around his waist and scent-marking him, letting others know he belonged to someone. I have heard it is both pleasing for the Omega and the Alpha when they scent mark, and all I wanted was to be wrapped up in his embrace, held tightly in his arms against his broad chest. Maybe he'd kiss me, and maybe we'd — NOPE, nope, stop right now. That is a fantasy, one that I'm not going to entertain at all!

My pheromonal scent began to leak into the room, mixing with the Alpha's scent, combining citrus and pine into a pleasing mixture, my body growing warm with my thoughts. Immediately shaking them from my head and dampening my pheromones, I cut off any interest I may have in Mr. Ellis as I set the Starbucks bag on the stack of filing cabinets beside the door. His eyes darkened, but he watched the movement, lingering on the bag before returning to my face. There was an emotion there that I couldn't quite read. I readjusted my backpack and looked at him, trying to focus on his eyes as they stared through me.

"Erik told me about the jacket and how you're the one that took me to the nurse's office. I'm sorry to have put you through such a hassle."

"Why are you not on any suppressants, Mr. Keller? The university requires them."

"It's...it's not that I'm not on them." I glanced at the floor. Having to explain why was such a struggle, and I hated it. Either I was believed or I wasn't, and there was no way of knowing who would accept what I told them. "I'm a dominant Omega, sir. I'm on them. The current one is technically my sixth; however, it's just an injectable form of the oral one I was taking. They don't work like they're supposed to. I have documentation that shows that I'm on them and that I'm registered as a dominant and being treated by a physician, but for some reason, the suppressants aren't doing their job. I'm working with my doctor to find a solution that works. It's just taking longer than I want it to, and the option he's suggesting isn't viable right now, not until break or graduation, at least. I have two more semesters, and I'm done in the spring. I just need to make it through and hope to find something that will act as a band-aid until then. I have an appointment with him on Friday, and we'll see what can be done. I still need to find something long-term for when I enter the workforce."

"A dominant Omega...but that's—"

"Rare, I know."

I gave him a small smile that I knew didn't reach my eyes. He stared at me; the unreadable expression on his face from earlier was replaced with surprise and wonder. It was strange. Of the roughly thirty-two billion Omegas out there, around ten billion are male. One in twenty thousand are dominants. I just had to draw the short straw in both instances, so most didn't believe me when I told them my true designation, especially since I was born to Beta parents. Yet, here Mr. Ellis stood, looking at me as if I were something akin to a miracle.

"Did the jacket help?" he asked, breaking the silence.

"Uh. Yeah. At least, I think it did. It was bearable toward the end, so thank you for that. And thank you for taking me to the nurse's office. I just wanted to return your jacket; sorry for keeping it so long."

I turned around, my cheeks flushed with embarrassment at how awkward I was and desires flooding my brain.

"The forest."

"What?" I turned around to look at him, my hand still on the door handle. He pushed off from his desk, moving toward me, and my lungs held their breath while my heart picked up speed.

"When I was a teen, my family took a trip to the Pacific Northwest, and we hiked through Mount Rainier National Park. My father planned it during our spring vacation, so it was cold and damp. I returned a few years later on my own in the summer. You smell like the pine trees and earth during those summer days. But when you're in heat, that scent is harsher, stronger, like those days in spring."

"I-I'm sorry."

Why was I apologizing for the scent my pheromones gave off? I can't control that! Mr. Ellis stopped in front of me, his eyes fixated on mine. My heart pounded against my chest, and my breathing picked up as I lowered my gaze. He slowly slid his hand under my chin, forcing me to look at him. He leaned in, and I squinted my eyes closed. Jesus fuck, what was happening?!

"It's the most beautiful scent in the world," he said softly.

He pulled away, and a sense of disappointment washed over me. It was as if he wasn't even aware of how he was affecting me right now; he reached over and grabbed the bag with his jacket, pushing it against my chest until I grabbed it.

"Keep the jacket. Especially if it's a comfort to you."

Aidyn

"Was Mr. Ellis not in his office?" Erik asked as I sat beside him, putting the Starbucks bag between us, his voice cutting through the fog of my thoughts.

"Huh?" I asked, distracted as the devil himself entered the classroom and placed his bag on his podium. "Oh…no. He was busy; I'll have to do it after class."

"Are you feeling okay? You look a little flushed; maybe it was too soon for you to return to class. I can skip—"

"No, no. I'm fine. Really."

I took my laptop out of my bag and gave him a slight smile. I opened my document of notes for this class like I always did, yet I found that I couldn't focus on a single thing he was saying, my thoughts scattered and still in Mr.

Ellis' office. My Omega didn't know what to make of the situation that took place in Mr. Ellis' office only a few moments ago, and I couldn't get the idea out of my head that he had almost kissed me. Would his lips be soft? Would they taste like honey to go along with that beautiful tea scent of his? I wonder if his beard would be prickly and how it would feel against my — Jesus fucking Christ, what was wrong with me? Getting a hard-on in a classroom full of Alphas being taught by an Alpha—who I wanted to do unspeakable things to me—was not a good idea. The neutralizer could only do so much.

Despite my thoughts keeping me trapped in a never-ending torturous loop, I noticed out of the corner of my eye that the Alpha from the debate last week, James Forester, was glaring at me as if trying to get my attention. When I would turn my gaze to glare back, he would immediately look away, and I would find Mr. Ellis staring at me. At the end of class, Mr. Ellis left quickly, refusing to look at me before he disappeared into the crowd of students. A low growl emanated from my throat, turning a few heads as I shoved my laptop and the jacket into my bag. My Omega didn't like this one bit. How dare he ignore us! I sprinted out of my seat without saying a word to Erik and practically ran down the stairs, searching for Mr. Ellis. I spotted him as he was headed for the back rooms where his office was, and a sense of déjà vu washed over me. Catching up to him as he entered his office, I pushed the door wider for me to enter, a look of surprise on his face. Apparently, that's his only expression when I'm around, and I want to challenge him to make others.

"Mr. Keller, what are you—"

I dropped my items at the door to his office, and my feet carried me to him, pressing my body against his front and pressing my lips firmly to his as if my whole being craved him. My Omega purred inside me with happiness and bliss but was immediately replaced with anger and rejection when Mr. Ellis pushed me away from him. A battle of emotions waged war across his features before one side lost, and he launched himself, taking my face into his hands and kissing me as if he would starve without me.

I wasn't aware we had moved until I was pressed against the door of his office, a hand on my hip as he held me in place, pulling me against the front of his body. His warmth seeped into my flesh as his citrus honey scent enveloped my senses, my pheromones rising to greet his, tangling together to drive us both to the edge.

Panting, he broke from our kiss, his forehead pressing against mine, his breath creating a fog across my glasses that were slightly askew from our passion. I leaned forward, trying to capture his mouth again, but he only shook his head, pulling away, looking at me with desire and a sense of longing.

"If you don't want this, tell me now, and I'll walk out of here with an apology," I said, my gaze moving from his eyes back to his red tinted lips.

"We can't. Teachers can't be with their students," he said softly, his thumb brushing over my lips and crossing my cheek to cup the side of my face.

"Then we don't tell anyone."

He gave a low chuckle. "Your pheromones are drowning me, little fawn. They will know."

"Then we just invest in de-scenter."

In the back of my mind, a nagging voice tried to remind me that this was wrong. He was my teacher, I was his student. There were rules against this, and the relationship was unethical, say nothing of the fact that I practically forced myself onto him. But I drowned out the voice by swallowing his half-hearted chuckle in another kiss, my hips acting on their own as they thrust forward, feeling how eager and happy he was to be here with me. A moan escaped him, and he pushed with me, grinding into my own length.

Losing all sense, my hands moved toward his waist, a sound of frustration echoing in my throat as I struggled to free him from his jeans. He chuckled again at my impatience, reaching down to assist me with his belt, its metallic sound loud in the room. Pushing his pants down just far enough to pull his cock free, hard and thick in my hand as I stroked the soft, silky skin, dragging the foreskin over the head, its tip disappearing in my fist. He pulled his face away, eyes closed, and I had a full view of his pleasure, his upper teeth sinking into his bottom lip as his head tilted forward to rest on my shoulder, obscuring my view of his cock. He began to move with my strokes, my thumb finding the bead of pre-cum that coated his tip, smearing it down his length to guide his movements.

With my free hand, I removed my own cock from my pants, and his large hand instantly wrapped around my length, stroking me in rhythm with my own movements before he pulled my hand off him. Pinning it against the door, he pushed against me, our cocks sliding against each other, and I couldn't help the groan that slipped from me, pleasure blossoming through my body, my knees buckling. His hand gripped us both, trapping us together in his fist as it created a channel for us to slide through easily. I began to match him, thrusting into his fist and against the heat of his cock, my smaller cock sliding against his larger one. It was an image that would be ingrained in my memory forever, entranced by the sight as I watched us race for release in his grasp.

I could feel slick begin to pool at my back entrance, and a whine escaped me, longing for him to fill the neediest part of my body. He released my hand and immediately covered my mouth as voices filtered through the corridor, my heart skipping a beat as I watched him through lust-filled eyes. I had never been so turned on in my life, and my hips began to shudder as I approached my breaking point, feeling the knot at the base of his cock begin to swell. He adjusted his movements to cover the knot, squeezing it tightly against my shaft as I grabbed onto his biceps, hoping it would ground me. Our movements became frantic, moving myself closer and closer to the edge until I muffled out a cry into his hand, exploding in his grip, covering his cock in my release, and setting off his own. He groaned into my neck, his voice deep with pleasure, our combined seed spilling over his fist and down his swollen knot. I removed his hand from us, lifting it to my mouth, and watched those piercing blue eyes regard me as I licked his fingers, cleaning our essence from him before kneeling before him. I gently ran my tongue over the sensitive bulb, cleaning him as it began to deflate, swallowing down his softening cock.

I had never wanted to taste another partner like I wanted to taste him, rolling my tongue across the sensitive head of his cock. I moaned around him, enjoying the salty flavor of our mixed seed, my Omega preening happily at having pleasured our Alpha. His kisses tasted nothing like honey, but I would swear that his essence had an aftertaste of citrus and honey.

Doing the best we could with the tissue box from his office, we attempted to clean up the mess we had created before we sat on the floor in his office, my head on his shoulder, our hands entwined. I found that I couldn't stop touching him. I wanted to feel the warmth of his body against mine and breathe in his scent as our pheromones calmed down, returning to a baseline. He had opened the window in his office to clear out our scents and pulled on the leather jacket again. His body radiated enough heat that I couldn't help but try to cuddle closer as a chill went down my spine, curling into him as he wrapped his arms around me in silence. We waited for the late afternoon classes to be fully underway before leaving his office, and when he felt satisfied, he escorted us through the side exit closest to the staff offices and walked me to his car. With the click of a button on his key fob, he opened the passenger-side door for me.

"Let me take you home," he said softly, with a smile.

I didn't know what to make of the situation. He hadn't said anything as we recovered and waited, and insecurity had begun to set in. Maybe I had overstepped, forcing myself on him. Maybe I had put him in a position where he let instincts take over, and he regretted what just transpired. Maybe he would put in a requisition to have me removed from his class. Silent, I got into the passenger seat, watching him round the car and get in. The panic and insecurity in me quieted immediately when he took my hand, entwining our fingers together once more, using his opposite hand to push the start button on the dashboard of his vehicle. I still wondered if this weird tug-and-pull feeling between us was one-sided, and I struggled in silence as he headed toward my apartment.

I tilted my head against the window and closed my eyes, drowning in my own thoughts and questions that remained unanswered as he pulled into the parking lot of my apartment. Refusing to let things feel more awkward, I mumbled a thank you before stepping out of the car, forcing myself to pull away from him. I hated how clingy I was being, as if this meant more than just sex. It was clear this was a mistake, and I would deal with the consequences as they came.

"Aidyn." His voice stopped me as he opened his car door and got out. My eyes watched him as he moved toward me to cup my face in his hand, forcing me to look at him.

"I want to be honest with you," Luke hesitated, and I braced for the rejection that I knew was coming. Conversations of begging me not to report him, how he'll do anything I ask except be in a relationship with me. That we both got carried away and this was nothing more than simple fun. "The cliché is always, this has never happened before, but it applies here. I don't know what that was back there, and the rules of the university are very strict. As long as you are my student, I cannot see you romantically. I should tell you that this was a mistake, apologize for letting things get so far, and tell you that it cannot happen again. But I've never met an Omega who calls to me like you do. We'd have to hide our relationship from the university, from our friends."

I stared at him with wide eyes. I called to him? Is that what this feeling was? My Omega never looked at the same Alpha twice, as if he had no interest in them. Yet, he wanted to be soft and affectionate with Mr. Ellis. Care for him, be by his side, and give in to the basics of being an Omega, something I never indulged in before. That's why I was so unnerved. We had our first official encounter, and my Omega was ready to make a nest with him. I had never built a nest in my life, but my Omega was consumed by the desire to start now and build it with him. The fact that I was returning to my apartment alone and that the person living inside it with me wasn't him made me upset. But this was too soon, too fast. Wasn't it? I barely knew him, and I was diving in feet first. There was a war raging inside me, and I couldn't think! I needed him, but I also suddenly needed to be away from him.

"I want to be with you, I want us to be together. I *need* us to be together, but I won't force you to hide this. Think about it." he said softly, shrugging off the jacket and wrapping it around my shoulders. I realized why he had been wearing it. The scent was almost gone when I gave it to him, but now it clung strongly to the material once more. He leaned down to kiss me and moved away, letting me step back from the car. I dug through the zippered pocket of my backpack in a daze, fumbling out my keys, and glanced behind me one last time. I was surprised to see Mr. Ellis leaning against his car, arms crossed over his chest, waiting for me to safely enter my apartment before he drove off. No one ever waited for me. I closed the door and couldn't help but peer through the peephole immediately. I watched his shoulders slump downward, a look of pain on his face as he got into his car. He waited momentarily, and I wondered if he was fighting the same war, too. With the roar of his engine, he drove off, and I instantly felt a wave of sadness, and what I could only describe as a dull ache settled in my bones. This was not good. This was not normal. **Fuck me.**

Luke

FUCK. FUCK. FUCK. FUCKITY. FUCK.

AIDYN

Omegaprincess: · 3 years ago · *34k views*

> Are fated mates real? I met an Alpha pack for the first time over the weekend, and I can't get them out of my head. I do feel more comfortable with one more than the other two, so I was curious if he could be my fated mate.

Caffineaddictedalpha: · 3 years ago · *34k views*

> No. There is no evidence that supports the existence of fated mates. It's just a story our parents told us when we were kids to make us feel better about being different and dealing with heartbreaks at a young

age, and Hollywood decided to capitalize on it. Sorry to burst your bubble, princess.

Beta4luv: · 3 years ago · *34k views*

Nah. While I do believe there is someone out there for everyone, even us Betas, I don't believe fated mates are a real thing.

Cupcakesnacks: · 3 years ago · *34k views*

YES! I believe my Alpha is my fated mate!

CheekyBeeky: · 2 years ago · *31k views*

Why are you asking the internet?? If you believe they're your fated mate, then they are. You won't get a real answer from the internet.

Knottedluv: · 2 years ago · *31k views*

I could be your fated mate if you want me to *Winky face emoji Eggplant emoji*

LonePack: · 1 year ago · *30k views*

No matter what little fairy tale your mommy told you, you're not special. Fucking Omegas, you show them a tiny bit of affection, and instantly they think you're Romeo and Juliete.

"Asshole," I mumbled, rolling over in bed and continuing to scroll through the message boards. I can't remember when I first heard of the term 'fated mates'. I think it was part of the cartoons geared toward children with fairy godmothers and happily ever afters. I never put much stock into fated mates, but it was the top explanation on Google for 'why do I feel a strong pull toward an Alpha?'. Some comments stated that it was simply biology and Alphas and Omegas call out to each other for the survival of the species. Others proposed the theory of fated mates, depending on how strong the pull was. So naturally I fell down a rabbit hole. I nuzzled the jacket that was scrunched up in my arms, breathing in Mr. Ellis's scent. Cuddling leather wasn't comfortable, if I was honest. The material was cold and stuck to me, and the zipper was hard and even colder against my skin, but it was all I had of him. If I had my choice, I probably would've stolen a flannel shirt or a sweater, but I was grateful for what I had, and I wasn't going to seem ungrateful and ask for something I had little right to.

Mr. Ellis had dropped me off at my apartment roughly three hours ago, and I still had about an hour left before Erik got home from classes, and while he couldn't sense pheromones, I still showered as a precaution. My body felt hot and tight, and my Omega was upset. He didn't care that it was only logical that Mr. Ellis would give me space to figure this out. All he cared about was that our Alpha left us, and we felt abandoned. I knew he hadn't; I knew that, but god, I was on edge. I could still feel his lips on mine, his tongue staking its claim as he pressed his body against me. Images of his cock flashed through my memories, and I groaned as my body rose to attention, my leaking cock straining against the pajama pants I put on after my shower. I reached down and gave it a firm squeeze, my hips thrusting forward, hoping to release some of the tension. My head dropped forward in pleasure as Mr. Ellis' scent engulfed my senses, my face buried itself in cool leather, inhaling his scent.

Clothing suddenly became too tight and restrictive, and I frantically kicked off my pajamas, freeing my cock to thump against my stomach, smearing pre-cum across my belly and the bedspread as I rolled onto my front. My Omega senses kicked into overdrive. Reaching for the toy that I usually kept stashed under my bed, I could feel my entrance dampen with need. Replaying the moment in Luke's office, I positioned the toy at my entrance, slowly pushing the smooth tip inside. Gasping at the unique pressure as the toy invaded the inner parts of my body, I couldn't help spreading my legs a little wider to reach even deeper. The toy slipped in with little effort, and I began to slowly move the toy in and out of my body before pushing backward into my palm each time the toy pushed into me.

But it wasn't enough. I knew the sound of Mr. Ellis' voice as pleasure took over his body, how much sharper his scent became the more aroused he was, and how hot his breath was against my skin. The sounds he made as he climaxed, his head resting on my shoulder as he struggled to slow his breathing and rein in his pheromones. The feeling of his knot against me. It felt huge, larger than any toy I had taken before. My body longed for him to be here with me at this moment, taking his pleasure from my body, using me as he filled me over and over until I begged for him to empty inside me. The orgasm I spilled across my bedsheets was one of frustration, knowing that masturbation wouldn't be enough now. I felt empty, frustrated, and a little angry, and I knew he was to blame. I didn't have a choice. I had to see where this went because being alone wasn't enough anymore.

Dr. Easton had a last-minute cancellation at the Omega Clinic Wednesday afternoon, so I texted Erik, saying I would be skipping the English lecture for the doctor and would probably head home after. When my name was called, I followed the nurse into the exam room, where she took my vitals, blood pressure, and weight. Over the past six months, the physical exam and lab work process had become second nature during these visits, and I just moved through the steps robotically. Dr. Easton entered the room shortly after the nurse had left, instantly reviewing my chart with a smile as he glanced over the latest paperwork.

"If it isn't the Omega who challenges my degree. Before we get into it, why don't you tell me the reason you're here less than a month after your last visit?"

I smirked at Dr. Easton as he took his place on the rolling chair next to the computer and laid my file down on the table, frowning at something on the chart before turning to the screen and prattling away at the keyboard. This was one of the reasons I honestly liked Dr. Easton. He preferred to listen to the patient's own words before creating a plan of action instead of basing it off of words on a sheet of paper. After countless doctors who refused to listen to me, it was refreshing to have one invested in my case as much as I was, even if it was out of medical curiosity. It helped create an understanding and a calm environment where I didn't feel like I was going crazy from the lack of answers.

"Apparently, switching to the shot suppressant didn't work, and I ended up in a week-long heat. Emergency suppressants didn't help either. This heat happened while I was at school. That cannot happen again."

"Mr. Keller, were you exposed to an Alpha during that time?"

That's a weird question. "I mean, I'm always exposed to them. They're everywhere, and I have classes with many of them."

"Let me rephrase. Were you intimate with an Alpha at all during that time?"

"Only yesterday," I blushed, "but the fever started before I got to class. I thought it was just a symptom of the suppressant. Sometimes I feel like I can't cool down my body temperature when I'm adjusting to new medications."

"So you weren't intimate with them before your heat?"

"No, sir. However, I was around them when I went into heat, and my roommate was able to get an article of their clothing halfway through the week."

Was I talking too much? Rambling about unnecessary details? It didn't seem to matter to Dr. Easton, who noted everything I said in my file on the computer.

"Did your heat last longer than normal or shorten after the clothing item?"

"Honestly, I'm not sure. The last heat I had was about eight days long. This one was about six days, and I don't know when I got the clothing item. I don't remember much. I remember not being in so much pain after a while, and then I came out of my heat."

"And during intimacy yesterday, was penetration involved?"

"No. Does that matter?" I could feel my Omega bristle at the question, as logic failed me again. I knew he was asking for a medical reason and not because he was a pervert or wanted the gory details about what transpired between me and Luke, but my Omega wanted to keep those details to himself. No one should know what happened between me and my Alpha.

"Per your last visit, you want to remain on suppressants until you finish college, and your Alpha knows this, correct?"

"He's not mine, and he doesn't get to dictate what goes into my body." I narrowed my eyes at Dr. Easton. Again, I knew he didn't mean to be rude, but it certainly came off as dismissive. He only smiled as he finished something on the screen.

"We need to discuss a few things, Mr. Keller, and it's up to you if you want to relay them to this Alpha. An experimental suppressant is available on the market right now, but very few Omegas have tried it. I didn't want to suggest it at your last visit because it'll take some work on your part, and it's still in the trial phase."

"What would I have to do?"

"Stop all suppressants. We use an IV drip to flush out their remnants in your system, like we had discussed before. Once the suppressants have left your system, you will go into heat; that's unavoidable. Once you've had your cycle, we can start you on the new suppressants, but they'll take time to adjust to your body. The side effects aren't really different from any others you've had in the past, but I'm hoping with you being a dominant, this will help you. But your Alpha will also need to help you through your heat. Even if you don't have penetrative sex, having an Alpha being intimate with you will help the worst of the symptoms. I think you went into heat while on the current suppressant because it wasn't strong enough to combat whatever Alpha you encountered. The spike in your pheromones leads me to believe that they were a very strong Alpha, and your Omega responded positively to that. Almost as if they, too, were dominant.

"I believe the perfect time to do this would be when you're not in school. If you want it done sooner, I suggest we shoot for your winter break, and then you return in the spring on new suppressants. You would stop the suppressants on the last day of your classes the week before winter break, come in the first day of your break, and we'll hook you up to the IV. You'll probably go into heat that night, if not the next day; after your heat is over, you'll take the first dose of the new suppressant instead of putting you on one you've already tried. But you're hyper-fertile during your heats being a dominant Omega, so even if this Alpha has the implant, it's best if they use condoms to be extra safe."

It was a big ask. I'd be putting a lot of trust in Mr. Ellis if I asked this of him. Did I have the right to do so? Technically, I could ask Erik to help me out. I could use the jacket Mr. Ellis gave me and the knot sheath we still had from the last time Erik helped me, but the idea made my skin crawl. My brain decided to zero in on a bit of information that Dr. Easton had dropped ever so casually.

"Another dominant?"

"It's rather rare to see two dominants in the same state, let alone in the same orbit of each other. I have a best friend that's dominant as well. The likelihood that three are in the same area is rather unusual. Like, I should go buy a lottery ticket at lunch, rare."

"I'll talk with the Alpha, but either way, I'll go through with this, with or without his help," I said, smiling at the doctor.

"Without will be painful and very difficult. Are you prepared for that?" Dr. Easton asked, eyeing me firmly.

"Yes."

"I need to talk to you about something," I said, storming into Mr. Ellis' office Thursday morning without so much as knocking before pushing the door open.

Luke's head snapped up at my entrance, but his eyes instantly softened when he saw me, making me stop in the middle of opening his door. No one had ever looked at me like that, and he didn't even seem pissed that I barged in like I owned the place. At that moment, I wanted to run to him and climb onto his lap, bury my face into his neck, and inhale his scent. I was so focused on asking this huge favor that I forgot who I was asking it of.

He wore a burgundy cardigan over a cream-colored t-shirt, and he had ditched the dress pants I last saw him in for dark denim jeans. God, he looked amazing, and all I could do was watch him as he moved toward me. He reached behind me and closed the door, his eyes not leaving my face. I wanted to lean against his body, stand on my tiptoes, and kiss him. But I fought the desire that burned like fire through me. I didn't want to be clingy; I didn't want to be a needy and pathetic creature after sharing a single moment of intimacy. That's how you scare people away, and I didn't want that. What I was about to ask for was something that I had no right to, given the nature of our relationship, or lack of relationship. Fear of rejection and offending him had my words stalling in my throat, unease creeping up my spine. It was a medical necessity, as far as I was concerned, and if this experimental suppressant worked, then I wouldn't have to worry about my future. I was also scared of uncertainty, considering my last heat left Erik wounded and bruised. He hadn't complained; in fact, he grinned proudly at the marks and showed them off to an annoying degree. It still made me feel like I was too much during my cycle, too feral. I didn't want to hurt anyone, and if Mr. Ellis couldn't withstand it, would I be able to move on if he decided I wasn't the one for him? My brain swarmed with 'what ifs' that had no place here. We were figuring things out, so why did my brain act like it was forever with Mr. Ellis? My Omega let out a soft whimper as I ran my hands over his chest, distracting myself as I admired the sweater.

"Can...can I have this after class? I don't like the jacket."

IDIOT! I quickly chastised myself. *Be grateful for what you have, and don't be stealing other people's clothing!* Before I could stammer out an excuse and correct my statement, Mr. Ellis chuckled and leaned down, nuzzling my neck.

"Only if you give me something next time," he muttered, his lips brushing against my neck, and I shuddered.

"Take me home again, and you can have anything you want."

"Hmm, anything, little fawn?"

My nose crinkled slightly, and I had a foggy memory of having heard him call me that before. He pulled away as I tilted my head upward towards him. "Why do you call me that?"

"You smell like the forest." He shrugged as if it was plain as that. "Your hair reminds me of a new deer with curiously green eyes that watches everything around you. It just seemed to fit.'"

I couldn't help but smile as I followed him, crawling into his lap as he sat down at his desk again, indulging in what I had wanted to do the moment I walked into his office. As if it was the most natural thing in the world, he leaned backward, giving me more space while also wrapping his arms around my waist to hold me in place. Jesus fuck, I didn't want to move from this spot ever.

"But I doubt wanting to steal my sweater is why you came today, Mr. Keller. Did you think more about my request?"

"It's Aidyn, Ade if you truly want. But yes, I have a counter request, and it will put you in a difficult position. I spoke with my doctor yesterday about my suppressants. We have a battle plan, but in order to try the new ones, I will have to go off mine and have a cycle. He suggested that I have you with me. Even if we don't have sex, he said that having an Alpha there will help."

"And you want me there?" Mr. Ellis' eyes were wide in surprise.

"I know it's a huge ask, and I know we're just trying to figure things out. But —"

"When will this happen?" he asked, cutting me off. "And is it safe?"

"Dr. Easton assured me that it was safe, and he thinks it's best to do it over winter break."

"Easton? Ryan Easton?"

My gaze immediately snapped to him, confirming his question as he regarded me, processing what I told him. Multiple expressions danced across his face as his gaze lowered to the ground. He released an arm around me to put his head in his hand as he thought about the information I had just dumped onto his lap. The scent of cloves cut through the air, though it was faint, alerting me to the fact that he was upset. And my Omega didn't like it, but I expected this.

"Forget I asked. It was unkind of me."

"I'll do it." Luke's head snapped up, panicked. "I'll help you in any way I can. If I'm not there, how do I know you'll be safe? I don't want anyone else to touch you. But I also can't have my best friend treating my Omega."

"You're the dominant he told me about?"

Now, it was my turn to stare at Mr. Ellis. While I was shocked to learn that my doctor was his best friend, who now knew I was intimate with, my Omega preened happily at being called his.

"The Eastons are family friends and have been treating the Ellis pack for as long as I can remember. But I don't need him to know every detail of my love life. I'll look into another doctor for you once you switch to the new suppressant. But we won't tell him that I know you."

"That's fine with me. I imagine that could make things awkward for you. He says you're powerful, though. He doesn't know it's you, just that I encountered a powerful Alpha. And that I was 'intimate' with him."

Mr. Ellis scrunched up his nose before chuckling and cupping my head in his palm. "That's because, just like you, I'm also dominant. I'll help you. I'm honored you asked, but what would you have done if I had said no?"

I shook my head, adjusting myself in his lap until I could rest my head on his shoulder. "I would've gone it alone. You were the only Alpha I wanted there. You'll have to wear a condom, though. Even assuming you have an implant, being a dominant Omega makes it really easy to get pregnant, and I can't have that happen right now. I want to try this relationship with you, even with this week looming over our heads. It's a huge ask and a lot of trust, but I don't want anyone else there."

"I could believe the suppressants weren't working for you because the implant didn't work for me. It was just putting something in my body that was rejected immediately, but if I have to double up on condoms, I'll do so. I don't want to put any pressure on you during that time, or on our relationship."

"There is something you need to know before you fully commit to this, though." A heated blush crept onto my cheeks, and I closed my eyes, as if it would stop the embarrassment. He needed to know what he was getting into, yet I didn't want to scare him away from me. "My heats can be intense. The last person I spent my heat with came out bruised and exhausted. He was covered in scratches and bites, and I swear he was about to keel over. I understand if that sounds intimidating and you don't want to do this with me."

Mr. Ellis pulled my head away from his chest, leaning in to kiss me softly until I opened up for him, wrapping my hands in his cardigan. Finally giving in, I straddled his lap, releasing pheromones to meet his as we embraced, drowning me in his cozy scent. Breaking from the kiss was the hardest thing I had to do when his phone's alarm went off, its irritating sound splitting through the room. Sighing, Mr. Ellis bumped his forehead against mine before standing up, effortlessly lifting me up with my legs around his waist. The swelling in his pants hinted at how excited he was to have me there, and I couldn't help but grind my hips on his length. He groaned and turned a harsh gaze my way, setting me on the desk to silence his phone.

"You're mine going forward, little fawn. Teasing your Alpha before he lectures a class isn't in your best interest."

All I could do was give him the biggest grin of my life.

Luke

De-scenters need to be banned and burned in hell, and rolling down the windows in my car only helped marginally air out the acidic scent surrounding us. At least I had the forethought to pull off the cardigan Aidyn liked before spraying us both with the heinous chemicals. I knew there was a reason we had to use it—to make less trouble for Aidyn. It made sense, but I didn't like it all the same. I hated that he sat in my class, listening to my lecture, and the only scent from him was chemicals. I knew other students used de-scenters or the fake pheromone spray that companies produced for people like Harllow, and normally I wasn't fazed by them. Today, however, was different. I couldn't scent the one person that had changed my life so much already.

I was so distracted that I honestly didn't remember what I taught in class, going through the lesson methodically with the notes from the previous years of teaching, hoping I had made the class interesting. But my head was back in my office with Aidyn wrapped around me, his body warm and soft against mine as he felt perfect in my arms. After class, I returned to my office for the cardigan when my phone pinged with an incoming email to my faculty address. There was no text to the email, just a simple picture of my car, and I couldn't help but smile. Without looking at the sender's email, I knew who it was from, and it reminded me that I needed to give Aidyn my personal number.

I couldn't help the big grin that spread across my face as I spotted Aidyn leaning casually against the side of my car. He had his eyes trained on the path to the parking lot, hoping to spot me as I approached, and a grin that mirrored my own spread across his face as he watched me. Instead of going to the driver's side, I walked right up to him, my eyes darting around us to make sure no one was around before kissing him. A surprised squeal escaped him before he leaned into the kiss, gripping the belt loops at my hips. Pulling away was practically torture, but I didn't want to increase the chance of being caught.

Unlocking my car, I opened the passenger door for Aidyn before placing my cardigan in his lap once he was buckled in. As I crawled into the drivers side, it didn't escape my attention that Aidyn instantly began toying with the buttons on the cardigan absentmindedly, feeling and petting the fabric as if it were a soft cat while I pulled out of the university parking lot. My Alpha stood a little taller, chest puffed out, at the happiness my clothing brought to the Omega, and I took his hand in mine, squeezing it lightly. We had rolled down the windows as we sped out of the inner community, the chemical scent beginning to overwhelm the small enclosed space between us. It didn't do much, but it made it easier to think, and my mild headache began to disappear.

Aidyn lived about a half hour from campus, but the trip seemed so much shorter as I pulled into a guest parking spot closest to his unit. Aidyn unbuckled himself before opening the door but turned to me when he noticed I was still buckled into my seat.

"Are you not coming in, Mr. Ellis? Remember, I have to give you back your jacket?" he grinned.

"Luke, please, when we're not at school. And I really shouldn't…" I breathed, shaking my head. I watched as disappointment flashed across his face before he slid a blank mask over his expression. "It's not that I don't want to. Lord knows I do. But I want this relationship to build on each other and not on sex. I'm not assuming that's what would happen, but I don't know if I can behave. Especially when I know Harllow won't be home for a few hours, and my Alpha screams at me to cover you in my scent to wash away those chemicals."

"And here I thought I was just being a needy Omega, wishing you would do exactly that the whole ride over. I didn't want to say anything that could possibly make you regret this or me. I'm already asking so much of you."

I raised my eyes to look at Aidyn, a slight blush on his cheeks. He was avoiding my gaze, looking down at the cardigan in his lap and fingering the material again as he fidgeted under my gaze. I reached over and brushed his hair behind his ear before placing my hand under his chin and forcing him to meet my gaze.

"I won't regret this or you. Ever. I want to do right by you and not force you to do anything you're not ready for or uncomfortable with. You're not asking too much of me, little fawn. I wish you would ask more if you have need of me, and if it's in my power, I will give it to you happily. I told you, you're mine going forward, and I want to take care of you."

"Sooo, if I asked you to come in and just cuddle on the couch with me for a bit, drown me in your scent, would you do it?"

"With pleasure. I know many Omegas turn their whole home into their nest. Are you sure you want me in your space so soon?" I asked, tilting my head to the side.

"I've actually never built a nest," Aiden responded, blushing and avoiding my gaze. "If I ever did, it would probably be in my bedroom since I don't live alone, but there is no real sanctuary. You wouldn't know I was an Omega just by looking at my bedroom. I don't want to rush this, either, but my Omega is trying to run before he can walk. You'll be helping me immensely in a few months, but I don't want my first time with you to be during my heat. I want to remember it. As you said, sex isn't what I'm assuming either, but how do I know that my Omega instincts aren't trying to rush this?"

Unbuckling my seat belt, I leaned across the middle console, pulling Aidyn to me. I pressed my lips against him, holding his face to me as I poured as much emotion and love into the affection as I could, releasing my pheromones to soothe the frantic look in his eyes as anxiety began to cloud them. This man was my undoing. It gave me an odd sense of comfort knowing that he was battling the same thoughts as I was. That we were on the same page, and it was clear that we needed to work on our communication skills so that we didn't isolate each other, drowning in our insecurities. I was holding back every Alpha urge I had for him because we just began whatever this was, and I didn't want to scare him away. I wouldn't survive it if he never contacted me again. Pulling away, I looked at him, running my hands through his soft blond hair, and smiled at the slightly dazed look in his eyes.

"You can't rush this; that is impossible. We go at our own pace, as slow or as fast as we want or need to go. I'll take my lead from you, little fawn."

"Then come inside. Please." I could hear the slight begging tone at the end of his sentence, and there was no way I was going to deny him anything.

The scent of Aidyn was *everywhere*. It mingled with the artificial scent his roommate wore, but my Alpha honed in on his scent the second I stepped into Aidyn's apartment. My Omega's scent clung to the air as if a candle burned in the room, filling the space and making my dick harden at its inviting embrace. This was probably a huge mistake. Probably. He mumbled something about making myself at home while he fetched my jacket and watched him move down the short hallway that was to the right of the front door, taking my cardigan with him. I looked around the small living room and couldn't help but smile.

The bookcase on which the TV sat held an assortment of books, its three shelves bowing slightly with their weight as if someone had run out of room and began stacking them horizontally across the vertical books. Every nook and cranny was filled with a book. Everything from romances to detective novels to sci-fi and mystery, with the occasional horror. I noticed a murder mystery book I enjoyed a few years ago. It was about a Beta detective who had lost his partner and had been experimented on in a lab, hoping to make him an Alpha. He had heightened senses but wasn't a complete Alpha, and he finds out that his partner had been murdered by the mafia, whose leader is an Omega, whom the detective falls in love with. I had stopped reading it some years ago, no longer finding the time, and the author had stopped writing a few years back due to health issues.

Another shelf beside the bookcase housed an assortment of DVDs and pictures. Pictures of Aidyn and Harllow on summer break at a beach, Aidyn graduating high school, and an image of a very drunk Harllow wearing a birthday crown. I knew they were best friends, but I wouldn't say I liked the implication that, to outsiders, they looked like a couple. I knew Harllow wanted that, but I got the impression that Aidyn didn't. And if he did at one point, he didn't now. A fresh wave of Aidyn's scent entered the room, and I turned around to find Aidyn standing nervously by the couch. He had changed into a pair of loose black lounge pants paired elegantly with a large, chunky navy sweater that gave him a cozy and snuggly vibe.

"You look comfy," I smirked, watching him blush under my praise.

"I wanted to get rid of the de-scenter. I don't have any clothing that would fit you, or I'd offer you a change of clothing too," he responded, depositing my jacket and a buttoned flannel onto the back of the couch. I recognized the flannel instantly as the one he had worn the day he had turned my life upside down. I wonder if he remembered, but he didn't say anything to suggest so. He moved to the couch, his hand resting on the spot he wished for me to occupy. When I sat down, he instantly threaded his fingers through mine, tilted his head onto my shoulder, and sighed contentedly.

My Alpha took pride in the touch, that his Omega was happy in my presence. I met his pheromones with my own, and I was grateful that Harllow was a Beta, so he would never know that I was here as we bathed each other in our scents, filling the room. Without having to be told, I could tell that Aidyn was perfectly content to sit in silence. Affection and touch were all he craved, and I was happy to meet that need. My thumb rolled little circles over the back of his hand, my head tilted backward, resting on the back of the couch, eyes closed.

Aidyn snuggled a little closer, settling into my body's silence and warmth before pulling his legs up onto the couch to curl them up beside him. I sunk further down on the couch, releasing my hand from his grip to drape my arm around him so he could nestle against my chest. He removed his glasses, setting them on the coffee table in front of us before tucking himself into my side, his face nuzzling my neck and breathing in my scent. My dick rose to attention, and I cursed its over-eagerness. It didn't give a damn that I wanted to take things slowly or that I was comfortable where I was with him pressed against me. I shifted slightly, trying to get my cock into a better and more comfortable position so it would stop straining against the zipper of my jeans, and Aidyn chuckled beside me.

In a single fluid motion, he straddled my lap, staring at me as he pressed his pelvis into mine, and I could feel his hard-on pressed against me. I felt better knowing that he was just as happy as I was to be in this moment with each other. He leaned forward, rubbing his face along my cheek before nuzzling my neck again, and it occurred to me at that moment that he was scent-marking me, just as he had done during his heat, and my heart melted. He was making it clear to anyone I may encounter after leaving this apartment that I belonged to someone. That I belonged to him. I reached for him, cupping his face in my hands as the beginnings of my Alpha's purr rumbled through my chest. I pressed my lips to Aidyn's, swallowing the low moan he emitted at our touch, devouring it as if it was the most decadent thing in the world. He opened his mouth to me so that I could taste him, my fingers slipping into his soft hair as our breaths mixed with one another. A slow external vibration rumbled across my chest, and I pulled back, surprised, staring at Aidyn with large eyes. He blushed as his Omega answered my purr with his own. Someone was purring for me. *He* was purring for *me*. Tears filled my eyes, and I let out a soft, relieved chuckle, my forehead pressed against his. A purr was important to an Alpha and Omega dynamic. It's used to calm each other down and to express anger, possessiveness, love, happiness, and contentment. I had given up long ago that I would ever purr and, in turn, that someone else would purr for me, to feel the vibrations of another.

"You have no idea the gift you have just given me." I breathed softly, looking at him with a smile.

Tucking my face into Aidyn's neck, my beard scratched against his soft skin, and his breath hitched at the sensation. A soft moan escaped his throat as I placed tender kisses on the sensitive skin, nipping slightly. His sound was a mixture of a chuckle and a moan above me, made foreign by the purr that still rumbled strongly. He ran his hands through my hair, tugging on the last strands at the base of my skull.

"I want to take you out to dinner. A proper date."

"I can't tonight." He shook his head, leaning into my body again. "But Erik has a family game night every Friday. He typically heads over there right after class, which goes into the early morning hours, so he spends the night."

"So there is a potential for a sleepover," I grinned wickedly at him, hugging him closer to my body.

"If that is your wish." He smiled, returning my suggestive grin.

"No, little fawn. I won't rush you into anything, even staying the night."

"I'll tell you what," he said, sitting up straight and looking at me with a sudden serious expression on his face. "Get condoms anyway. If we use them, great; if not, we have them for when we do."

"Mmm, very logical of you."

"I try." He reached over, grabbed his phone off the coffee table, and handed it to me. "Put your number in. I don't want to have to send you an email every time I want to speak to you."

"For the best. Those emails are monitored."

I'm grateful he remembered because it had completely slipped my mind. We exchanged phone numbers before realizing that Harllow was due home within the next half hour. Aidyn walked me to my car, our hands interlaced with each other. I was already missing him and hadn't even left the damn parking lot. Longing and sadness filled his eyes as he looked up at me, and I took the opportunity to scent him once more, rubbing my face along his neck and face, followed by the inside of each wrist. I held him in my arms again, cupping his face and kissing him softly before bumping our foreheads together.

"Tomorrow?" I whispered.

"Tomorrow," he confirmed, nodding.

Luke

Even the differences between the designations are visible in the types of condoms you can buy. Betas have access to fancy condoms that are 'ribbed for their pleasure' and 'ultra-thin, barely there' or 'additional lubricant' to spice things up a little. Alpha condoms come only one way, with a slight difference and no extra lubricant or ribbing. Regardless of designation, all condoms come in the standard sizes of small, medium, large, and extra large; however, Alpha condoms were designed with extra latex around the base to accommodate the swelling of a knot. The size of the condom correlates with the size of your knot at full swell, and I have never measured something that never existed until now.

Large seemed to be the standard for Alphas of my proportioned size, but as a dominant, that meant my knot was bigger. Unable to decide, I grabbed a box of twelve in a large and an extra large, just to be safe. I checked my watch as I got in the car, and nerves rattled through me when I realized it was almost time to pick up Aidyn. I hadn't gone on a date in years and wanted this to be perfect. Aidyn was right; sex didn't have to be on the table, and I was okay with that. I just wanted to show him a good time and treasure him the way an Omega should be treasured. The way I wanted my Omega to be treasured.

I sent Aidyn a text, notifying him that I was down the street and should be there in under five minutes, only to find him outside his apartment. He was dressed in a pair of dark navy jeans, gray shoes, and a gray sweater that zipped up at the breast. He had layered it over what appeared to be a cream-colored button-up. His hair was pushed back like he had run his hands through it with some product to give it a casual yet styled look, and the light in his eyes, when he spotted my car, made my heart melt. Fuck, he looked amazing.

I hadn't done so badly myself, pairing black jeans with black ankle boots and a forest green sweater that reminded me of the color in his eyes. He climbed into my car, and I couldn't help but lean over, kissing him in greeting. He deepened the kiss, sliding his tongue into my mouth, exploring my taste until I groaned. When he pulled away, I was breathless and hard as hell, and he had a large, smug grin on his face.

"Careful, or I'll spank that smug look off you," I mumbled, putting the car into gear.

"My safe word is tea," he teased back, and my cock throbbed at the challenge.

"Why tea?" I knew he was joking, but I was curious if there was some truth behind it.

"It's what you smell like. Citrus and honey, like a comforting cup of tea."

I was his safe word? Lord, give me strength! I gave him a side eye as I turned onto the main street, making a show of palming my cock to readjust it and noticing Aidyn watching the movement, his eyes transfixed on my crotch and the noticeable swell there.

"You get to choose how tonight goes," I said, pretending as if I didn't want to find a hotel or take him back to my place and sink into him immediately. At least I have the condoms for that now. "Fancy date or not-so-fancy date."

Aidyn grinned as he thought about it. "And you have plans regardless of what I choose on such short notice?"

"Yep!"

"Less fancy then. I'm not a big fancy person, not someone to go all out for."

"That's where you're wrong," I mused, turning to ensure I could switch lanes safely, and headed to our first destination.

I pulled into a local revolving sushi restaurant that I frequented often. I loved this place. The little dishes of fish and rolls moved along a conveyor belt, each plate a different color that correlated with the price of the dish based on the quality of the fish and the amount of food. Anything Asian is a comfort cuisine for me. If it's not breakfast food, it's probably Asian. If I'm having a bad day, I'll order from a local Chinese or Korean place for a fix, but if I'm having a really bad day, then I'll get sushi. Something special? I'll get sushi. Want to spend time with someone special? Sushi. Suffice to say, I'm in a constant state of craving sushi. After discussing it with Aidyn, we decided that there was no reason for two people to take up a booth, and we were escorted toward the bar in the corner. It was somewhat early, with most people still getting off work, so the restaurant wasn't very busy, allowing us to converse without difficulty. Once we sat down and ordered our drinks, I couldn't help but grin when he requested a set of children's chopsticks.

"I have tried several times to master the skill," he explained. "I've even watched videos on how to teach kids how to use them, and nothing. Growing up, I spent a lot of time at my grandparents' house. My grandfather was a carpenter by hobby, something he picked up in high school, he said. My grandmother often made veggie stir-fry because it was quick and easy, and she used the vegetables in their garden. He once crafted a set of chopsticks for me, gluing two pieces of wood to a clothespin. I loved that set. Sadly, it got lost when they had to move into a care home. I would use a fork, but you can't really do that with sushi."

He shrugged, reaching up to the conveyor belt, and choosing a plate with a look of excitement. It was an odd choice, and I tilted my head in confusion. On a bed of rice, wrapped in a belt of seaweed, sat a spongy yellow substance, and in all my years of eating sushi, I had no idea what on earth it was. He found the eel sauce that was on the bar next to the soy sauce and drizzled it across the yellow sponge.

"What on earth?"

"Try it," he said, picking up one of the pieces with his child-sticks and cupping a hand under it to catch anything that may fall.

I looked at him curiously before leaning in and taking the item into my mouth. My brain couldn't make sense of what I was eating. First, the yellow product was cold, while the rice was warm. It had a spongy yet fluffy texture, its sweet flavor enhanced by the eel sauce, and yet the flavor was also familiar in a way I couldn't place.

"Like it?" he asked hesitantly. I nodded, looking around for more and seeing that it was a ways off. I'd make sure to grab a plate when it came back around. "It's Tomago. Basically, it's a Japanese rolled sweet omelet. Every place makes it slightly different, but it's just seasoned beaten egg. My favorite kind is made with sake. It's one of my favorite things to get when I get sushi, even though it's not actually sushi. I attempted to make it at home a few times but always failed, so I gave up. If I can find blocks of it at Asian-international markets, I'll snag a few blocks and force myself to cut it up so that I'm not just munching into it. Erik leaves them alone because he thinks it's cheese, and he's lactose intolerant."

While I know Harllow didn't stand a chance, not with me in the picture, I still didn't like the idea that someone living with Aidyn was also in love with him and could only smile as Aidyn mentioned his roommate. I wonder if Aidyn knew how Harllow felt, but I couldn't bring myself to ask because, honestly, I didn't want to know the answer. But at the same time, Aidyn was here with me, so the answer was meaningless.

When our stomachs had become exotic aquariums and were too full to add more, we stacked our plates up by color, ranging from least expensive to most expensive according to the charts they had posted, and I paid the bill before Aidyn had a chance to reach for the clipboard. He wrinkled his nose at me, and I smirked as I signed the receipt, and we left the restaurant.

The sun was beginning to set as we made our way back to the car, painting the sky in shades of purples, pinks, and oranges. Unlocking the back driver-side door, I grabbed the bouquet I had picked up earlier, instantly nervous as I awkwardly handed them to Aidyn. Growing up, my parents always told me to bring flowers to the person you were interested in, and I had debated a great deal on whether or not I should purchase them. Aidyn stared at the flowers as he got into the passenger seat. They weren't anything special, just a mixture of white flowers that I didn't know the name of, with a few blue daisies placed for a pop of color. Moving to the driver's seat, my brain was rather unkind to me, insisting that he hated them and that it was weird to give another man flowers.

"It's okay if you hate them. I didn't know if you liked —"

"I once read that the only time a man receives flowers is at his funeral, and they don't even get to enjoy them. I remember thinking how accurate and depressing that statement was, having never received flowers myself. Men don't really give each other flowers, so I simply wasn't expecting them. They're beautiful." He reached for a daisy, pulling it out by the stem and breaking off a part to shorten it before tucking it behind his left ear and smiling at me. "Blue daisies are actually my favorite flower. Thank you."

"You look beautiful," I said softly, touching the petals lightly to avoid ruining them. My heart swelled with affection as he blushed at my compliment. I loved watching him react to me as if no one had complimented him or cherished him before. "B or C?"

"What?" Aidyn asked, suddenly confused.

"Pick a letter. B or C."

"B?"

"B it is!" I grinned at him before pulling out of the restaurant parking lot, ignoring the curious and confused look Aidyn gave me. I was having fun. Maybe a little too much fun, but it's been amazing. I enjoyed planning out the date locations and being with him. We didn't have to worry about anyone knocking on my office door or Harllow coming home early and catching us. I got to be in the moment with someone I liked and felt like my heart would burst from overjoyment.

Pulling into the bookstore parking lot, I checked the time on my watch to ensure they didn't close soon before stepping out of the car. Aidyn was already out of the car again before I could open the door for him, but he moved to my side, sliding his hand into mine.

"B for Bookstore. Clever. What was C?"

"Cat Cafe." I smiled. "I love animals, and I thought it would be fun to pet cats and drink coffee after dinner."

"Either way, I would've walked out with something. This way, we didn't have to make any unplanned stops for pet supplies."

A deep laugh rumbled through me, briefly picturing what it would be like to raise a cat with Aidyn. The images brought on an odd warmth that blossomed through my chest, and I had to shake it from my mind as we entered the bookstore. As children, we grew up being told to whisper in libraries, and I feel this carried over to bookstores as well, noise dampened by the pages of books. As long as you're not being obnoxious, you can talk at a normal volume level, but you forget that when you see how quiet bookstores are. You feel you have to whisper.

"Alright," I said, looking at him. "I assumed the books in your apartment belonged to you, so I thought we could come here. But the idea was, I could pick a book out for you, and you pick a book out for me."

Aidyn's eyes brightened at the idea. "But what if I pick something you hate?"

"Judging by your bookshelf, that's not possible. But if you do, I'll still love it because you picked it out. I have no trigger warnings to avoid, and I read everything."

"Same, but I am a sucker for a good dark romance. No triggers here either."

"Sounds good. Let's meet at the register in twenty minutes?" I suggested.

He smiled. "Make it thirty. I want to take my time."

Before he could run off among the stacks, I stepped into his space, lifting his face to mine. I couldn't resist the urge to scent mark him, dragging my nose along his cheek, down his neck, and down into his hair. The scents of the forest mixing with the daisy in his hair caused my Alpha to release a pleased sound from low in my chest. Somewhere along the way, my eyes had closed, and I opened them to find Aidyn had closed his as well, enjoying my marking. With his eyes still closed, I leaned forward and placed a tender kiss on his soft pink lips before stepping away. He opened his eyes, slightly unfocused as he glanced at me, and I headed for the romance stacks with a wink.

Over the past few years, the romance genre had blossomed, making other sections a little smaller so that romance could take over. Despite this, outside of Pride Month, when certain titles were pulled from the shelves to display, it was rather hard to find gay romance readily available. Not to say I read only gay romances, but it was something I easily identified with and enjoyed the romances that I never thought I'd have. It was a way for me to explore my sexuality. I never feared coming out to my parents. Bringing home a man was treated the same way as if I had brought home a woman. However, I was forced to have a conversation with my parents upon entering adulthood, that it was expected of me to set aside my preferences for the sake of duty. Male Omegas were rare, and in our social circle worthy of my parents' status, they were practically nonexistent.

Glancing up to search for Aidyn, I located him by the blue daisy still tucked behind his ear as he wove through the fiction shelves. We had known each other less than a month, and I felt like I had known him my whole life, as if I had been waiting for him. Internally, things were progressing quickly for me, yet something was drawing me toward him. When we were apart, it felt like there was something missing inside me. But I was also afraid. Of him, of myself. He had the power to destroy me, and I was often irrational and obsessed with him, so I wondered if I was going insane. My Alpha was sure he was ours, our mate, our everything. My Alpha cared little about the timing and pace of a relationship, eager to mark him, form a Mates Bond with him, and tie us together for the rest of our lives. My Alpha was ready for that bond the moment Aidyn stepped into my classroom.

But what if he didn't feel the same way I did? What if these feelings were one-sided? He mentioned he was worried about rushing us, but that didn't quite mean he felt the same way I did. My parents wouldn't accept him. Keller wasn't a name I had grown up hearing, so I knew he didn't run in the same circles we did. The size of his apartment, with the addition of a roommate, meant that wealth wasn't in his background, unless they didn't want to offer too much financial support. But none of those things mattered to me. I love him for who he is, but I knew telling my parents that I might've found a partner would be a pain in the ass. I didn't need them to like it, just to accept that I can make my own choice.

Shaking away my thoughts, I return to the books before me. Instead of just pulling the books out to look at them, I tilted my head, straining to see the titles as if that was easier. If a title catches my attention, I'll pull out the book anyway, checking out the cover before reading the description. Some people have said not to judge a book by a cover, but it's a window into that world. However, I personally will pass on a book due to character names. I once found a book where the love interest was a man named Jason who was enraptured by his best friend, Teagan, and I couldn't help but gag at the thought. Not interested in the trauma that would be handed to me by two characters sharing the same name as my dad and sister.

The title caught my eye first, but it was the cover that kept my attention once I extracted it from the shelf. A shirtless male surrounded by pine trees covered in fog stared back at me, the faint outline of a wolf's paw print in the background. It was dark blue with the title 'Fated Alpha' in scripted font. It appeared to be a wolf shifter romance about a lower member being kicked out of her pack for refusing the advances of her pack leader and running into another pack that was traveling through the state. The summary alluded to some big secret the visiting pack was hiding and if the female main character could handle it while things heated up between her and the leader of the visiting pack. While I thought Aidyn would devour this, I wanted to double-check if the book was part of a series. The only trigger I truly had was that I hated books ending on cliffhangers, so I always double-checked in case I needed to grab the second book. Pulling out my phone, I entered the book's title into the search bar. The reader community never fails to let me down, and I instantly found that it did not end on a cliffhanger and that there were also several spicy scenes that readers went crazy for. Apparently, the visiting pack leader was 'amazing and a big cinnamon roll' in regards to the main female lead. However, another tag caught my eye as I was about to put my phone away.

Fated mates.

When you're a kid, you often fantasize about finding your one true mate, your fated. They were your mate, but the bond was supposed to be stronger and unchanging, and you couldn't fight the pull you had on each other, an instant attraction that neither could fight. I looked up at that moment to see Aidyn walking toward me, flower still in his hair, a smile on his face as our eyes met. But fated mates were fiction, right? No way something like that existed. Right?

"Find something?" Aidyn asked, reaching out to me.

I realized then that even if it were fiction, it explained my pull toward Aidyn. Why I had been feeling the way I did. I may not be his fated mate, but he was mine. I looked for him first in a crowded room before giving it my attention, sought out his touch often because it calmed me, and I loved the feeling of his body against mine. Maybe that was why I could scent his pheromones, despite the neutralizers, but not that of other Omegas. I wasn't broken; I was waiting for my one. He is my mate, and I have to hope I am his. The second I thought about it, it felt like the last puzzle piece had been slotted into place.

"Yea, did you?" I smiled at him, sliding my hand into his, and moved toward the register. He showed me the cover of a rather thick volume with a tall stone tower and an elf and human standing at its base.

"Apparently, they have to save the world from a high-elf wizard who believes that humans are less than the bugs beneath their feet. The human on the cover displays magic, but mages died out eons ago, and this elf is sent to kill him but can't for reasons he doesn't understand."

When Aidyn talks about something that excites him or interests him, his eyes change to a bright meadow green, and I love that elated expression, how bubbly he gets. It's addicting. I showed him the cover of the book I grabbed for him, and he snatched it from me instantly, practically bouncing on his toes in excitement, explaining that this had been on his 'TBR' pile for a while. I wasn't even aware that the book community had its own set of acronym code words until he explained that it's a short way to say 'to be read', and that it is simply never-ending for voracious readers like him. I wondered briefly if getting him an e-reader in the future would be a smart investment. We made our way up to the front counter, greeting the sales associate kindly, where Aidyn refused to hand me the book he picked out for me, stating that there was no way in hell he would let me buy my own gift. All I could do was laugh at him until the sales associate stared at her computer dumbfounded.

"Sir, you have roughly $80 in rewards, but you can only use $35, did you—"

"No, I'm saving it, but thank you!' Aidyn said, blushing when he caught my eye. "I read, sue me."

"Saving them for what, though?" I asked, dumbfounded.

"Sometimes I use them for textbooks, but honestly, I enjoy gifting books at Christmas, and that's when I use the points."

I was flabbergasted and also kind of in awe of him as we exchanged books before getting in the car. For someone who reads as much as he did, I couldn't imagine the level of self-restraint not to use the discount for books. His eyes held such excitement as he flipped through the pages, listening to the soft shuffle they made as they flipped into place. His happiness was so visible that it warmed me from the inside. But then reality crashed into me as I realized the night was over. I had an idea of one more place to take him, but then what? I couldn't keep him with me the whole night, and I was worried that proposing that he come to my place would be too much.

"What's the matter?" His voice dragged me from my thoughts.

"If I'm honest, I don't want tonight to end, and I don't want to take you back to your apartment."

"Who said you had to take me to my home?"

Luke

Pinning Aidyn against the foyer wall, I pressed my body against his, slipping my tongue into his mouth. He moaned in greeting, looping his fingers through the belt loops on the front of my jeans, pulling my body closer against him. Aidyn had pushed himself against me, stepping on his tiptoes to kiss me on the elevator ride up to my condo apartment, and the kiss had become laced with need by the time the doors opened onto my floor. He winked at me, pulling away, slowly releasing my hand.

"I've always wanted to make out in an elevator," he teased.

Smirking at him, I loved the fact that he had no issues making demands of me, teasing me, or being the first one to make a move. He was clear about his desires and needs, and with the pass in the elevator, it was very clear what would happen the second we stepped into my apartment. Thank

God I grabbed the box of condoms from the back of the car when we got out.

No sooner had we stepped into the foyer of my apartment did I have my lips on Aidyn again. I kissed him like a dying man, desperate for an oasis in the desert. He released more of his pheromones, his forest scent mixing with the damp rain of his arousal, and I couldn't wait to sink into him. But he needed to know something important about me first before this became really embarrassing. I pulled away from him, my forehead pressing against his, and he panted from our connection, his green eyes watching me.

"Before we go any further and I embarrass myself, I need to tell you something." I breathed, soaking in his scent. "I haven't had sex in about two years."

Aidyn's eyes grew wide as he looked at me. "Two years, are you serious? My Omega practically served himself to you on a silver platter two weeks ago, and you hadn't had sex in two years?"

"An Omega in heat can't give adequate consent. I would be lying if I said I didn't take care of myself later, though." I grinned sheepishly.

Aidyn took my face in his hands, leaning forward to kiss me tenderly before smiling at me. "You have my full consent, my overly patient Alpha."

Picking him up was effortless, and he wrapped his arms and legs around my body, his ass seated on my hard length. I couldn't help but rub against him, which made him moan into my neck, his tongue flicking over my collarbone, causing me to shudder.

"I wanted to explain in case everything was over too quickly. I've...I've also never knotted anyone. As a dominant –"

"It can be on the larger side; I've felt it against me. I'm not worried. If things are over too quickly, we'll rest, and then we'll go again."

He nuzzled my neck, surrounding me with his scent, and I breathed a sigh of relief. I thanked whatever God was in heaven that this Omega was brought to me. I carried him through my apartment to the bedroom, lowering him to the bed before pulling my sweater over my head and draping my body over his. Aidyn had already removed his glasses, setting them on my nightstand before he had taken the opportunity to pull off his own shirts and now lay beneath me, bare-chested and beautiful. His skin was pale like cream with a sprinkling of fair hair that dusted across his chest and ended in a small trail that disappeared into the waistband of his pants.

A smile quirked on my lips as I saw the silver bar pierced through his left nipple, and I ran a thumb over the nipple; his body shuddering under me. To find that he had a piercing was a surprise. Aidyn didn't really give off the vibe that he would be covered in tattoos and piercings, and I couldn't help but lean down, running my tongue over the metal and the raised flesh. He moaned softly, his back arching as I wrapped my mouth around the bar, flicking my tongue across it once more.

"Rumor has it, the pierced nipple is more sensitive than the other," I murmured, moving to the neglected right one, running my tongue across it before biting the nub. "Is that true?"

"I—I wouldn't know," Aidyn huffed. "I lost a bet. The loser had to get a piercing of the winner's choosing. And I refused to get my dick pierced, so we went with the nipple."

"Who was the winner?"

"....Erik."

"Mmm,"

I wasn't exactly thrilled that the Beta got to choose what happened to my Omega's body, but I also had no place to say anything of the sort. It was his body. If he consented to it, then I had no choice but to let it go. That doesn't mean I won't reap the benefits of the gift this Beta had unknowingly given me, though. I took his unpierced nipple into my mouth again, sucking on the tender flesh while rubbing my thumb across its pierced counterpart. His breath hitched in his throat, and I didn't miss his fingers digging into the bedsheets, trying to find a perch to hang onto. Holy fuck, he was sensitive, and I couldn't wait to witness his responses to the things my Alpha wanted to do to him. Reaching for his jeans, I unbuttoned them single-handedly, pulling them with his underwear down his body, before staring at the naked Omega before me.

He was soft and pale, paler on my dark sheets. His soft rose nipples were the same color as the tip of his smaller cock, which twitched under my gaze. He was large for an Omega, most likely because he was a dominant, the same way my designation gave me a larger knot than most Alphas. Size wasn't important to me, all that mattered was him and how affected he was by me. The last time we had been intimate, our instincts took over, and I hardly remember what his body looked like, only the feel of his cock against mine, his breathing labored as we both frantically sought release. I could see everything now, and I wanted to take my time to devour him completely.

"Jesus fuck, you're beautiful," I whispered, drinking him in.

"Ha! Hardly," he scoffed.

"Mmm, but you are. As if a sculptor carved you from marble. Soft, pale, and perfect, with a cute cock begging for my attention."

I took his hard cock in my hand, running my thumb across the bead of pre-cum that rested on his tip. I could tell by the puddle of slick beneath him that he loved my compliments and praises, and I stored that in the Aidyn file that I kept in the back of my mind.

"You know," Aidyn moaned, his hips thrusting upwards as I lazily stroked his length. "Most guys would hate it if someone called their cock 'cute.'"

"Mmm, true," I agreed. Moving southwards, I settled my face between his legs. I nipped at the flesh on his inner thigh, causing him to jump and writhe above me. "However, you're not most guys, are you?"

This time, I bit down harder, my teeth sinking into the flesh of his inner thigh, and my Alpha urged me to break the skin. But we had discussed nothing of bonding, and now wasn't the time when we were both drunk on each other's pheromones. A fresh wave of slick seeped onto the bedsheet, letting me know how much my teasing was turning him on.

I released the flesh between my teeth, licking over the mark that I knew would bruise. Without warning, I flipped Aidyn onto his stomach; his surprised yelp had me chuckling as I pulled him up by his waist, forcing him to present to me.

"So wet for me, little fawn."

He attempted to bury his face into the blankets as if shy at my commentary, but my Alpha was elated at the sight of him presenting. It's a natural Omega response to produce slick, something that makes mating easier, but it felt good to believe that I was probably the cause of the amount that ran down his thigh and tight ball sack.

Unable to resist anymore, I leaned forward to lick the slick from his thighs, licking over my bite mark and up the seam of his sack. Aidyn moaned into the comforter, his hips swaying slightly, begging me to move to his core. I chuckled softly at his impatience, moving just close enough that the breath from my words teased him even more.

"So goddamn perfect."

His moan ended in a cry as I surged forward, my tongue flat against his eager hole, the sweet flavor of his slick bursting across my tongue. Using my hands to spread him further, to give me more access, I devoured his core as if I were kissing him, my tongue teasing over his entrance before sliding inside briefly. His moans had turned into a needy mewling, his hands moving between his legs to reach for his aching cock before I swatted at them and growled.

"No. Hands in front of you on the bed." I commanded, tracing his rim with my thumb. Aidyn let out a frustrated and needy whimper but did as he was told, shifting his body to stretch his arms out in front of him, clasping his wrists in the opposite hands.

"Good Omega," I smiled, biting his ass cheek firmly.

I didn't know how much longer I could tease him. I reached out and caressed the swell of his ass, my hand moving over the gooseflesh and fine body hair that existed there. It was clear that Aidyn provided grooming maintenance for his entrance, and while I enjoyed the smooth, soft view, I can't say I would've minded either way. Though I'm sure hair and slick were a fucking nightmare combination, so I couldn't blame him. Unable to resist any longer, I discarded the rest of my clothing, tugging on my cock for a moment before reaching for the box of condoms from the bag that I'd dropped on the bed, tearing into the cardboard box and pulling out a plain foil packet.

"Want my help?" Aidyn asked, his green eyes focused on me.

Why was him offering to put a condom on me so fucking hot? My cock twitched in response as I handed him the packet. He tore it open with his teeth, pulled the condom out, and slipped it between his lips. He gave me a smirk before he gripped the base of my drooling cock in his fist, sliding his mouth over my tip and sealing the head in the condom, using his mouth to work the prophylactic down my length. I have never had a partner orally put a condom on me, and Jesus fuck, it was so hot to watch him. He used his fingers to roll the condom down, but it stopped halfway down my length. Aidyn sat back on his heels, staring at it before he let out a full laugh, its sound echoing around my bedroom. God, I wanted to bottle that sound, perfect and melodic. Once he stopped laughing, he reached forward, pulling the condom off me.

"Someone told me that when an Alpha tells you he's too big for a condom, he's lying. They've apparently never met a dominant Alpha. It appears that it's not just your knot that's larger." He chuckled.

He grabbed the bag the condoms were in, pulling out the box labeled 'X-large', and then proceeded to repeat the process, slipping the prophylactic between his lips once more and applying it to my eager cock, rolling it to my base, his tongue twirling around my head until I moaned in pleasure. When the condom was firmly in place, he squeezed and rolled my balls in his hand for a moment before lifting off my cock, a smirk on his lips, knowing full well that he was driving me crazy. Ass.

"Present for your Alpha," I said hoarsely, my throat dry with desire. "Arms back in the stretched position; I don't want you coming without my permission."

His eyes widened as he moved back into position, knees bent, ass raised, and arms stretched forward. Despite my dominant nature, I was nervous. It had been a while since I slept with anyone, and of course I had never knotted them. The pressure of it and being with someone I cared about was starting to get to my head. What if I was a terrible lay? What if it did nothing for him, leaving him feeling disappointed and unsatisfied? What if I hurt him? What if he couldn't take my knot and would need someone else for his heat? What if this was a complete and utter disaster? Aidyn lowered his hips, resting his entrance on my tip. I glanced up at him, and his forest green eyes watched me, a reassuring smile on his lips. He broke his stretch long enough to reach a hand behind him to squeeze my thigh.

"You got this, Alpha."

His trust and reassurance fought the dark clouds of my spiraling thoughts, and I smiled at him, leaning forward to kiss his spine in thanks before lining myself appropriately. Pushing forward, I slowly sunk into him, and a low moan erupted from my throat, echoing his own. The self-lubrication his body created allowed me to push in with little resistance, his body accepting me easily and clinging to me tightly, desperately trying not to let me go. I retreated slowly before pushing back in, his body clenching around me. There was no way I was going to last.

"Jesus fucking Christ,"

Leaning forward while trying not to put my full weight on him, I cupped his chest, my fingers toying with his piercing. His head bowed between his arms while I pulled the metal away from his body, mixing a little pain with his pleasure. Aidyn kept his arms firmly planted on the bed, not moving as I had instructed. His body shook while his breath hitched. He began to push back against me, meeting me halfway through each thrust, pushing me deeper inside him until I reached the end, my cock sliding along his prostate with each thrust. Our pheromones permeated the bedroom, drowning it in a perfume that was completely us. I could feel my rut on the edges of my being, and the base of my cock began to swell, catching on the rim of his hole. I could feel his body wanting to accept me, preparing to expand as I did.

"W-wait!" Aidyn cried out suddenly, his knuckles white as he gripped his wrists, nails digging into the skin.

Panic laced through me. My Alpha went into high alert, responding to his sudden change in response. He hadn't used his safe word, but I didn't know if he had been joking when he said it was 'tea'. I immediately pulled out of him and backed up, my knot deflating as my heart thudded loudly in my ears. I immediately leaned over, taking his face in my hands, my eyes dancing over his face for some sign of discomfort or pain, but all I found was a glazed look in his eyes as he tried to form a sentence to help me understand what he needed.

"Sorry. Mirror."

"Mirror?" I asked, my heart pounding loudly enough that I wasn't sure I heard him properly.

"Watch you. Knot me."

Dear God.

Relief was a bucket of cold water over the feverish panic I had just experienced. He wanted to watch our first knotting and scared the shit out of me in the process. I immediately got up from the bed, padding into the bathroom to grab the portable shaving mirror that hung on the wall. Aidyn watched me, his expression full of lust and desire as I returned, dropping it beside him. He hadn't moved, his ass still in the air as slick ran down his legs from his swollen hole.

"Such a good boy, not moving," I whispered, positioning myself behind him again, kissing his back before smacking his ass cheek suddenly. He gasped in surprise as my cock sunk into his dark pink hole, swollen from our desires. I glanced down to watch him swallow my cock, smirking at the red handprint across his fair skin.

"However, you scared your Alpha. Not a nice thing to do, is it?"

He shook his head, and I smacked his ass again, smacking close enough to the first spot that his breath caught with the sensation. "Is it?"

"No, Alpha! I'm sorry."

Humming in approval, I soothed the warm red flesh beneath my hand. I leaned forward and lightly wrapped my hand around Aidyn's throat, pulling him off the bed and against me as I plunged upward into him. He let out a sharp cry, his hands gripping my thighs to steady himself, his nails digging into my flesh. His body struggled to adjust to the sudden tempo I had created. Harsher and rougher than before.

I ran my nose along his neck, kissing him and nibbling the flesh there and leaving small red marks in my wake. Reaching down with my free hand, I placed it just below his belly button, feeling my cock just barely under the surface with each thrust of my hips. My Alpha purred at the thought that one day, the womb that lay beneath my touch could be filled with our pup, and I growled at the pleasure that thought brought me. My knot began to swell once more, teasing the edges of his hole, desperate to be pushed into his heat. I released his throat, pushing Aidyn onto all fours. Reaching for the shaving mirror, I shoved it underneath us, desperately hanging onto what little control I still had. Rut began to clog my vision, fading the edges of my sight, but it chased away the insecurity I had about knotting him for the first time.

"Can you see us?"

Aidyn looked under us and moaned, nodding his head. I couldn't see under us as well as he could, but leaning back, I could watch from my own point of view, realizing if I didn't do it soon, my dominant knot would never fit.

"Does my Omega want to watch himself get knotted? Locked with his Alpha for hours?"

Unable to trust his voice, Aidyn nodded, but I let out a growl.

"Tell me," I growled.

When he didn't respond again, I leaned forward, my right hand slipping under him to encircle his throat again, deepening my growl as I squeezed slightly, biting his shoulder.

"Please let me watch you knot m—fuuuck!"

At his words, I pushed my almost full knot into him, forcing his body to stretch around me so I could seat myself deep inside and lock us together. His body convulsed around the larger intrusion as my knot rubbed against his prostate, and I groaned into his neck, exploding inside the condom.

"Please, Alpha!"

I heard the cry in his voice as he pushed against me, eager for something more as he grinded against my knot, my cock still hard inside him. I reached between us to realize his cock was still hard, heeding my words that he wouldn't come without my permission. Taking his sweet cock into my fist, I began to move it down his length while he rode my knot and shaft, his body squeezing and clenching around me as he fucked his cock into my fist.

"That's it," I murmured. "Be a good Omega and come for your Alpha."

His whimper turned into a moan as he came, his release splashing across the shaving mirror and bedspread. I hadn't expected to come again as he had, my body eager to match him as I pumped another load into the condom. His body seemed to relax, and I adjusted us into a more comfortable position, moving us on our sides, my leg sliding between his thighs. He let out a very contented sound when I pulled him closer by his waist, scenting him and kissing his neck, lulling us with a purr that was soon joined by Aidyn's.

"Best show ever," he whispered lazily, but all I could do was chuckle.

AIDYN

Sleeping with male Betas poses a low risk to Omegas. There has never been a record of male Betas impregnating Omegas, male or female. The biggest risk in sleeping with a Beta is the potential for STIs. Because of the fact that there is no fear of impregnation, my partners over the past few years have been Betas, with the most recent one being the night before I entered Luke's classroom, and my life changed. The last time I was knotted was by a sheath Erik used when I went into heat between new medications, and it was an emergency, but that was a year ago and a necessary mistake I would never repeat again. So when Luke pushed into me the next morning, everything felt different. My hole was sore from the stretch his large knot had given me the night before, and the line between pleasure and pain blurred before finally giving way to pure pleasure. I must've dozed off after sex, and I had been sleeping on my stomach. Before he pressed into me, Luke had applied some lubricant to the condom, and it took a moment for my body to register what was happening before it finally provided slick for Luke, allowing him to slide in deeper.

"I'm sorry, little fawn," Luke moaned above me, kissing my shoulder and resting his forehead between my shoulder blades. "Waking next to you naked in my bed made me want to claim you again."

I let go of the pillow that I was clutching tightly and reached out for his wrist, finally opening my eyes to look at him behind me, my hips arching upwards into him, opening my body to him.

"Never apologize for claiming what's yours," I moaned.

"Fuuuck," he groaned, his weight dropping onto me. I tilted my head back so that he could press his face into my neck, covering the flesh in licks and kisses. "Your hole is so soft and greedy for my cock, it doesn't want to let me go."

Using my inner muscles, I squeezed around his cock, enjoying the stutter to his breathing as I did so. I did it again, and this time, he pulled out, flipping me over onto my back and hitching my legs into the crook of his arms before sliding back in, pushing deep into my body until I saw stars. The position lowered my hips, and his cock hit familiar places differently, my channel slightly tighter. It also meant I was facing him directly, his eyes watching me intently as his hips bounced off mine. I reached up to cup Luke's face, my Omega purring at seeing his Alpha take pleasure in our body, and his Alpha responded with his own call, leaning down to nuzzle into my neck, scent marking me.

My Omega loved him already, but I couldn't bring myself to say the words openly. A little voice in the back of my head laughed at me, calling me pathetic and naïve. That I was falling too fast, and it would burn out quickly. He would grow tired of the novelty that I was, and after he helped me, he would leave me. My chest felt tight, and my moan sounded more like a heavy whimper as a wave of anxiety washed over me, clouding the pleasure he gave me.

Luke raked his nails across the underside of my thighs, his nails digging into the flesh and leaving red lines from my ass to the back of my knees. It was a feeling I had never felt before. No other partner had done this, and my body shuddered in response, squirming slightly until he did it again, and I wiggled. It was strangely pleasurable, my body lighting up at the touch.

"Come back to me, little Omega." Luke hummed, raising my leg to nip at my calf.

I hadn't been aware that my insecurity had caused my purr to go silent, the first indicator that my brain wasn't allowing me to be in the moment with him. He was still inside me, but he had stopped moving, watching me to make sure I was okay and waiting for me to tell him to stop, his eyes full of concern. I shook my head and smiled, leaning upwards to kiss him, slipping my tongue into his mouth to deepen the kiss. He grunted in surprise and began moving again, slowly as he pressed into the kiss and gave my leaking cock something to grind up against, smearing pre-cum across our abdomens, tempo slow and intimate. His pheromones engulfed me, and I released mine in response, drowning us in our scents as I reached my climax, my seed erupting between us and triggering Luke's release. I could feel the knot at the base of his cock, outside of my body, but pushed snugly against my opening as he held himself back from pushing it into me.

I ground my ass against it, desperate to be filled by him, until he gripped my hips tightly, forcing me to stop, a slow, exasperated chuckle erupting from his throat. He withdrew from me slowly, peeling off the condom and tying a knot into the end before he leaned over to kiss me. He instructed me not to move and that he would be right back before stepping off the bed and disappearing into the adjoining bathroom. I immediately felt his absence. My body felt empty without him inside me, and when he stepped into the bathroom, my Omega panicked when we couldn't see him again.

Sex often leaves one feeling vulnerable, and a kaleidoscope of emotions washed through me. Logically, I knew we weren't being abandoned; he was tossing the condom and would be back like he had said, but my Omega wanted to watch him, see him. The echoing of the emotions and thoughts I had only a moment ago fueled the uncertainty. We had said a lot of things in the heat of the moment, I rationalized. I told him I was his to claim, and he called me beautiful and his. There was no way he seriously meant any of that. He'd say the same thing if it was any other Omega, wouldn't he? After all, he didn't knot me just then. Did he not want to, or did he have his first knotting and decided it wasn't for him? Can you be horrible at being knotted?

When Luke stepped back into the room I felt my Omega relax slightly, comforted by the sight of him, now in clean boxers and a wet washcloth in hand. However, it did little ease the panic that was inside me, fearing I had done something wrong. Sitting beside me on the bed, I watched his movements as he gently cleaned my stomach free of cum with the warm cloth before taking my cock and cleaning it off as well. Instructing me to roll over onto my stomach, he continued to clean me, sliding the cloth between my ass to remove any traces of lube and slick. Never, in the history of my past lovers, including Erik, had they cleaned me up afterward. It's as if etiquette and care go out the window when it's a one-night stand, yet here Luke was, doing the basic level of care. Burying my face back in the pillow, I was unable to suppress the purred moan that escaped me as he pressed the warm cloth against my entrance. Once he was satisfied I was clean, he tossed the cloth into the laundry basket by the door and got back into bed, pulling me into his arms as he kissed the back of my neck, his low Alpha purr rumbling against my back. I was so full of emotions and thoughts that I was numb. I didn't understand what was going on with me; the only thing I could do was curl up against him. Matching my position, he curled around me, molding to my body shape.

I didn't know when I fell asleep, but I woke to the scent of coffee. Sitting up, I reached for my phone to discover that it was a little after ten in the morning and a text from Erik that read that he would be staying at his parent's place until the evening to help his father out with some yard work. Setting my phone down on the bed, I looked around the bedroom, finally taking in his simple decor.

The bed sat against the far wall, with the bedroom doors almost directly across from it. A dresser sat beside a wall of windows that led to a balcony, and from the height, I estimated that we were about three or four floors up, on the top floor. There was a bathroom that I noticed earlier to the left of the bed, with a full-length mirror on a sliver of wall between the bathroom door and the bedroom door.

At the foot of the bed was a set of cushioned benches, and I found a set of clothing folded on one of them. Pushing back the sheets, I grabbed my glasses off the bedside table and put them on. Reaching for the clothing, I found them to be a navy undershirt and a pair of boxers. I lifted the clothing to my nose and inhaled Luke's scent. The bedroom smelled of us and sex. The idea of washing him from my body created an emotion that I couldn't quite put words to. Irritation? Annoyance? Offensive? Either way, it didn't make me happy, and I was grateful that Erik couldn't smell pheromones so I could wear Luke's scent home.

Catching my reflection in the mirror, I noticed a series of light bruises and bite marks decorated my collarbone and breast, bruises marrying my hips. The largest bruise was on my inner thigh and the slightest imprint of teeth lay in the middle of the bruise. My fingers danced across this one, wincing at my weird brain telling me to poke it, and I listened to it. The mark was in a position that hinted I would feel it if my thighs brushed each other. Our Alpha had marked us, and my Omega loved the idea.

Following the scent of coffee, I found Luke at the stove. The sound of eggs and breakfast meat grilling echoed through the room as the coffee pot sputtered out the last of its brew. On the kitchen bar that overlooked the living space was a vase, the bouquet of daisies he had given me the night before resting inside with clean water. I don't remember grabbing them from the car, which could only mean Luke went out to get them at one point. In front of one of the chairs sat the blue daisy that I had in my hair, wilted but still alive enough to press it if I wanted to.

"Coffee mugs are in the cupboard above the machine, and creamer is in the fridge. If you like to froth your creamer, the frother is in the cupboard with the mugs." Luke said when he noticed me, a smile on his face.

The whole moment felt rather domesticated to me, and I couldn't help but smile, moving into the kitchen to discover that Luke had a serious mug problem upon opening the cupboard. It had two shelves, and every inch of it was stacked with mugs of various designs, sizes, and widths. Some had Halloween themes, others had Christmas, with a random seasonal one thrown in for good measure. Some had no design and were simply a solid color but rounded to fit in one's hand perfectly. There were even a few that I would deem too small for coffee; anything below 18 fluid ounces was a water cup and should not be used to siphon the life-giving liquid into my system. They were fine for tea or even hot chocolate, but I need large cups for coffee.

I selected a teal mug for myself and a white one with a raised pumpkin on it for Luke before pulling out the frother. I didn't own one myself, but my parents did, and I was a sucker for frothed cream on top of my coffee, and it was one of my favorite parts about heading home for the holidays. That reminds me, I must let them know I will come home late this year due to my heat. I wonder what Luke is doing for Christmas. Does his family live in town? Ignoring my thoughts, I move behind Luke to the fridge, unable to resist the urge to trace my hand across his lower back before grabbing the creamer, grinning at the pumpkin spice flavor.

"Ah, I see you're a basic bitch too." I teased.

"What can I say? It's not fall without it. Can you please make enough foam for both of us? Just fill the frother to the max line."

Nodding, I filled the frother to the line as directed. I started the machine while Luke began to plate breakfast, setting the dishes on the island next to each other. When the machine had done its job, I poured our coffees before topping them off with the thick, fluffy spiced foam and took them to the island before taking a seat. As Luke sat down, I moved my portion of bacon to his plate before taking a sip of coffee, moaning at the bliss sliding down my throat. Very few things were better than the first sip of good morning coffee.

"Don't like bacon?" he asked, raising an eyebrow.

"Not really. I'll eat it if I have to, like if it's already in something, but if I can, I'll substitute it."

"I don't know if I can be with a sinner *and* a heathen."

"One of us is a teacher who is sleeping with his student. We're already sinners. However, you're looking at this all wrong. If I dislike bacon, that means more for you."

Luke stared at me for a moment before bursting outwards in laughter that rumbled in his chest. "Touché."

We ate in comfortable silence. We didn't feel the need to talk as we enjoyed the morning, but we were both acutely aware that our time together was coming to an end. The kitchen clock mocked us, loudly ticking away the seconds we had left. I hated that clock. Who owns an analog clock these days anyway? I wasn't aware I had been bouncing my knee on the bar stool until Luke reached over, resting his hand on my thigh to settle me.

"Did you know I wasn't even supposed to be in your class?" I rambled absentmindedly, unable to stop the influx of word vomit that flowed from my lips. "I had my first heat at seventeen. Both my parents are Betas and couldn't prepare me properly. Obviously, they knew what a heat was, but there was essentially nothing they could do, and being seventeen, sex wasn't an option since we didn't want to risk a pregnancy so young. The suppressants didn't work, and I was lucid enough for my first that I was aware of how much pain I was in and how scared I was. I begged my mom to stop it from hurting while I was curled in bed, crying. I felt alone, and no one knew what to do. My mom worked with another Omega who had an Omega daughter around my age. Typically, when an Omega goes into heat, we rarely want another Omega near us unless they're pack. Our Omega brains see them as a threat, and we don't want to fight for the attention of a potential mate, so my parents didn't know what would happen if they invited this strange Omega into my space. Having her close by, helping me through my heat and soothing me, calmed my fear. It did nothing for the pain, but I came out of it better than if she hadn't been there.

"When I was born, my parents knew I was an Omega, but at the time of my birth, little was known about dominants and recessives, so it didn't really occur to the doctors and nurses to test for those. After my heat, my mother booked an appointment, and we found out I had the dominant markers. I will never forget what that Omega did for me, and I wanted to be that for someone else. While it's not a common practice, clinics are opening up positions for Omega specialists that can help the newer generation through their heats. There is always the potential for rejection, and generally speaking, suppressants work. But there is a chance that they won't, and there is a chance there are more like me out there. So I took a minor degree in nursing with a focus on Omega studies."

I turned to Luke to find him staring at me, focusing on my words. His hand had slipped into mine, our fingers intertwining. He said nothing, allowing me to explain why I was in his class. Taking his class had been by chance, something I had done for me. I couldn't get over how well chance or fate lined up perfectly for me for last night even to happen. I took a sip of coffee before continuing.

"Your class wasn't on the list for my degree that the advisor gave me. Erik wants to be a psychologist, which is why he's taking it. I remember reading the syllabus and summary of your class in the handbook, and I decided to take the class for myself. I knew how the Omega brain worked, but I wanted to see it explained from an Alpha's point of view. I thought that if I took the class, I could better understand how the world sees us and how I could use that to help those I'd be in charge of. Prepare them better for a world where they're viewed as a hindrance to society and lesser than others. The majority of the world thinks the way Betas and Alphas do of us Omegas, as nothing more than weak baby factories, so I wanted to see what the biology and psychology of it being taught by an Alpha would be like."

"And?" Luke asked. There was an odd look on his face, one that I couldn't place. I could tell he was holding his breath, worried about how I would critique his class and inadvertently judge him. I gripped his hand tightly, giving him a soft smile.

"I expected you to be aggressive in teaching. Most Alphas are and do, in fact, push the narrative that we're the weaker beings and should spend our lives in submission. There are some people in the world who believe that if you go into heat at seventeen, then you're old enough to find a pack and start breeding, regardless of the age of consent. It's been a fight in the Supreme Court for nearly a decade, and with more and more presenting earlier than expected, it's become a hot topic. So imagine my surprise when I found a class taught by someone unbiased who treated designations as equals and spent the same amount of time on both sides. You allow fair debates, and you teach in a way that makes us think and even open the floor to critical thinking. Even if a silly Alpha didn't appreciate an Omega stepping in. I don't know why your class wasn't offered to me, and I'm trying not to take it personally. I'm trying not to think it's because I was an Omega. This is just a long way of saying that I'm happy I'm in your class. I don't know what the future will be for us, but for now, I'm happy."

"I wanted to teach the facts, even if it went against the common belief. I don't know if I believe in fate either, despite the fact that I've been thinking more and more about fated mates. I don't know if I believe in the idea; it's one I've never entertained. But you being in my classroom, you echo every fear and worry that I possess as well, and me being who I am, it just makes too much sense. It's too coincidental. I'm not saying that to rush anything or force you into an uncomfortable position. I want to take our time still, but everything's adding up in ways I never thought possible."

"What do you mean 'me being who I am'?" I tilted my head, turning to look at Luke directly. He bowed his head, avoiding my eyes.

"Unlike you, my parents didn't know what my designation was at birth, though it was assumed I would be an Alpha, considering our family line. There hasn't been an Omega born in my family in centuries, but I was tested at puberty like everyone else. It came with dominant markers, but I hadn't presented appropriately yet. Once I started college, I noticed something was off, and by society standards, I'm essentially broken." He took a breath before glancing at me, but his eyes didn't meet mine. "Until the day you entered my classroom, I had never scented an Omega. I can't tell the designations apart, everyone smells like a Beta to me."

I blinked at him, processing what he was saying. All my life, I could detect the pheromones of an Alpha. But to present and not know if the person beside you was an Omega or a Beta…I couldn't tell if that was a blessing or a curse. However, now I understand the hesitancy behind his movements around me. I was the only person that produced a scent for him, so he didn't want to scare me off and lose his only experience. It explained why he kept rubbing his face and nose on my neck when we hugged and breathed deeply because it was something so new. Something he could finally experience.

"So...last night when you said you had never knotted someone, it was because you never produced a knot?" I asked carefully.

"Until you, I have never produced a knot. I had a partner leave me in college because I couldn't give him what he needed." He looked at me then. "I was so worried that I couldn't be what you needed either. Plus, how we're acquainted certainly didn't help matters. Teachers can't be with their students. But you were the first knot that mattered."

"Mattered?" I tilted my head. "You just said that you had never produced a knot until last night."

"Mmmm, technically correct," he laughed, his cheeks turning a deep crimson. "I told you I had to take care of myself after your heat. I, uh, ended up being stuck to a sleeve I was using. You were the cause."

I tried not to laugh. I really, really did. This was a serious conversation, and I needed to be understanding and kind, yet I couldn't stop the laughter from inside me. Luke's blush deepened, but he smiled at me anyway. "Why didn't you knot me this morning?"

Luke's cheeks flushed an even deeper red. "I wanted to, Lord help me, I wanted to. But I was worried you would be too sore; as a dominant, my knot is bigger. The position we were in would've made it more difficult, though not impossible, I just didn't want to hurt you. And I didn't know if we had the time to be stuck together again."

That made a lot of sense to me, easing the underlying fear that had settled in my stomach from the lack of his knot this morning. I hopped off my stool, spinning him toward me to place myself between his legs, and kissed him. Our kiss tasted of eggs and coffee, and I couldn't help the feeling of domestication again.

"You're not broken, Luke. But that toy will be if you ever knot it instead of me again."

This time, he laughed, pulling me close and nuzzling my neck before kissing my collarbone. "I promise never to knot anything but you again."

"Good boy."

I was fully aware I was being a fucking brat. I was on edge, fidgety, pissy, and snapping at Erik over the stupidest shit. I was being an asshole, but I couldn't seem to stop. I wanted Luke. I hated that our time together was so short, and now I was pissed that Erik was sitting next to me on the couch instead of him. It was Sunday night, and I still had yet to shower, refusing to wash his scent from me. Instead, I was curled into the corner of the couch, under a throw blanket, wrapped in the cardigan I had stolen from Luke. Erik sat a cushion down from me, opting not to be so close after I snapped at him earlier. He was focused on his fried rice with beef and broccoli. The latest episode of some superhero show playing on the TV, but I couldn't focus. I hadn't been able to focus since coming back to the apartment. I had even attempted to read the book Luke bought for me, but my attention span couldn't absorb the words, and I kept reading the same sentence repeatedly before I finally gave up. The pocket of the cardigan vibrated, and I pulled out my phone, unlocking it to read the text message that came through while another two followed it.

> *I didn't leave my bed until late afternoon.*

> It still smells like you. It makes my dick hard and my heart ache.
>
> I miss you. Is it too soon to say that?

I put the sweet and sour pork container onto the coffee table before texting out a reply to Luke, smiling down at my screen.

> I can't bring myself to shower yet. I'm wearing your cardigan, and I miss you too. Keep those balls full for me?
>
> I don't know if I can completely prevent myself from self-pleasure, especially when thoughts of you invade my dreams, but for you, I shall try.
>
> I can't wait to suck on those full balls.
>
> You're lucky Mr. Harllow is there right now; otherwise, I'd come and use that teasing mouth of yours.
>
> I don't view that as 'lucky,' Sir. That is the very definition of 'unlucky.'
>
> Fuck, I love that you called me sir. I eagerly await when we can be together again.
>
> As much as I enjoyed your cock in me, I can't wait until I can feel your arms around me again.
>
> And I can't wait to hold you, little fawn.

I found that I couldn't control myself around Luke; filters were not installed, and I just said whatever popped into my head at the moment, and not once has Luke made me feel like I was being too much or too forward. When nothing more came through, I put the phone back in my pocket and grabbed my pork. I glanced up to find Erik staring at me, his expression blank.

"Who's that?" he asked slowly.

"Classmate from another class. He couldn't remember what pages we needed to read before Monday. Dumbass waited until the night before." I lied easily.

Erik made a sound in his throat as if he didn't believe me but left it alone. He mixed his food before standing up, stating he was full. He packed up the food before taking it into the kitchen to put it into Tupperware and placing it in the fridge. I smiled at him as he walked past, handing me the TV remote. He mumbled 'good night' before disappearing into his room. I couldn't help but sigh at his absence. I could tell by his response that he didn't really believe me and he was upset, but there wasn't anything I could do about it. He knew where I stood on our relationship and was only setting himself up to be hurt. I pulled out my phone again, unlocking it.

> *Are you comfortable with me telling Erik I'm seeing someone?*

I watched the dots appear, disappear, and reappear before disappearing. Luke had read my message, and he was struggling to respond. Finally, a response came through.

> *I don't want to hide you. I want to openly kiss you and hold your hand and tell everyone you're mine. But the university has rules against dating students. As*

> long as you're in my class, I cannot see you romantically, so I have to hide you. I'm sorry, but does Mr. Harllow need to know?

I wasn't angry. I understood. He and I being together was a danger to his job as an educator and violated several ethics laws. I would honestly hate myself if he were to lose his job over us, over me. I wasn't worth that at all. However, Erik needed to move on. Mentioning that I was seeing someone would solidify the idea that I had found my own happiness; it was time he found his.

> I wouldn't ask if I didn't think it was important. He needs to stop hanging onto the idea that we'll be partners, that I will ever love him the way he loves me. He deserves his own happiness, but it's not with me. I won't mention who, just that I've started seeing someone. It might even allow me to stay at your apartment for an extra day. Come home on Sunday instead of Saturday. [winking face emoji]

> I see; manipulate me into saying yes [winking face emoji] Leave me nameless. I promise it won't be forever. Once you're no longer in my class, we can tell everyone.

> Even then. There is no rush to tell anyone anything until we're ready. Until you're ready.

Taking a deep breath, I unfurled from the couch. Tossing the empty food container and wandering into my bedroom, I set my alarm 15 minutes earlier than normal so I would have time for a shower before class. Stripping off my clothing except for my boxers, I pulled the cardigan back over my bare shoulders. Now I knew what it was like to lay in my mate's arms, his front pressed against my back as he tucked me close against his body, his warmth and scent enveloping me and creating a place where I was safe, protected, and loved. Without him, I felt cold and alone, and I think it is time my brain and anxiety stopped fighting what my Omega was telling me. *Luke was my mate.* It was okay to miss him. It was okay to want and crave him. We move at our pace; he even said so. And if that meant coming off as desperate and obsessive, then so be it. If it makes Luke uncomfortable, I'll back off, but until then, I'll give in to my Omega. Let him do what he wants. And the first step is telling Erik.

Luke

I pinched the bridge of my nose while my mother practically screeched in my ear. My parents are very traditional. My mother was in charge of raising me and my sister, as was her place dictated by my father as her Alpha, with little to no power in the relationship. She couldn't make financial decisions, have her own bank account, or make long-term decisions for the household, such as servant employment or decor. Everything had to be run by my father first. His word was absolute and never questioned. He was the head of our household, and I hated that my mother ranked lower than I did. I wasn't a 'mama's boy'; I just felt she deserved better, and I generally gave in to her a lot simply to make her life easier and out of pity.

Over the past few years, my relationship with my parents had strained due to their refusal to accept my choices and their ability to turn every event into a matchmaking opportunity. Normally, I would have a preplanned excuse as to why I couldn't attend my fathers birthday parties, but with the sudden development of my relationship with Aidyn, it had slipped my mind. By not showing up, I had unintentionally made things rather difficult for my mother, and there was no doubt in my mind that my father took his disappointment out on her and blamed her for her inability to keep her kids in line.

"I just don't understand why you weren't there." She sighed finally, her voice in a more normal tone.

"I got sick, I'm sorry," I lied. "I meant to call, but I barely had the energy to do anything."

"Then you need to make it up to your father at Thanksgiving. We're inviting the Richards over; their daughter is an Omega, and she'd be perfect for you. Good family."

"A female. I'm into men, Mother, you know this."

"I'm fully aware. However, finding a male Omega from a good family is like looking for a needle in Central Park after a blizzard."

"And if I've met someone?" I inquire, my knuckles turning white as I grip the armrest of my chair.

A knock on my office door distracted me, and a wave of relief washed over me as Aidyn entered my office, his forest scent calming me instantly. We didn't have class together today, so he stopped by just to see me because he wanted to, and my Alpha preened under that knowledge. He sought me out because he wanted me, and I breathed a sigh of relief just having him in my space. A look of concern washed over his face the moment he could sense how tense I was. I pushed back a little from my desk, switching the phone to my other ear, and smiled up at him as he came to me, crawling onto my lap without asking. The chair protested under our combined weight, but I could finally breathe again when he touched me. He nuzzled into my neck, releasing pheromones to help calm my agitation;

a low rumbling started in his chest as he began to purr, smoothing away my anger so I could calmly respond to my mother.

"'*Met someone?*' Who? I don't know of any prominent family with a male Omega available."

"Jesus, Mother. It shouldn't matter who his family is, this isn't the 1700s. It should matter that I'm happy."

"Luke Aaron Ellis! It does matter. You have a duty to the Ellis name and lineage. If he is not from a prominent family; fine, even your father has mistresses. Just close your eyes, pretend you're knotting him, and do your duty."

"Jesus fucking Christ. I would never do that to him. I want him by my side, not treated like some whore who must remain in the shadows and I can't have a proper life with. He deserves better than that."

"Watch your language!" my mother scolded, as if she hadn't just told me to close my eyes to knot.

"If that's all you have to say, Mother, I'm going to hang up now." I could hear her voice still coming from the call as I clicked to hang up. I immediately set my phone to 'do not disturb' so I wouldn't get any incoming calls from her.

I tilted my head onto Aidyn's as his head rested on my shoulder. I wrapped my arms around him, pulling him closer and burying my face into his neck, breathing in his scent. I don't actually hate my parents; I just hated how they forced their ideals onto us, refusing to let us be our own people. Even my sister was set up to marry someone of their choosing, though I didn't get the impression that she was in love with the Omega they chose. I'm sure Emily was sweet, but seeing as she rarely spoke and interacted with the family, I couldn't say for sure. I closed my eyes and let out a pleased sound when Aidyn began to run his fingers through my hair.

"So your mother thinks I'm a prostitute?" Aidyn asked, finally breaking the silence, a playful pout on his lips.

Chuckling lightly, I bent down to kiss him before answering with a sigh. "The Ellis family is a very prestigious family. We're among the elites in big houses. We hold balls for all the major events and holidays, and the Christmas and New Year's parties are invite-only, and everyone wants an invite. It's a life I grew up in and one I don't care for. I'm the black sheep, so to speak. They want me to stop dragging my feet, settle down, marry a good Omega, and continue the line. My mother has tried to set me up with every Omega she deems worthy, regardless of gender or my sexual preference, and I have refused everyone."

"And I'm not worthy."

My eyes flashed open as a wave of anger seared through me. Aidyn didn't sound upset or offended, just indifferent, as if he knew his place. But his thoughts were wrong. His place was beside me, and I would fight for that right, regardless of what my mother said.

"You listen to me, little fawn. Yes, you are. She doesn't get to decide that for me. She suggests that I keep you as a lover but have a marriage and produce offspring with another to keep up appearances and what she deems to be 'my duty.' But fuck that. That isn't the life I want, nor is it the life I want for you."

He said nothing, lost to his thoughts as he brushed through my hair, his fingers snagging occasionally on a tangle. I leaned into his touch, tilting my head against the back of the chair. I found I was perfectly content, enjoying the feel of him on my lap, pressed against my side. I knew we would have to use the descenter when we left the classroom, but it was like my office had become our own little world. Everything beyond that office door could wait while we hid from it all and enjoyed each other's presence.

"When do you have to leave for your class?" I asked quietly, my eyes still closed.

"Soon," he responded. "Is it wrong that I want to skip?"

I couldn't help but smile at that, squeezing his thigh as I finally opened my eyes to see him watching me.

"What kind of teacher would I be if I let a student skip their classes?"

"The kind that sleeps with his student and would take advantage of the extra time."

I chuckled and shook my head. He's right. I would love to bend him over this desk and bury my cock in his eager hole, claiming him again. God, the weekend couldn't come soon enough. This reminded me of our conversation the night before. He had made a decision, but I had to wait for him to bring it up on his own.

"I didn't get a chance to talk to Erik," Aidyn said as if he could read my thoughts. "He had left by the time I woke up this morning, and he left my text on read, which bodes well for the conversation we're going to have tonight. It's my turn to make dinner, so I'll make a favorite dish as a peace offering. I was feeling anxious, so I came to find you; I'm sorry if I'm intruding."

"You could never intrude, little fawn. I wanted to see you but had no excuse to."

"I want to stop fighting, you know. I don't know if what you said about fated mates is real, but I'm done fighting whatever this is. My Omega wants to give in to you, and that scares me. What if, by doing so, I rush things or make you uncomfortable? What if I'm too needy and become borderline obsessive? What if I lose who I am?"

"Baby," I sat up straighter in my chair, moving him effortlessly as I readjusted. Enveloping him in my scent and pheromones, I soothed the panic he was clearly experiencing. "You and I are fighting the same battles. My first and last thoughts of the day are of you. I seek you out when I enter spaces you frequent; I check my phone constantly, thinking it vibrates with a new message from you. You consume my very being in ways no one else ever has. You're my mate, and I won't believe differently. I'm only uncomfortable when we're apart. You could never be too needy because your desires are the air I breathe. You could never be obsessive because I already worship the ground you walk on. You can never lose who you are because your Omega is part of you. His desires and wants are yours; you must let yourself have them. You are my biggest weakness and greatest strength, and it is my duty to cherish and love you. And it will be a blessing to do so."

Aidyn blinked at me; his cheeks tinted a soft pink as he processed my words, reading between the lines. "You love me."

He presented the statement like it was also a question, cautious of my response. I don't know when I actually realized I had fallen in love with him, though I suspect it was around our bookstore date. Smiling down at him, I opted for the truth.

"From the moment you walked into my classroom."

His lips crashed into mine, surprising me briefly. He pressed into my body, pouring his emotions and unspoken words into our kiss. His cheeks were damp with tears, their saltiness mixing into our kiss. He released his pheromones as his purr returned, telling me without words that he happily returned my affections. He was mine, and I was his. And no one, not even my parents, could take him from me.

"Where the fuck did he go?" I mumbled to myself, going down the condiment aisle of the grocery store.

I don't want to say that Aidyn had been distracted lately, but I could tell that something was making him rather flighty. He suddenly got the impulse to make me his favorite dish during his stay with me this weekend, and since I needed to pick up groceries anyway, it was the first stop we made after class. Except halfway through our shopping, Aidyn exclaimed he had forgotten something and had run off to grab it, but he never came back. So here I was, wandering through the grocery store, looking for my lost Omega.

I found him standing at the seasonal display at the front of the grocery store, where they sold a few decorations for the upcoming holidays, which happened to be Halloween. I had actively been avoiding this section, if I was honest. Every year, I drop hundreds of dollars on Halloween décor I didn't actually need, purely because Halloween was my favorite holiday and I'd take it over Christmas any day of the year. While I was not actually a fan of horror movies — and let's be real, today's "horror" is just someone throwing around as much gore and blood as they can in a scene — the holiday was still my favorite, and I had a certain set of movies I watched every year.

As I approached him, I noticed he was staring at a group of plushies sitting on the shelf beside a carton of chicken broth. A throw blanket with bats on it was in his hands, and I watched him repeatedly squeezing the fabric, running his thumb over its texture, and something clicked in the back of my brain. Aidyn's Omega was looking at potential nesting material.

"Hey," I said, smiling as he jumped at my voice, pulling him from whatever trance he was under.

"Oh, hi!" he said, rushing to put the blanket back on the shelf, grabbing the broth carton, and putting it in the cart. "Sorry, that should be all I needed. Did you get all you needed?"

"Not exactly," I said. "I realized that you don't have a nest at my place. Did you want to build one there, too?"

"What do you mean 'too'? I don't have one at my own apartment, remember? I don't even know how to build one."

"There is no right or wrong way to build one, Aidyn. Just let your Omega take over; he knows what to do. If you see anything you'd like, put it in the cart."

He shook his head. "I don't have the money for it right now."

"That's not what I said. If you like it, put it in the cart. We can go to a larger department store this weekend if you'd like. They have stores specifically for nesting Omegas. If you feel safe in my apartment and want a place, we can ensure you have a nest; I won't move it when you're not there."

Aidyn looked at me before turning to the decorations. Hesitantly, he grabbed the throw blanket again and put it into the cart, watching me to see if I'd tell him no. I smiled at him, encouraging him, while he began to study the shelves, finding the perfect items, and finally letting his Omega instincts take over. I wondered, and not for the first time, if he had ever given in to his Omega. He had told me he had grown up with Beta parents, so I was curious how much his lineage impacted his life like mine did. I couldn't imagine resisting what I was or feeling that every instinct I acted on as a dominant Alpha might be wrong.

With each item he put into the cart, I could see a sense of contentment change the expression on his face. His shoulders lowered, slowly releasing the tension he was holding, and it occurred to me that I had been a shitty Alpha. I hadn't noticed how stressed and worked up he was, how he was pretending to be okay so he didn't come off as high maintenance and a burden. He would be staying with me until Monday evening, since it was a holiday, which meant he had already told Harllow that he was seeing someone and didn't need to hide the fact that he wouldn't be home for a few days. The Halloween decorations also signaled that we were halfway through the school term, meaning we would spend his first unmedicated heat together at the end of it. I couldn't imagine the stress, anxiety, and uncertainty he must be experiencing. Nests were places where Omegas could decompress and feel safe and protected. It bothered the fuck out of me that he didn't have one in his own apartment, so he was just carrying this weight around with him every day. I needed to do better.

Glancing at the cart, I noticed that Aidyn had added two throw blankets, string lights with mesh bats on them, and two candles and was currently looking at the plushies again. He had moved a squishy ghost beside a squishy bat together, eyeing them both as he decided which one belonged in the cart, his eyes dancing between the squishy creatures as if the others on the shelf didn't exist. Only these two were making the cut, apparently. He reached out his hand, letting it hover above the bat before it darted forward quickly and grabbed the ghost instead, making its way into the cart. He began to walk toward the check-out lanes but stopped long enough to cast a second eye at the bat, now sitting alone on the shelf, smiling it's weird, soulless smile. He shook his head, tugging on the front of the cart to wheel it toward the lanes.

Jesus fucking Christ, could he be any more adorable?

As I moved past the shelf, I grabbed the bat, settling him beside the ghost on top of the groceries. Aidyn watched its movements; his eyes zoned in on the plush like a cat, and I could see the fight in his eyes. He was worried it was too much, that he was too much, and he would put it back if I gave him the option, which is why he didn't have it.

"We can't leave his friend behind. That's rude. He'd be lonely," I reasoned.

Aidyn raised those beautiful green eyes to me; the battle was still there, but the large smile that spread across his face was fucking worth it.

Aidyn

I wasn't a crier. It wasn't really something I did, so why did I feel like crying now? Something felt off, and I couldn't place what it was. We arrived at Luke's apartment, and I helped him put away the groceries before he instructed me to start on my nest while he worked on dinner. I deposited the plushies onto the corner of Luke's U-shaped sectional before taking the blankets and lights into the bedroom.

The last time I was in this space, I don't remember seeing a nightstand on the right side of the bed. It was a different color than the one on the left, which led me to believe that he had gone out of his way to purchase one for me. My heart melted at the idea, but the fact that the color was different from the other made me itchy. I would try to ignore it since Luke went out of his way for me. I placed the candles on the nightstand and found a phone charger plugged into the wall on this side for me to use. I couldn't help but smile.

I unboxed the lights and opened the package of small Command hooks, placing them in a loose zig-zag pattern above the headboard on my side of the bed. Once that was plugged in, I unpacked the throw and placed it on the right side of the bed to avoid disturbing Luke. Luke assured me that I could do what I wanted, but it still felt wrong, like I was an intruder. This wasn't my home, and I shouldn't act like it was. If I gave in to my Omega, it would be too much, and he would think it was stupid. My Omega struggled because I didn't feel comfortable here. Not really. I could feel the desire to build a nest, but also insecure about doing so. The only reason I was comfortable here was because he was here. I was safe with Luke, but my Omega was unsure if he was safe in his Alpha's space. Maybe that's why everything looked wrong. I tried researching other nests, but mine looked nothing like the one on the internet. Maybe it was the way the lights were strung. Maybe it was the one Halloween blanket I didn't wash before putting it on the bed, so it smells faintly of the spiced candles that were around it at the store. Maybe it was the mismatched nightstands. Maybe it was because I was defective and had no idea how to build a nest because I had never had the instinct to make one before. The ones online looked beautiful and were put together in a round, nest-like shape made up of clothing and blankets, and mine looked like someone just decorating for the holidays.

This is how Luke found me, kneeling on the bed, tears running down my cheeks, as I berated myself for being totally stupid and defective and having zero idea what the fuck I was doing. He crawled onto the bed behind me, wrapping his arms around my waist and pulling me against his body. The second his citrusy scent hit my nose, my body released the tension it held. I sagged against his chest, brushing the tears from my face as embarrassment flashed through me. God, I was pathetic.

"What's wrong, little fawn?" he asked, nuzzling the side of my face.

"I don't know. Something feels off, and I can't place it. Maybe this stuff doesn't belong here. Maybe I don't belong here."

"That's nonsense. If I had my way, you would be moving in, not staying a weekend. You belong here. Maybe it feels off because there are only a few items, which we'll fix tomorrow. We'll go to a nesting store and find the perfect items."

"Luke, I can't afford it."

"Let me take care of you. I thought you said you would give in to your Omega a little more. Doing that means relying on your Alpha to care for you, no matter what it is."

"No offense, but teachers don't get paid that much. If you keep trying to buy things, you'll go broke."

"Is that what this is about? You're worried about my finances?" he chuckled softly. "Sweetheart, I own this building. I also own several commercial buildings, both for businesses and residential. My parents didn't like me becoming a teacher and openly informed me that they would not support it. Teaching wasn't the family business, so I started saving and investing before I started college. I teach because I want to, not because I have to."

"Oh." What else was I supposed to say to that? Even if he claims to be financially better off, my anxiety would still tell me that he's spending too much, and what if he grows tired of me? Fated mates, be damned.

"Now, I know it's your nest, but would it be okay if I changed a few things?"

I could only nod and allow him to drag me off the bed. I stood where he instructed so that I could watch him attempt to fix my mess and correct him if something didn't seem right. My Omega, however, was over the moon. We were building a nest together. He was thrilled that his Alpha was changing what we had and wanted to actively be a part of its construction. I watched as Luke unstrung the bat lights, removed the hooks, and applied new ones to hang the lights in a swooping design above the headboard instead of a zig-zag. Once that was done, he moved the throw to the middle of the bed as if it were a centerpiece on the comforter. He opened the other throw and folded it over the foot of the bed so that both had a home in his space.

He looked at me then, seeing what I thought, and I nodded, feeling as if things were finally clicking into place.

"Are the lights too bright for sleep?" I asked, tilting my head.

"If they are, we can pick up some of those plugs that will turn lights on and off with a mini remote or an app on our phones. You can keep it by your nightstand. But I don't think they're too bright."

"Speaking of stands," I glanced at the two nightstands, and Luke must've caught me looking because he started laughing, a rumbling sound that started in his chest.

"Yeah, I was in a hurry and couldn't find one like mine on short notice. I hate them. They need to match."

"They do." I smiled, relieved.

"But is this a little better?"

"Yeah. I'm sorry. That was embarrassing as fuck."

Luke smiled at me before coming around the bed and taking me in his arms again. "This is new for you; you're listening to an urge you didn't acknowledge before. If something is wrong or off, we'll fix it."

"Would you be okay with continuing to help me build my first nest?" I asked, tilting my face towards him.

He blinked at me for a moment before leaning in and kissing me tenderly on the lips. "Nothing would make me happier."

Well. That was a lie. Apparently, his cock in my mouth made him really happy as I took him down my throat, flexing the muscles there to squeeze around him. His hands pushed their way into my hair, grasping at the strands. He applied a little pressure to the back of my head, but not enough for me to choke or prevent my movements. It was rewarding for me to watch him come undone, to give in to the pleasure I provided him. Every time I twirled my tongue in a certain way over his head, he would squirm, and his breath would catch in his throat. His knuckles dug into the comforter as if he were looking for anything to ground himself into.

"You keep that up, and I won't last long, little Omega," he hissed, his head tilted backward against the pillows.

"So let me taste you." I ran my tongue over the slit of his cock, catching the droplets of precum that leaked down his tip. The scent of his Alpha mixed well with the saltiness of his gift, spreading across my taste buds and exciting my Omega.

The bedroom was dark except for the bat lights that hung from the wall, illuminating the pleasure on his face in a soft glow. Shadows danced across his skin, making the moment more erotic than it had any right to be. I was falling in love with him. I didn't have a choice not to love him. He was my mate. I wanted to be around him. I thought about him constantly. I wanted him to love me the way I loved him. I was so fucking fucked, but at the same time, I was starting not to worry. He soothed the fear of my own Omega, and I wasn't afraid to be in his care. I was learning that it was okay just to be.

I moved off his cock, focusing my attention on his balls that hung heavy before me. I couldn't help but rub my face into his soft, velvety sack, his Alpha scent strongest here. I carefully cupped one of his balls with my tongue, pulling it into my mouth, and sucked gently before moving to the other one; his face flushed in pleasure as he watched me. He ran his fingers through my temple, tucking my hair behind my ear, and smiled down at me.

"So beautiful with my cock filling your mouth."

Fuck, could he be any hotter? I stroked his cock, my motions rough and hard, bringing him off the bed as his back arched into my touch before I swallowed his cock again. He gasped as I used my hand to twist around his shaft, bringing him closer and closer to his climax. He couldn't help himself, his hand digging back into my hair, pulling at the strands, and he began to move his hips with my ministrations, pushing his cock deeper down my throat. I opened myself to him, allowing him further than he had ever been before, breathing becoming more difficult as my eyes began to water, and yet I was more turned on than ever before. He used my mouth for his own pleasure, coming undone and taking from me what he wanted. He wasn't cruel about his actions, just desperate for the release I was attempting to give him. He erupted in my mouth, his salty flavor exploding on my taste buds and sliding down my throat in hot, aggressive bursts. I moaned as his taste hit me, his hand leaving my hair, but I continued to swallow him, making sure I had drawn out every last drop. He began to twitch and groan as my tongue flicked across his sensitive and overstimulated tip.

Without warning, he climbed on top of me, pinning me beneath his body and capturing my mouth with his, his tongue removing all traces of him from me. His hand cupped my hard cock, and I reached down to stop him, shaking my head as I interlaced his fingers and brought it to my chest.

"That was for you, not for me. I don't want anything at this moment except to bring you pleasure. You've changed my life so much in such a short time. All I can do is show you my gratitude and please you."

He looked at me momentarily before burying his face in my neck, nipping at the skin softly. "You could never displease me. You are a gift, Aidyn, one I never thought I'd receive."

AIDYN

The last time I stayed over in Luke's apartment, he had woken me up, taking what he wanted from me. Now, lying awake beside him as he still slept, I took what I wanted. He lay sprawled out on his stomach, his right leg hitched up between my thighs, facing me, and I drank in his profile. Being here beside him still felt like a dream. It has only been a few weeks, and my world has changed so much because he was in it. I couldn't express this emotion properly, yet he was still here. Still wanted me.

His body changed, no longer relaxed with sleep, alerting me to the fact that he was awake before he pulled me closer to him, rolling onto his side and cuddling me. Our legs switched places, my knee going between his thighs as I wrapped my arms around his waist, snuggling against his chest.

He gave a contented sigh, pulling me as close as he could without squeezing me. My Omega began to purr, his song filling the space.

"I will never grow tired of that sound," Luke said, his voice thick with sleep.

I didn't want to move. Even though our nest was small, being here in his arms was all my Omega needed. Luke had other plans. I protested as he pulled out of my grasp, the warmth of him leaving my body. He chuckled, kissing me before encouraging me to get out of bed. Luke was a nude sleeper, which meant that I got a gorgeous view of his firm ass as he dug through his dresser looking for clothing. He smirked at me before pulling on a pair of boxer briefs, and I let out another sound of disappointment.

The autumn rainy season had begun, and I was grateful that I had chosen to pack my favorite mauve chunky sweater, decorated with a set of tan buttons that went up the left side. It hung just a little past my ass and was made from a soft, fluffy yarn that felt nice against my skin, making me feel warm and cozy when I wore it. I typically paired it with black skinny jeans or leggings and a pair of boots, but I chose to leave the boots at home. The rain pounded heavily against Luke's car, the windshield wipers working on overdrive as our first stop of the day was at a local coffee house near Luke's apartment before he pulled into the parking lot of the nesting department store.

"We could've stayed home, you know," I said, unbuckling my seat belt and grabbing my coffee. I put my thumb over the mouth hole so rain wouldn't get into the cup before I moved to open the door.

"Not gonna happen," he said, grinning at me. "No need to cancel plans for a little water. Now, stay in the car until I get the umbrella open."

"But it's just a little water," I mused, looking at him with a grin.

"Brat,"

He opened his car door and opened the large umbrella he had grabbed from the back seat before leaving the car. I grabbed his coffee from the center console, and together, we huddled under the umbrella until we reached the building's overhang. Closing the umbrella, he shook off as much of the rainwater as possible before pulling a trash bag from his hoodie pocket and placing the wet umbrella into the bag.

"Clever."

"I thought so," he said, grinning as if he were the only one who had ever come up with the idea.

I rolled my eyes and handed him back his coffee before he led us into the store. I was instantly overwhelmed by what I saw. I had never been in a store specifically designed for Omegas nesting; after all, I had never built a nest, so I hadn't really needed to. It was essentially a one-stop trip for anything I could need. Blankets and throws of different styles and materials lined the closest shelves to our right. Beyond that were pillows and other bedding, including special sheets for heats labeled as 'slick resistant'. Stuffed animals of all sizes came beside candles, lighting, and clothing; every item had a tag with a number associated with the product. It was all too much, and anxiety began to take hold.

"This is a bad idea. Let's go home. I'm happy with what I have."

"Hey," Luke responded softly, pulling me away from the door so we weren't in the way of incoming customers.

He slid the umbrella into the crook of his elbow before cupping my chin with his free palm, forcing me to look at him as the restlessness and unease made my body shake. A low purr rumbled from his chest and made my heart quicken, my belly flip-flopping as the anxiety began to cool. The shaking stopped almost as quickly as it had appeared, and I sagged against him, using his body to hold myself up.

"We'll take each aisle one at a time. If you don't find anything you like, that's okay, but at least you looked, and I'll make sure to reward you for putting up with your silly Alpha later."

He kissed the back of my hand, his eyes full of the desire and promise he was making. Hesitantly, I sighed but nodded, and the large smile on his face reassured me that this was okay. I watched as he grabbed a piece of paper and a pen that sat on a small display by the door before explaining to me how the store worked. Each item had a number that coincided with one in the back of the store. While the store had pheromone neutralizers, items were kept in the back in protective packaging to prevent any damage or scents from being attached to the products. No Omega or Alpha wanted to go home with an item that smelled like someone else. The products on display were so I could touch and feel them and decide which would be perfect for me and my nest. The only exceptions to this rule were the plushies in display bags and candles. We started with the closest aisle to us, and I reached out to touch the fabric of a nearby blanket, instantly withdrawing my hand with a wrinkled nose. Why do people even think that scratchy and crinkly blankets are ideal? How does that even remotely feel nice against your body? I heard Luke chuckle behind me, and I threw him a look before continuing.

Reluctantly, I wrote down the number of items I approved of on the piece of paper, adding a dark navy weighted blanket to the list, along with a checkered green and white soft throw. It was rather awkward as fuck as I touched everything that seemed remotely interesting. I squeezed and felt up fuzzy pillows to ensure I liked the feel before deciding one or two could go on the list with the blankets.

However, buried among the pillows, something caught my eye. An otter plush animal lay nestled in the back of gray and purple pillows. He lay on his back, front paws clasped on his tan belly, with a wonky whisker that stuck out at a different angle than the others. I picked him up, discovering that he had a bit of weight, much like the blankets on the list. I looked down at him, lightly booping him on the nose before smiling softly. The otter was unwrapped and smelled of something stale and forgotten, but I couldn't help but hold the plushy close to my body.

Otters were my favorite animal. Growing up, I often asked to go to the aquarium for my birthday and would sit and watch the otters for hours as they danced through the water, chasing each other. I loved to hear the chirps they'd make in excitement when it was feeding time and when they would sometimes sleep against the glass in a little alcove so I could watch them. I don't know why I stopped attending the aquarium as I got older. I didn't need an excuse like my birthday to go, especially since we stopped celebrating outside of a dinner at a restaurant of my choosing, but I had stopped around fifteen or so. I glanced at Luke, who was watching me with interest, but there was no judgment on his face as I held the otter.

"Would you ever be willing to go to the aquarium with me at some point?" I asked, turning the otter around so that his back was pressed against my front, and I wrapped my arms around his stomach under his little clasped paws.

"Pick a day, and we'll go," he said, smiling.

I couldn't help but smile back, taking the otter with me as we continued shopping. I found a set of slick-resistant bed sheets in a deep forest green and a pastel lavender, adding them to the list with my upcoming heat in mind. By the time we headed for checkout, I had added another set of bed sheets, four hoodies in various colors that I could rotate Luke's scent out with, more string lights, and a matching set of nightstands in a dark cedar. When we got to the register, I realized I had to hand over the otter, and I didn't like the idea at all. He had been abandoned before, and it was as if it was the only thing grounding me through the anxiety of buying nesting material. To give him up felt like a dam would break with me. Inwardly, I chastised myself. I'm an adult and needed to act like one, yet I couldn't bring myself to put him on the counter.

As if seeing my inner turmoil, the associate leaned across her counter with a handheld device and scanned the tag attached to his ear. She put the device back into its holder and took the list of items from Luke and began to tally them up on her register. My eyes widened as I heard her ring up the total. $1580?! In what world was that price reasonable for something deemed supposedly necessary for Omegas? Jesus fuck. There is no way I'll be able to pay any of that back, not for a while at least. Maybe this was all too much. He'll realize how expensive it is to have an Omega, how expensive *I am*, and he'll get rid of me the first chance he gets. Maybe we should put all this back and get a refund. I shouldn't have said yes to this.

"No." Luke's firm voice withdrew me from my thoughts.

Luke handed the woman his card as she looked at him questionably, but his eyes were on me, addressing me. He was watching me spiral, clutching the otter so tightly against me that he'd be choking if he were real. Luke reached out to me, pulling me tightly against his body. I inhaled his scent, clutching the fluffy fabric of his hoodie, burying my nose into the material. He purred softly, taking his card from the woman and slipping it back into his wallet. The associate gave me a sympathetic look before turning to Luke and informing him that he could take his car around to the loading dock, and the employees would load our items in the back of his car for us.

"We're returning nothing, and you're not paying me back. I want to do this, Aidyn. It's okay. You've made me the happiest Alpha in the world today, letting me take care of my Omega."

I looked up at him as we stepped into the cold autumn air. It had stopped raining, but the world still smelled fresh and damp, a light breeze occasionally blowing by. The clouds overhead hinted at more rain, and I hoped we were home when it did. I wanted to lie on the couch with Luke, wrapped in a throw with him and this otter, listening to the rain while we watched a movie or read our books. I just wanted to be cozy with him. It was so strange how he consumed my life and infiltrated my very being in such a short time.

"Did I really make you happy?"

"In ways you'll never know." He kissed the top of my head as we headed toward the car.

Aidyn

It took three trips to get everything into Luke's apartment. We sat the bags and boxes on the kitchen bar so that it was easier to riffle through them and dispose of the sales tags and packaging. Luke stopped me from immediately digging into the bags by wrapping his arms around me and kissing the back of my neck, causing my body to shudder at the intimate touch.

"You have five minutes to strip and wait for me on the bed. It's time I reward my Omega for being so good today."

I stared at him with large eyes, his eyebrow raising the longer I stood in my spot. An inhuman sound left my throat as I dashed to the bedroom, pulling my sweater over my head as I went. Kicking off my jeans and underwear, I crawled onto the bed, pushing the blankets out of our way and kneeling on the sheets facing the door, my hands on my thighs.

And waited.

I could hear Luke rummaging around in the kitchen, pulling items out of the plastic shopping bags before throwing the bags away. I could hear the tearing of plastic and cardboard and the soft snip of scissors as he prepared each item for nesting. When he was done, he entered the bedroom with two of the new throw blankets draped over his arm.

"Take your glasses off and place them on the nightstand, and turn around, facing away," he said softly, moving toward the bed.

I quickly moved to obey him as he set the blankets on my side of the bed, laying them down and tucking the edges under the mattress before crawling behind me and running his fingers down my back as he did so.

"We're going to try something new. Are you okay with that?"

"Yes," I nodded, licking my lips.

He opened the draw on his nightstand before he moved behind me, his front pressing against my back as he slid the blindfold over my eyes, blocking out the world.

"I want you to experience nothing but pleasure, but I don't want you to know what I'm doing to you until we're done. I want you to focus on my voice and what I'll do to you. You once gave me a safe word. What was it?"

"Tea," I croaked out, my throat suddenly dry.

"Good boy. Use it if things get too much or if you become over sensitive. I want you to also use the color system. Green is good, yellow tells me to slow down or you're reaching your limit, and red stops, no questions asked. I will be checking in with you and making sure you're okay. Understand?"

What in God's name would he do to me that required me to use colors? I wasn't new to the color system. I'd read about it in books and seen it in a few movies, but I never used it with partners. I nodded, vocalizing my understanding of the situation, my heartbeat loud in my ears. I heard him digging around in the nightstand again before I felt the weight of a few objects being placed on the bed beside me. The sound of the condom packet opening echoed loudly through the room. He touched me then, his arm circling my waist to pull me against his front, and I could feel how hard he was against my ass. I couldn't help but groan slightly as I moved my ass against him, stopping only when he pressed his fingers firmly into my hips.

"Arms behind your back, cross your wrists for me. That's it."

Complying easily, I could feel the scratchy nylon as he placed something across my wrists, velcroing them in place. Instinct told me to test the material, and I found that while I could move my wrists, they were still locked behind my back, and I couldn't do more than wiggle in the binds. Luke traced his fingers lightly down my spine once more, and I couldn't help but arch into his touch, my body shuddering at the warmth of his fingers against my feverish skin.

"Color?"

"Green," I whispered. "How long have you been planning this?"

"Mmm, not long," Luke admitted, pushing between my shoulder blades to push me forward onto the bed, my ass raised in the air. "If you let me, I want to explore all sorts of things with you, maybe get better restraints than these. But this is a two-way street; if you don't want to, that's fine too."

"Well, I don't hate this so far."

Luke ran his hands down my sides and over my ass, his thumb rubbing against my exposed hole, and I jumped slightly at the sudden touch.

"I can tell," he breathed. "You're so wet for me already."

Wiggling my ass in anticipation, I could hear him chuckling behind me. Luke began to move my hips, spreading my knees apart to force me into a position he was happiest with. This placed my ass high in the air on full display, the side of my face on the new throw blankets, and I realized he was using sex as an opportunity to scent some of the new items. My Omega drew pleasure from the knowledge that our Alpha was putting in the effort to improve our nest.

Slick began to run down my thighs, my senses on high alert without my sight, making me more sensitive to touch and sound. I flinched at the sudden feel of Luke's tongue on my inner thigh, trailing the line of slick to its source, his tongue flat against my twitching hole. I pushed back against him, impatient and craving more, but his fingers dug into my thighs, pushing me back into place as he growled against my skin.

Once he was satisfied that I was back in a position he liked, he resumed his teasing, sliding his tongue over my center until I squirmed at his touch. Slowly his tongue entered me, and I could no longer hold back the moan that escaped from my throat, his hand sliding downwards to cup my tightened sack before moving upwards along my shaft. My legs began to shake while I fought not to give in to the pleasure, to not thrust into his grip or push back against his tongue as he extracted pleasure from my body.

He suddenly pulled off me, my body sagging slightly at the sudden emptiness of no longer being touched. The whimper escaped me before I could even stop it, my breaths coming out in pants. Everything felt more intense. I couldn't tell what he was doing or what he would do next. I needed something to ground myself, but my wrists were bound, and I couldn't touch him; I couldn't reach for him, and it was driving me crazy. He grabbed something off the bed before something cold touched the edge of my entrance.

"Breathe in for me, little fawn." Doing as I was told, he worked the tip into me, opening me up slowly. "Good boy, now breathe out."

Upon exhaling, he slid the rest of the toy into me, and I could feel the bulbous areas pressing in against my body, stretching me as I groaned against the blankets. I honestly loved the sharp, sudden pain of being stretched to accommodate my partner, and the bulbous shaft of the toy stretched me to the edge of almost pain, tears prickling the corner of my eyes. I moaned again, wiggling my ass a little as I waited for my body to adjust to the toy. Once adjusted, I resumed my position, no longer moving. Luke pushed on the toy, securing it in place and moving it against me before he readjusted once more, parting my legs to make room for himself as he slid under me, his shoulders pushing my legs impossibly far apart.

He licked his way up my abdomen until he couldn't reach anymore, biting at my sides before licking the tip of my wet cock. My breath hitched in my throat, and I moaned out in pleasure as his tongue swirled around the head. Without any more warning, he swallowed my cock, and the toy inside me kicked to life, vibrating against my insides, hitting the pleasure center buried deep within me.

"Oh, sweet fuck!"

Luke chuckled around my shaft, vibrating against me and mixing with the other vibrations, sending my senses into overdrive. I fought not to collapse onto him, my body shaking as pleasure consumed me. He tugged on the toy, extracting it from my body before pushing it back inside, repeating the movement and slowly fucking me with the vibrator. My moans turned into cries and expletives, thrusting myself into his mouth each time the toy entered me. My body teetered on the edge of orgasm, threatening to give way any second before he suddenly withdrew the vibrator all the way and removed his mouth from my cock.

"I thought this was supposed to be a reward, not torture!" I exclaimed, panting heavily, my body shaking, covered in sweat.

"Oh, it is," he mused, his voice heavy with lust. "Color."

"Yellow. Take me, Alpha."

The toy had done its job in preparing me, opening me up to receive him in one thrust, burying his cock deep within me, our groans echoing around the room. I heard the popping sound of a cap opening before the cool feeling of lubricant being applied to my aching cock. I shuddered at the temperature difference, my body feverish with need. Once satisfied I was ready, Luke slid something over my sensitive tip, encasing my cock in a new toy. I buried my face in the blankets, a strangled cry erupting from my throat as my body reached its limit for stimulation, my body torn between thrusting forward into the toy and pushing back on my Alpha's cock.

Luke began to move, pulling at my resolve, desperation for release clawing at me. With each thrust of his cock, he hit my already sensitive prostate, sending waves of pleasure through me, heightened by the toy he forced me into, the toy squeezing and gripping my shaft. When I thought I couldn't take any more, a new wave of pleasure crashed into me as I could feel his knot forming at the base of his cock, catching on my rim as it threatened to swallow him while it pushed against me.

Tears ran down my cheeks under the mask as his pace quickened. Before I could warn him, I erupted into the toy, the orgasm pulling from my overstimulated body, grateful for the release it had been craving. Luke followed quickly, his cock twitching as he reached completion, his cock buried deep in my ass, his knot pushing into my body and locking us together. My brain was consumed by a thick, hazy fog, blissed out and incapable of thought while he quickly undid the cuffs, massaging my wrists and shoulders, stiff from being in the same position too long. He removed the toy from my sensitive cock, a whimper escaping my throat. Luke pulled me against him into a seated position, my back pressed against him as he cradled me in his lap. The shifting of positions had his knot brushing against my prostate once more, resulting in a dry orgasm and me begging him not to move. Luke chuckled softly while I tilted the back of my head against him as he slid the mask over my eyes, smiling down at me.

"Hey,"

"Hi," I answered softly, nestling closer to him.

He had turned off all the lights except for the bats on the wall, creating a soft glow in the room that wasn't too bright for my adjusting eyes. Reaching for one of the throws that was close by, Luke wrapped it around me, his purr filling the room. My Omega joined in on his song shortly after, showing him how happy and content I was. My eyes slowly began to adjust to the world around us, and I looked at the bed to find the nylon cuffs, a bottle of lube, a condom wrapper, and two sets of toys on a towel. One was the toy he had inserted inside me with a bulbous tip before tapering off in the middle and widening again at the base. It was remote-controlled, which explained why I didn't know it vibrated until suddenly it did. It had a ring at the end of it so that he could easily remove it. The other was a clear masturbation sleeve, nothing special until I recalled something he had said prior.

"Is that —"

"The sleeve I knotted? Yes. Another last-minute addition. I had intended to get you a new one, so we didn't use the same one, but I saw it in the drawer when I grabbed the other stuff."

He groaned as laughter vibrated through my body, squeezing and vibrating along his cock as it remained nestled inside my body.

"It will never know the knot of an Alpha again, only the cock of an Omega," I smirked, eliciting a rumble of laughter from him.

"How are you feeling? Too much?"

"It was perfect, Alpha," I mumbled, suddenly exhausted.

Luke held me, kissing my forehead softly as sleep took over.

Aidyn

Erik has all but stopped talking to me unless it was necessary. He has even gone so far as to move seats in the classes that we shared, no longer sitting beside me and being the petty, pouty asshole that he was. I was done trying to talk to him. If he wanted something like this to come between us, it was on him. I never led him on, and I established that my heat with him was a mistake and he had no chance, yet he had it ingrained in his skull that I was being difficult and would see the error of my ways eventually.

Being 'friend-zoned' is a myth. Forcing someone to like you isn't how affection and attraction work. If someone felt that being placed in the friend category is the worst thing in the world, then they weren't a real friend and didn't care about the person in the first place. Erik was quickly proving that we were nothing more than his attraction and lost to me—and I won't lie, it fucking hurt. Making friends has always been hard, and being an Omega made it harder. Society has taught the world that Omegas are nothing more than baby factories and we're fragile creatures. We're always on guard to protect ourselves in case something happens, and most Betas viewed us as competition for partners. We're either a fetish or instinct.

I thought Erik was different, but apparently not. Luke noticed right away because, of course, he did. He never asked questions; he just told me to contact him if I needed him or to leave the apartment. Within a week of Erik giving me the silent treatment and ignoring me, I contacted Luke. I packed an overnight bag, and he was at my place within the hour, and now I was rarely home. It occurred to me one evening that I didn't have a reason to go home anymore when my mate and nest were all at Luke's apartment, but I still felt like I was intruding. I waited for Luke to tire of me, but he hadn't said anything.

He didn't say anything when I vented about Erik, only comforting me as the pressure got to be too much, and I broke down, realizing I was losing someone important to me. As if I was mourning a family member, and despite having Luke, it was very isolating. However, when it had passed, I was left with only anger. I was angry that Erik felt that this was how he could treat me, angry that he would rather throw years away simply because I didn't like him back. That our friendship meant more to me than it did to him. Fine. That's on him and not on me. I had more important shit to worry about.

Midterms had passed, but the workload increased the closer we got to finals. Many of the teachers had quizzes prepared to ensure that we were ready for the final, and others had multiple projects that were due. My stress levels were at an all-time high. Luke helped me study, but it felt peculiar to study for a test given to you by a teacher whose knot had been inside you only moments before. I did enjoy his reward system, though. He had also gone the extra mile, giving me some of the quizzes he had done over the previous years to fill out and test my knowledge. I used them as study guides for the midterms, highlighting key information I would need to pass. Most nights, Luke made dinner while I sat at the kitchen bar, my notes and guides spread across the countertop. Though my brain was foggy today, and I struggled to focus.

"You alright? You keep spacing," Luke asked, interrupting me from reading the same sentence six times.

"Yeah, just struggling to concentrate, and I can't figure out why or how to focus."

With a sigh, I gathered my notes and the quizzes, placing them inside my textbook before pushing them off to the side and out of the way. The brain fog was getting worse, becoming too exhausting to fight through it in hopes that something I was studying would stick. I watched as Luke seared the salmon fillets he had sitting on a plate before re-plating them. He then started working on a Parmesan sauce, starting with sautéing the garlic and sun-dried tomatoes.

"I've been meaning to talk to you about that, but I didn't know how to bring it up," Luke said cautiously, adding white wine to the pan and letting it simmer before adding heavy cream and Parmesan cheese to create a thick sauce.

"Bring what up?"

Again, he was silent as he added the salmon back to the pan, letting it simmer for a bit as he spooned the sauce over it. Finally, he plated the salmon with asparagus and placed the dishes on the bar, but he didn't move.

"I haven't noticed a change in your pheromones, but I have noticed a change in your behavior as of late. You're spacing out in class, when we talk and when you're studying. You've been coming over here for the past month since Harllow stopped talking to you, and I've noticed you've been antsy. Spending more time in your nest, you've even brought some things home from your apartment to place in the nest."

"And?"

Where was he going with this? Have I begun to overcrowd him? I realized recently that we've been acting more domesticated than usual, as if we were already living together, even though I knew that wasn't the case. I had forced my way into his home and left things here. The second we walked through the door, I would change out of my daily clothing and into a pair of pajama pants and his hoodie. He had been kind enough to let me stay, but maybe I was starting to become too much.

"Hey," Luke reached over the counter to take my hand, forcing me to look at him. "None of that. I'm mentioning this because I'm worried about something you said before. Your heats haven't followed a set schedule, and you went into heat while on suppressants in my office. With the stress of Harllow, the past midterms, upcoming projects, and you spacing out, I'm worried your heat will show up unplanned like it had in September. I want to be prepared in case that happens."

Holy fuck. Fuck fuck fuck fuck fuck. It hadn't even occurred to me that I was experiencing pre-heat symptoms. I had been on suppressants so long that I didn't even recognize the signs. Once I get to this point, it could happen either tomorrow or weeks from today. It was so unpredictable that I was a ticking bomb, ready to go off any second. Fuck! Panic spiked through me as my brain began to move a mile a minute, affecting my breathing as the panic attack began to set in.

"It's okay." Luke made his way around the counter, taking me into his arms and holding my head against his chest. "I should've brought this up sooner. I noticed the spacing out only this week, but I didn't want to say anything in case I was wrong. Lately, once dinner is over, you curl up on the couch in my scent and your blankets with one of the plushies, something you haven't done until now. If I'm correct, I know this is a really bad time. But I want to have a plan in place. Do you want to hear my ideas?"

I silently nodded, my brain fighting through the fog and going into overdrive as I thought about the next few weeks. Should I contact Dr. Easton and tell him plans have changed? Could I get on the trial medication as soon as this heat is over? If I was going into heat, was it too late to stop it? I made a mental note to ask in the morning.

"You will continue to stay with me as you have been. We'll swing by your apartment later if you need anything more for your heat. If you go into heat, I'll call in sick. I have plenty of sick leave saved because I never actually use any of it. If I am not with you, I want you to text me the fire emoji before it gets to be too much, and wherever I am, I'll come to you. There is an app that can track friends, and we can set that up. You can watch me come to you. I will be there, regardless of what I'm doing."

"What if it happens if I go into heat during a different class? Or even if we're in the middle of your lecture? Or what happens if you're not here to let me in?"

Luke pulled away and set a key ring on the counter. There were two sets of keys on the ring. One had the letter O stamped on the front beneath the window cutouts, and the other had an H. He pushed the ring closer to me.

"One is the key to this apartment, and the other will get you into my office. Regardless if you're at school, you need to leave that classroom any way you can. Head straight for my office, and lock the door behind you. I left some of your blankets in my office this morning; they're in the bottom drawer of my desk. Stay there until I can come get you and bring you home."

My eyes widened, and I turned to look at him, his face serious but determined. Not only had he picked up subtle hints that I might be in pre-heat before I did, but he had also made spare keys and tried to make his office a safe place until he could reach me. Wrapping my arms around his waist, I pulled him into a hug, burying my face into his chest so my Omega could drink in his scent. I wanted to tell him how much I loved him, how grateful I was that it seemed he had thought of everything while I was oblivious to what my Omega was telling me. Yet, as I opened my mouth to tell him, those three words were replaced with a "thank you," and I was left struggling to find a reason why I couldn't tell him how I felt, while also wondering how on earth this man could be so good to me.

The following morning I woke to an empty bed and Luke's muffled voice from beyond the bedroom door. I found a sweatshirt he had left for me at the foot of the bed and pulled it on before leaving the bedroom. I was instantly hit with the scent of burnt cloves and citrus, his pheromones indicating that Luke was agitated and angry. I had left my glasses in the bedroom in search of him and found his fuzzy frame in the living room, pacing, his phone to his ear, with his back turned to me. I slid my arms around his waist, resting my head against his broad back as I pulled him against me.

Instantly his body relaxed, leaning into my touch while I released some of my pheromones to taper the burning anger within him. My Omega's purr rolled out of my chest, vibrating against his back as his arm clutched mine.

"I really don't know how many times I have to tell you that I'm simply not interested in Miss Richards. I have a mate, and I don't give a flying fuck if he's not good enough for you because he's more than good enough for me. I don't need your approval on my life partner, and I'm going to stay with him until I know that his heat has passed."

The last time Luke spoke to his parents, it had also been a fight about me and insecurity clutched itself tightly around my body. Attempting to pull away from him, he clung to me, refusing to let me go. Luke turned around in my embrace, cupping my face in his free hand, exhaustion and sadness on his face.

"A mistress does not come before family and duty. You *will* show up for Thanksgiving, or I'll drag you out of your apartment myself. Do you understand me?" His father's voice was loud over the phone's speaker, while his tone suggested that he viewed Luke as a problematic child.

"Mistress?" I whispered, smiling at Luke. "They do know I'm a guy, right?"

Luke gave a halfhearted smile and rolled his eyes, but there was a war raging behind his gaze. Like Luke mentioned last night, my heat didn't give a damn about holidays or families. Luke's family didn't give a damn about anyone he saw as his mate, and it was clear that I wasn't invited to their holiday dinner. That didn't bother me. What did bother me was that I was coming between him and his family. I wouldn't be the reason they fought.

"Go," I whispered, placing my hand on his cheek and stepping on my tippy toes to kiss him.

"I can't, you need me here."

"Go. Please," I insisted. "I'll be alright, and I'll be here."

Luke's eyes searched my face before he replied, "One hour. We'll have dinner, and then I need to leave. My duty is here."

Despite the plan, the closer to Thanksgiving we got, the more mini heat spikes I experienced. I doubled up on my suppressants, carried de-scenter spray everywhere, and ignored Luke's look of concern. I just needed to get through the next few days.

I spoke with Dr. Easton the week of Thanksgiving about the change of plans, and Luke filled out the form to take a leave of absence for the week after, citing a family emergency. The issue was that not many could teach his class, so he left behind a list of documentaries the substitute professor could show with a quiz to review the information learned and required reading for his return. In the five years that Luke had taught at the university, he never took a leave of absence, so he was confident the university wouldn't deny his request.

Dr. Easton explained that, unfortunately, there was nothing that could be done to stop my impending heat, but he said that it might mean I won't go into one when we flush the suppressants out of my system in December before the winter holidays. He couldn't find a reason as to why I was still having a heat, despite being on suppressants, and he apologized for the inconvenience. Which had me laughing, because holy fuck was this an inconvenience, and the idea that I might have a second heat next month just irritated the hell out of me.

We had gone shopping for water bottles, boxes of protein bars, and a box of Alpha condoms in preparation for my heat, and I placed them in the bedroom near the foot of the bed. It made sense to do so since my nest was likely where I would spend my heat. Luke had already left for his parents' Thanksgiving dinner, and the apartment felt quiet without him. I tried to focus on homework, finishing a project that was due next week, but struggled once more. God, this was annoying. Sighing, I entered the bathroom, turning the shower on to let it heat up. Stepping under the spray, a heat spike surged through me, and I groaned in need, using the wall to prevent myself from collapsing to my knees as the wave crashed into me.

I could feel slick gathering at my entrance as I reached behind me, inserting two fingers easily into my body. I groaned in frustration, my fingers not quite reaching the spot within my body that would provide temporary relief. I had grown so used to having Luke assist me that my Omega became greedy for him, desperate for him to make us feel good. But I had to handle this alone. Grabbing my cock, I ran my fist along the velvety skin of my shaft, my back arching slightly in pleasure. Visions of Luke and me together flashed through my head, bringing my release quickly, splattering across the tile surface. But it wasn't enough, and my body felt tight and unsatisfied, agitated. I turned the nozzle to cold, letting the water cool my feverish skin. This wasn't like my previous heats. I had never spiked like this, and I couldn't help but wonder if it was because I had access to another dominant.

The desire for my mate was quickly replaced by fear. Fear of the unknown and fear of my cycle changing. I trusted Luke; I wouldn't have asked him to spend my heat with me if I hadn't, but I couldn't help the anxiety that welled up within me. Somehow, I knew that my Omega would take over soon, I would be going into heat soon, and I could only hope that Luke would be here when I did.

Luke

I arrived at my parents' estate for Thanksgiving dinner, only to be forced into the guest bathroom by my mother, with strict instructions to shower before coming to the living room. I wanted to get out of this evening as conflict-free as possible, so I did as I was told. I could drown in Aidyn's scent when I returned to the apartment in an hour. However, my Alpha mourned the scent of our mate as it spiraled down the drain in a soapy mess that smelled strongly of coconut. When I stepped out of the shower, I found my suit was missing, replaced by a new one in a dark gray. I looked around to find my phone, panic surging until I found it on the floor under the bathroom sink.

I turned it on and was immediately greeted by the photo that Aidyn had taken of our hands, our fingers interlaced together on his lap. I had hundreds of photos of us together, but this was the most discreet one I had that was safe to display to the world. My heart hurt looking at it, and I could feel myself teetering on the edge, fighting my brain to leave and return to my mate. He needed me. Aidyn's spikes were coming closer and closer together, and I needed to be at the apartment when the heat became too much for him, but he insisted I come tonight. It was my idea to have him scent-mark me before I left, and now I had only the image to try and settle me.

Sighing, I pulled on the fresh suit and growled in irritation to find that the jacket was slightly too small in the shoulders. I would have to watch my movements to ensure I didn't split the seams down my spine. Exiting the bathroom, I could hear the voices of my parents and someone I didn't recognize, allowing it to lead me to their location. I found my parents, cocktails already in hand, sitting across from a couple, with a smaller woman in a navy blue dress between them. She didn't speak but smiled politely as my parents greeted me. She was rather small in frame with long blond hair that had been dressed up for the occasion but still fell down her back. Her large blue eyes watched me as I entered the room, framed by thick dark lashes. She looked like a carbon copy of the woman beside her, just younger and more timid. By his presence, I could tell the man beside her was an Alpha, so I could only assume that the younger woman was either a Beta or an Omega. Factoring in my parents, I could easily deduce that she was an Omega from a worthy lineage.

I noticed my mother's annoyed look when I refused the alcoholic beverage one of the household staff members offered me, requesting a soda or water instead. I pulled out my phone again, realizing I still had about forty-five minutes left. Fuck me. I told Aidyn I wouldn't be here any longer than an hour. I told my parents the same thing over the phone a week ago. And dinner still hadn't been served.

"What time is dinner, Mother?" I inquired, shoving the phone into my pocket and taking the Coke bottle from the staff member.

"You're being very rude to our guests, Luke. Sit down," Father instructed, his face blank of expression.

I narrowed my eyes at him and sat in a chair away from my parents, turning my attention to the family my parents had invited.

"I'm sorry, but I have a prior engagement I must leave for soon. I'm Luke." I leaned forward, shaking hands with the gentleman and smiling politely at the woman.

"Alexander Richards. This is my mate, Emilia, and our daughter, Anna. Jason has told us so much about you. He says you're a teacher for now?"

"For now?" Tilting my head and casting a side eye to my father.

"Your father said you will take over the firm when he retires in five years."

"I know nothing about that," I chuckled forcibly. "My sister, Teagan, would better fit that role. I enjoy teaching."

"And what is it that you teach, Mr. Ellis?" Emilia piped up.

It didn't go unnoticed that Anna remained silent between her parents, letting them control the conversation.

"I teach ABO Psych and Biology. It's the study of how our designations can potentially affect our psychology. My class is required for students going into the various medical fields. I enjoy what I do."

"There's not much money in teaching, though," my father said, lips pursed. "Now that you have had your fun, you can set your sights on the real world and take over the firm, as I raised you to do."

"I'm doing just fine, Father. I never agreed to take over the firm and I have never shown an interest in it. I've told you to give it to T; it's her dream, and she won't run it into the ground. All your hard work won't be for nothing."

I watched the sour look of annoyance cross my father's face with a sense of delight. My phone chimed loudly in the silence, and I fished it out of my pocket, glancing at the screen. My stomach dropped, my blood freezing in my veins, as I saw the simple fire emoji from Aidyn. Fuck! I stood up, handing the bottle to the staff member, my eyes focused on the screen.

> I'm coming, baby.

I quickly typed out my response before sliding the phone back into my pocket.

"I'm terribly sorry, but I must leave. As I said, a prior engagement needs my attention. It was lovely meeting you."

"Where do you think you're going?" my father snapped, standing up quickly.

"I'm needed elsewhere. I already told you I would be here for no more than an hour." I leaned over and kissed my mother on the cheek before unbuttoning the suit jacket, loosening its fit across my shoulder.

"It hasn't even been an hour yet, regardless, you are needed here." my mother said, her tone even. "I invited the Richards here so you could meet Anna."

It finally clicked in my head, and I sighed. I knew the last name sounded familiar, but I was naive enough to believe that my parents would actually listen to me when I told them I had a mate, and a mate that would be entering his heat. I shook my head, frustrated but agitated to get out of there.

"Have my parents told you that I'm gay?" I asked, looking at Anna directly.

Her eyes widened, shaking her head.

"I guess they also failed to mention that I have a mate."

"You do?" Alexander asked, looking toward my father.

"He does not!" my father countered back.

"I do!" I said, lacing my words with a growl. "His name is Aidyn, very intelligent. He wants to be an Omega Specialist, graduating in the spring. They also probably didn't tell you that I can't scent you. Without making any assumptions, I probably would've thought you and your parents were Betas. I can't scent a damn thing. But I can scent him. He smells like the forest on a warm day."

Anna looked at me with her large blue eyes, an unreadable expression on her face, while I could feel my parents fuming beside me. I knew if I could scent them, the room would be thick with toxic smoke, but I couldn't muster up the energy to feel sorry for them. My mother knew about Aidyn, and since she told my father everything, so did he. But they continued to push. I stared directly at Anna before I spoke again.

"They don't think he's worthy because he doesn't come from a family like yours or mine. They even told me to keep him as a mistress, but that isn't fair to him, and that isn't fair to you. I'm sure you're a sweet girl, but you deserve to be loved and cherished like all Omegas do. Not used as a pawn in an archaic mindset that you have no say in. You should get to choose, like I have. I have already chosen Aidyn. I did the moment I met him, and they refused to acknowledge that. I'm sorry that you got dragged into their game. I've already met my fated mate, and I hope you meet yours. But you won't if you're tied to me and this way of thinking. Now, if you'll forgive me, my mate needs me."

I bowed my head and began to leave, moving toward the front door, when my father's voice stopped me.

"You're too old to believe in fairy tales! Fated mates aren't real. This family is. You have a duty to this family and will do as you're told. Don't you dare walk out that door, or —"

"Or what?" I growled, eyeing him. "What could you possibly do? Cut me off? Disown me? That's fine. I don't need anything from you, and I haven't since I was sixteen. Aidyn is my family, and my duty is to him. You don't get to decide whether the offspring you chose to have gets to be a part of your life when it suits you most. You don't get to decide if you want to be a part of ours; I do. I came today because Mother asked me to, and I told her how long I could stay. I have been very upfront about Aidyn. You have chosen to lure the Richards here under false pretenses, and that is not my responsibility. That is on you and your bigoted ideas. My Omega needs me, and I'm done here."

I entered my apartment and could smell the scent of Aidyn's heat everywhere. The lights were off except for a soft glow from the bedroom, where the door was cracked open. Hastily kicking my shoes off in the entryway, I pulled off my tie, ditching my dress jacket over the couch, leaving a trail of clothing behind me. I turned off my phone and set it on the kitchen counter before using the guest bedroom to rush through a shower, washing off the scent of my parents and the Richards. Aidyn's scent called out to me, but I didn't want to contaminate his nest with them.

When I was showered, I moved toward the bedroom, naked. The scent of pheromones and slick was so strong that I let out an involuntary moan, shutting the bedroom door behind me and sealing out the outside world. Aidyn had stripped the sheets and blankets from the bed, arranging them into a nest of his own design at the foot of the bed on the floor. The border of the nest was a combination of my hoodies and t-shirts woven around stacks of books to create a wall that I would have to step over to enter his domain. The nest floor consisted of the weighted blankets he had chosen, with the Halloween throws placed on top to create a cloud-like cushion. Aidyn lay in the center of the nest, cell phone by his head with his back to me, curled into a ball and clutching my pillow close against his body. He was naked, his glasses gone, his skin pink with heat. He had moved the bottles of water and the protein bars closer to the nest, and mixed emotions washed over me. We knew his heat would happen quickly, and I knew it would happen while I was with my parents, yet he still pushed me to go to them. I should've been here with my mate, and instead, I had to fight a battle that I knew I couldn't win. How much pain was he in while he got everything ready? Did he wait until he couldn't bear it anymore before texting me?

As if answering my thoughts, Aidyn groaned, clutching the pillow closer to his middle as the petrichoral scent of his slick hit my senses. My Alpha hyper-fixated on our mate, our Omega, who slowly rolled over to look at me, a lazy smile on his lips as he reached for me. By the look in his eyes, I could tell he was struggling to regain awareness as his heat began to take over. Soon, I would lose him to the basic instincts our designations possessed. I moved toward the nest, and stepped into the circle. I took his hand, interlacing our fingers before I cupped his cheek with my other hand and kissed him softly.

"I'm here, little fawn. I got you."

A low purr started in his chest as he rubbed his face against mine, then nuzzled my neck, opening his legs so that I could nestle close against his feverish body. When he was done scent-marking me, he raised his glazed eyes toward me, struggling to focus on me. His body relaxed into my touch, releasing the tension it held. He ran his hand through my hair, and I smiled at him again before his features twisted into pain, and the fresh scent of slick reached me. I never knew what it was like for an Omega to be in heat, only the things that I have read and that were described to me, and it hurt my heart to see him in pain.

"My Alpha," he whispered, bumping his nose against mine and grinding his hips against me.

I couldn't help but meet his motions with my own, my cock leaking precum to mingle with his as they moved against each other. I struggled to pull away from him to find the box of condoms he had purchased, his nails digging into my skin as we broke apart. Tearing into the foil packet and rolling the condom down my length, I angled my cock, pushing into his entrance slowly, only to find that his body was ready for me and presented no resistance as I slid forward into his depths. He cried out in relief, head tilted back when I bottomed out, and I nuzzled his neck, kissing his sweaty shoulder.

"Such a good Omega, taking your Alpha so well," I whispered.

His skin was hot and clammy as if a fire raged within his body. His eyes glazed over, and his legs opened wider, willing me deep into his core. I leaned forward, cupping his face in my hands and watching him as I moved in and out of his feverish body. I could see Aidyn fighting to remain in control, struggling to stay in the moment and not let his Omega take over, but we both knew he would lose the fight. Every Omega did. But he needed my reassurance that all would be okay before he could let go.

"I got you," I whispered, kissing his throat and nipping at the skin gently. "Let go, I got you."

His nails dug into my arms as if trying to gain a perch, something to hold onto so he didn't lose himself, as if he was worried he wouldn't return from where he went when his Omega took over. His panicked whimper was low in his throat but high-pitched in sound—almost like a wounded animal—as he struggled, and my heart broke at the fear that I could see on his face. My Alpha's purr boiled to the surface, and I released more pheromones into the nest, surrounding us with my scent, calming the panic. Aidyn closed his eyes as another whimper of panic escaped his throat while he listened to my purr. When he opened his eyes again, my Aidyn was gone.

Luke

Despite all the preparation we had done for his heat, I hadn't anticipated how exhausting and draining they were for dominants and all the things that could go wrong. The first offense was the shower I had taken after Aidyn's first spike, wanting to wash off the sweat and sticky precum while he slept. This only made him furious when he woke up, a deep growl low in his throat when he smelled the soap and shampoo. He had tackled me the moment I reentered the nest, straddling my hips while an angry purr rattled in his chest. He immediately scent marked me, his face rubbing aggressively against my skin like a cat while biting into my neck harshly in punishment. I didn't shower between the spikes after that. His heat spikes occurred every two to three hours, with Aidyn sleeping between them, and by the second day, my balls ached in protest.

The second offense was trying to get Aidyn to eat when he wanted to sleep. I had to practically force the food down his throat, but getting water into him was easier, abusing the fact that he enjoyed kissing to push the fluid into his mouth. At first, he choked, not expecting it, but he caught on quickly, exploring my mouth with his tongue as if he were trying to get every last drop. I decided that if there were a next time, I would buy protein shakes and fruit, easy foods that I could get him to eat.

Being with Aidyn was nothing like being with my ex, Anthony. Anthony was lucid and in pain during his heat that we spent together, screaming at me that I had failed him. Insisting that I bring him a "real" Alpha. Aidyn, however, called out for me, demanding my knot, my scent, my presence. Despite the fact that he had warned me, I wasn't prepared for how feral he would be. He had warned me, even went as far as telling me his last heat partner came away with scratches and bruises. My arms and back were covered in scratches, caked with dried blood, and every inch of me he could reach had bite marks. It was like he was trying desperately to crawl into my skin, as if I wasn't close enough to him. Without my mating bite, the wounds on my body would heal, and there would be no evidence of the marks, and my Alpha fucking hated it. The marks made us proud, honored, and a little turned on. They were left by our mate in the throes of heat. It symbolized his desire for us, his need for us.

Aidyn slept, often curled in a ball around the otter plush we had picked up. Have you ever had sex with the beady eyes of a stuffed otter looking on like some weird-ass voyeur? I understand it's an inanimate object, but it's a little weird. Every time there was a lull in his heat and my knot had deflated enough to extract me from his body, his hands would search for the plush, pulling it close against him when he found it. Dark circles had appeared under his eyes, and I could tell he was just as exhausted as I was, if not more. Little was known about Dominant Omega heats, and the information I did find scrolling through my phone between spikes was mixed about how much longer his heat would last.

But while Aidyn slept fitfully, he was unaware of the battle I was fighting with my Alpha. My Alpha had tried to move to the driver's seat and dominate the situation more than once, letting animalistic need take over. The longer Aidyn's heat went on, the more I struggled—my Alpha found things to hyperfixate on, his anger growing the more I remained lucid and my thoughts were left to their own devices. I became more agitated, my brain entering the first stages of rut. This wasn't like when I was solo and dug my teeth into my arm. This was much, much worse. It was violent and unpredictable, and I began to lose cognitive thought.

I tentatively reached out my hand, my fingers running down the smooth skin of his neck. My mark should be here. I released more pheromones, pumping my scent into the stifling room, muggy with the scent of forest and rain. He should be constantly showered in my pheromones, but because of the fucking university's policy, he had to wash any traces of me from his body with that chemical spray, offending my nose with its scent. I *finally* had someone I could scent, someone who made me feel like a true Alpha. I wasn't broken when I was with him. And everything was against us. The university, my parents, his roommate. I was in love with him, and I had to hide him like he was something dirty. No one accepted us, and there was nothing that outwardly showed that he was my mate.

A low rumble started in my chest as I moved, pinning Aidyn's body under me as I towered over him on my hands and knees, looking down at my sleeping Omega. I lowered my head, nuzzling his hair, marking him with more of my scent. I'm sure I was drowning him, suffocating him with my scent, but I struggled to care.

Aidyn opened his eyes slightly, a purr rolling through his chest as he saw me before rolling onto his back and bringing his knees upward to allow me access to his body. I growled in approval, nuzzling his neck as I slid into his abused hole, words long abandoning me. His body welcomed me into its embrace, and the sound of pleasure vibrated through his throat. For once, he was calm, having just woken up, and I took advantage of his submission, withdrawing from his body slowly before pushing back in, his body shuddering at the impact.

I trailed my nose down his neck, licking at the junction between his collarbone and throat, brushing my Alpha canines against the skin. Aidyn moaned and tilted his head to the side as if daring me to cave to my thoughts. I needed the world to know. I need them to see that we were bonded for life, that he was my fated mate. Regardless of whether it was a myth. That I would not leave him for anyone, that leaving him would kill me. But without my scent or mark, he appeared to be available, and anyone could attempt to take him from me.

Below me, Aidyn mewled in pleasure, his hands gripping my biceps as my pace picked up, my rhythm more forceful than I had intended, but I couldn't stop the thoughts in my head. Aidyn slid his legs to the back of my thighs, trying to pull me into his body and locking me into place. His face flushed in pleasure, and my Alpha roared, knowing we were the cause. My Alpha slid into the driver's seat of my mind, finally giving in to his rut, and a haze settled in my brain, numbing any thoughts that tried to surface. Aidyn was all I wanted; he had come to me from out of nowhere and changed my life, and I refused to let him go. Not now.

My teeth sunk into his flesh, and the metallic taste of blood exploded across my tongue. I focused on my pheromones and willed them into my mark, starting the bonding process, tethering him to me. A gasp escaped from his throat while a faint tether connected us, locking into place. However, it felt heavy, unfinished, and frayed. It was blurry, and I couldn't determine the end of the tether, but instinctively, I knew he was at the other end. With a final thrust, I pushed my knot into his body, licking at the blood that ran down from the mark at his collarbone. My tongue licked over the bite, my Alpha purring at our claim. Aidyn shuddered beneath me, and I nuzzled him gently as sleep took over his exhausted body, the haze of my rut receding and my thoughts began to clear. I felt calm. Calmer than I had felt in days. I couldn't help but lick my mark again.

When my knot settled, I withdrew from his body, moving away after placing the otter in Aidyn's arms. Grabbing a bottle of water, I uncapped it before reaching down to remove the condom. Except, there wasn't a condom. I looked down at my cock, bare and coated in my seed and Aidyn's slick, my heart plummeting. Suddenly, I could taste the coppery tang of Aidyn's blood in my mouth, and swallowing made me sick as reality finally settled in. The immeasurable fuck-up that I just committed went undetected by my sweet Omega, who was curled before me around his otter plush. Completely oblivious to the fact that not only did I mark him against his will, but I knotted him without a condom. I am so fucking fucked.

AIDYN

I opened my eyes to find the sun streaming into the bedroom through a crack in the curtains. I was on the floor in the nest I had made while my heat spiked, and my Omega was desperate for Luke. I had texted him when the spikes became too much, and he had come to me, and then I remembered nothing. But now, something felt wrong.

I knew what it felt like to come out of a heat alone and what it felt like to come out of a heat after spending it with someone. This was different. There was no groggy feeling, my body didn't feel sore, but my Omega purred happily within me. It was content about something, and it took me a second to realize what it could be so content about.

Oh fuck. Fuck fuck fuck fuck fuck fuck.

Panic sliced through me, and I scrambled out of the nest as if it were on fire, only to realize that Luke wasn't beside me. Under the scent of Luke's pheromones, I found a lighter, softer scent. It was floral and subtle, faint enough that I had to really strain my senses to pick it up. My heart plummeted, and I needed to find Luke. I needed to know what happened because, clearly, something went wrong.

I reached for my pants and pulled them on before grabbing one of his hoodies from the nest. As I reached, a sharp pain shot through my shoulder, and I hissed at the sting. Standing up, I looked at my reflection in the mirror, and a sob caught in my throat. A fresh set of bite marks sat in the junction between my shoulder and the base of my throat. I covered my mouth with my hand as the sob finally escaped me, tears filling my eyes. If he had asked, I might've said yes. My Omega already acknowledged him as our mate, but Luke attempted to bond us together without a discussion. Like I was property to claim.

I no longer wanted to find Luke, not right now. What I needed was to get the fuck out of here.

Dropping his hoodie to the floor, I desperately searched around me for a shirt that was mine, pulling it from the nest and dragging it over my head. Panic and anxiety began to drown me, making it harder for me to breathe as I moved throughout the empty apartment, void of any sound from its owner. Grabbing my backpack, I slipped into my shoes and left, the laces dragging along the floor as I hadn't put in the effort to tie them.

Omegas could sometimes detect their pregnancy at conception, the same time their Alpha notices, but it was common for us to realize a few days later as we're disoriented from our heats as we come back to ourselves. But my heat broke abruptly without it tapering off like it should've. I knew what that floral scent was; I wasn't stupid, yet I still insisted on stopping at the pharmacy less than a block from my apartment. The woman who sold me the three boxes of tests had eyed me, looking around to see if anyone else was with me, and when she only saw me, a look of pity had crossed her face.

I was embarrassed, annoyed, and angry and grabbed the bag aggressively from her when I left. Pushing my way into my apartment, I dropped my backpack and keys off at the door on the floor, not taking the time to hang them up on the hooks in the entryway. Entering the kitchen, I grabbed a plastic cup from the cupboard and immediately made my way into the bathroom, shutting the door behind me before pulling the three boxes out of the pharmaceutical bag in my hands. Now I stood over the toilet bowl with an alcoholic wipe that I used to wipe the tip of my cock with before grabbing the cup and urinating into it. Opening each test, I dipped the ends into the cup, per the instructions, recapped them, and set them on the counter. And waited.

I jumped as my phone began to vibrate on the counter, and I glanced at the screen to find Luke calling me, but I couldn't answer. I watched the call go to voicemail, only for Luke to try to call again. I grabbed my phone in a panic, immediately turning the vibration off and setting my phone to Do Not Disturb so that I couldn't see his calls. I noticed he had also sent me a text, but I couldn't open it when my eyes landed on the tests and their results.

Pregnant.

Oh God. No, no, no, no, no. I knew I was; I could tell by the floral scent and the absence of waking up groggy. But knowing and having it confirmed were two different ways of thinking. Pregnancy was the risk of spending a heat with another dominant, especially since the implant and suppressants didn't work for us. But Luke had assured me that everything would go well. He had assured me I would be okay and we'd be fine. Yet I came out of it partially bonded and fucking pregnant! The floodgates that held my panic at bay disintegrated, and my chest tightened. I clawed at my hoodie, suddenly unable to breathe.

"Aidyn?"

Erik's voice reached through the other side of the door, and my panic increased. He was the last fucking person I needed right now. He knocked before opening the door, his eyes instantly landing on the tests on the counter.

"What have you done?"

"What do you mean 'what have I done'?!" Anger flashed through me, giving me something to grab onto even as it began to flee instantly. "I didn't fucking ask for this! I didn't ask to be a dominant Omega! I didn't ask to go into heat! I didn't ask for normal medication to do absolutely fucking nothing! Do you think I wanted this? You think I want a —oh god."

I dove for the toilet as bile climbed up my throat, and I vomited everything I had in me. I began to hyperventilate and didn't notice Erik had left the bathroom only to come back with a glass of water. He sat beside me, a look of concern on his face. I couldn't hold it together anymore, and tears began to fall on my face, sobs racking my body violently as Erik pulled me against him. I clung to his shirt, unable to stop myself. It felt like my whole body was in pain, and I just wanted to curl up and not think.

A baby was supposed to be a joyous occasion, something to celebrate and be excited about. If this had been a year from now, I would be running to Luke with the positive tests, elated at our news. But this wasn't in the future; it was now, and my heart broke. I had been bonded and impregnated without a single say in its process. Luke and I had a plan. I trusted him to see me through my heat; we had gone over it dozens of times. I bought condoms. Did they break? Why wasn't he there when I woke up? He had abandoned me in his apartment as if he thought I wouldn't fucking notice.

I wrapped my arms around my stomach, my sobbing slowly morphing to soft hiccups as I tried to recenter myself, closing my eyes. Silence enveloped us as Erik and I sat on the bathroom floor. I shuffled to reposition myself more comfortably and thought about what would happen next. Obviously, I couldn't keep it, but finding a doctor who would terminate the pregnancy of an Omega was going to be difficult. I couldn't go to Dr. Easton. Luke had said they were friends, and I don't know if he's aware of our relationship, but I couldn't take that risk. I'd have to look into reputable locations outside of him.

"Do you know who the father is?" Erik asked softly, interrupting the silence.

"Of course," I replied, hurt at the implication.

"Did he force you?"

"Nothing like that, Erik. I loved...love him."

"The guy you've been seeing?"

I was silent and only nodded, tightening my hold around my middle. A loud thumping came from the front door, and my body went into panic mode as our silence was disrupted, my heart pounding loudly in my ears. I sat up, eyes wide, and glanced at Erik, who was on alert, standing up from his spot. A fresh wave of tears flooded my eyes, running down my cheeks, my Omega calling out to our Alpha with a low, alien-like rattle that echoed along the bathroom tile. Even from the bathroom, I could hear how distressed Luke was by the tone in his voice as he called out my name, pounding on the door again, causing it to shudder on its hinges. He was probably panicking like I was, but for a different reason. Did he notice the change in my scent when he left me in our nest? As much as my Omega wanted to soothe the panic in Luke, he was also upset, demanding to know why we had been left alone, but I couldn't bear the thought of seeing him right now.

"That's our ABOPB teacher!" Erik looked down at me in horror. "Is he the father?"

I could only nod, and he let out an exasperated sound. "Jesus fucking Christ, Aidyn!"

"I know!" I groaned.

"What do you want me to do?" Erik sighed.

"T-tell him I don't want to see him. Or that I'm not here."

"Aidyn..."

"Please, Erik! I know I'm a terrible person, and I know I'm asking a lot, but please. I'll never ask you to get involved again, I promise. I just...not right now. Please."

Erik's eyes danced across my face before sighing and nodding. He left the bathroom, and I could hear him open the door, acknowledging Luke in a monotone voice.

"Mr. Ellis? What can I do for you?"

"Aidyn," the pain in his voice gripped my heart. It was laced with desperation, and I could only imagine how frazzled he must have been. I wrapped my arms around my body, curling into myself in my spot on the floor, trying to make myself smaller as a whimper escaped my throat.

"Why are you looking for Aidyn? What makes you think he's here?"

"He...we....have an app to track each other's location. It was for emergencies. This is...I need to see him."

"He doesn't want to see you right now, Mr. Ellis. And if anyone from the university found out you were here to see a student —"

"I don't give a fuck about the university!" Luke's voice rose angrily, and I could hear the growl punctuating the expletive word. "I just need to see Aidyn. Please, I need to know that he's okay and that he's safe. I just need to make sure my Omega is okay."

"*Your* Omega? Do you have any fucking idea what you've done? Do you realize the level of fucked-up you've caused him? He's ruined now because of you."

Anger boiled through my system. Ruined? I was not fucking ruined, and how dare Erik think I am. I obviously can't keep this baby, but even if I did, that doesn't mean I'm ruined. Letting the anger fuel me, I pushed up from my spot on the bathroom floor and walked to the front door. Erik stood in front of the doorframe, his hand still on the door, and Luke had his hands on the doorframe, trying to enter the apartment. When he saw me, his face softened, but the look in his eyes showed me how desperately sorry he was, how guilty he felt. His eyes strayed to the incomplete bonding mark at my neck, and he let out a low, pained sound that my Omega responded to with a whine at his distress. Erik turned around and spotted me before seeing the mark. He hadn't seen it earlier, and now that he had, rage consumed him.

"You fucking bastard!" Erik seethed, his fist pulling backward before slamming against Luke's cheek.

Unprepared for the blow, Luke's head was knocked sideways against the doorframe with a thunk before he fell to the ground.

"Erik!" I screamed, moving forward, my eyes on Luke.

Erik whirled around to face me, storming toward me and pulling down my shirt collar.

"He fucking marked you too?! What the actual fucking fuck, Aidyn?"

"Why do you care?" I snarled at him, pulling out of his grasp. "I'm ruined, so why does it matter?"

The color drained from Erik's face as I moved toward Luke, but he had already gotten off the ground, and I stopped in the doorway. My Omega begged me to run to our Alpha and tell him we were okay, to scent him before telling him that we should go home to our nest and revel in the fact that we're going to have a pup. But I wouldn't do any of those things.

"Go home, Luke," I said softly, my Omega protesting. "Go home and leave me alone."

And I shut the door.

Aidyn

I'm not sure which woke me up first, the searing headache from crying myself to sleep or the screeching sound of my alarm. Last night, I had pulled the sheets off my mattress and used what few articles of clothing I had that still held Luke's scent in an attempt to craft a nest on the floor at the foot of my bed. It felt incomplete and pathetic, but it was all I could do to provide myself with a little comfort.

Putting on my glasses, I glanced at my phone screen, ignoring the multiple missed calls and texts from Luke, and noticed a text from my mother inquiring about my health and if I would be home for Christmas. Even though my world felt like it was in shatters, life moved on, and I needed to move with it. It didn't stop just because I was in a crisis. I typed out a quick response, lying to my mother, saying that my health was good, classes were going well, and I would like to come home for Christmas. That last one is not a lie, though, I needed my parents.

"Why are you on the floor?"

I lowered my phone to find Erik standing in my doorway, two mugs of coffee in his hands.

"What do you want?" I snide.

I watched Erik move into the bedroom as he approached my nest. He moved to sit beside me, and I growled at him, teeth bared like a wild animal when his foot stepped into the nest itself. He quickly retreated, looking at me with large eyes as I sat up. I didn't blame him for not knowing it was a nest. I had never built one before, and it was pretty poor compared to the one I had crafted for my heat before losing my senses. He sat on the edges of my nest as I sat up, taking the mug of coffee he offered.

"You built a nest?" he asked, surprised. "But you've never built —"

"What do you want, Erik?" I repeated.

"I wanted to apologize for yesterday," Erik sighed and ran his hand through his hair.

"Which part? Punching Luke or telling him that I was ruined?"

Erik had the decency to look ashamed as he stared into his mug, his nails clinking against the porcelain. I don't think he realized I heard everything; our walls aren't very thick.

"I'm sorry. I let my thoughts and emotions get the better of me, and I shouldn't have said that. Or punched him."

"Your thoughts and emotions? This isn't happening to you, Erik, it's happening to me! I'm the one that's pregnant. Pregnancy doesn't mean I'm ruined. In what way am I ruined? Or have I finally ruined myself in your eyes so that you're no longer interested in me? Or is it the idea that I'm carrying some Alpha's child and not yours?"

He flinched at my accusation, and I had my answer. I placed my hand on my abdomen, where I knew the little creature was growing within me, and sighed. Despite me constantly telling him I wasn't interested and that he should find someone else, he still held out hope that I would change my mind. Being pregnant changed that. It also told me more about his character and that he loved the idea of me, but not me specifically. I was ruined because it wasn't his child, and he couldn't accept that. He wouldn't raise another man's child, and that was fine. I didn't want him to, but it finally, *finally* hit home for him. I stood up without saying a word, setting my coffee cup on my dresser by the door, and turned to look at Erik, crossing my arms over my chest.

"I'm going home for winter break. My mom asked if I was coming home for Christmas, and I told her I was. I'll be back a few weeks before the spring semester starts, but I think I'm going to move out."

"What?" Erik's head snapped up in surprise, the hurt evident in his eyes. "You don't have to —"

"No, Erik, I do. You ignored me for weeks after I told you I was seeing someone, going so far as to sit on the other side of our classes so you weren't beside me. You barely spoke to me, acting as if I hurt you or cheated on you despite the fact that we were never together."

"Then why did you let me sleep with you?" Erik shouted, jumping to his feet.

"That night was a mistake. I told you I would be okay, and you kept pressing to help me, saying nothing would change for us. I wasn't in my right mind and I caved. It was clear that things had changed. You acted as if you had some claim to me, and you didn't! I made it very fucking clear that I thought of you as nothing more than a friend, a brother even, and you didn't even have the decency to act like one. Now, when I need a friend the most, I realize that we're nothing more than roommates. Something you have made abundantly fucking clear over the past few weeks. So, as roommates, I'm moving out. Find someone else."

"And if I can't?"

"Not my problem."

"It's not like you can afford to live alone, Aidyn, especially not with a baby on the way. Assuming you don't terminate it. Don't be stupid! And by the sounds of things, you ended it with Luke yesterday."

"What I do or don't do with this pregnancy will not involve you, nor affect you in any fucking way. Whatever happens between Luke and I going forward is our business," I replied, narrowing my eyes at him.

He didn't need to know that I was already contemplating termination. He was right, I can't have this baby, but he didn't have the right to that information anymore. Our friendship was over the second he decided that I was nothing more than what was between my legs and that he couldn't have me. Maybe our friendship ended the second I said yes to sleeping with him. I should've considered his feelings for me, but my heat was spiking, and I wasn't in my right mind when I gave him an answer. I refuse to blame my designation and how my body works. I was still lucid enough that I could've told him no and locked myself in my room, but I hadn't. I'm part of the blame, and I'm aware of that, but I could also be an adult about it and acknowledge that it was a mistake, and I thought we could move past it.

"It's for the best," I said finally. "Now, please, leave so I can get dressed for class."

Erik blinked at me before stomping out of my bedroom, muttering 'go fuck yourself' under his breath as he left.

I was tired before I even got to school. Fighting with Erik this morning, saying my peace and ending a five-year friendship took more out of me than I expected it to, and I couldn't help but wonder if it was because I didn't have access to my nest anymore or because the creature inside me was already zapping my energy. But there was still one more person I had to visit before my school day started.

I didn't know if my relationship with Luke was over. I still felt drawn to him, and my Omega missed him terribly and was practically urging me to go to him. But what he did was inexcusable, and the bite on my collarbone throbbed under the bandaid I had placed over it, as if to remind me of his betrayal. I didn't know how we would move past this or if it was possible. I went to Luke's office and froze in the hallway, already smelling his citrus tea scent, except this time, it was tinged with spice and stronger than it normally was. The last time this happened, he had been pissed off at the Alpha in his class, and I hesitated at his door before knocking.

When I opened the door, I couldn't help but gasp at how much stronger his scent was in the room, thick and choking, coating my nose and throat. The strong scent was mild compared to what I was scenting now, and my Omega let out an inhuman sound as a response. Luke looked up from his desk, and there was a look of shock on his face, but something was wrong. Very, very wrong. He looked gaunt as if he hadn't slept in days, which I knew wasn't true. He had dark circles under glassy blue eyes, and his skin took on an almost ashen complexion, save for a purpling bruise on his cheek. It was very clear that he was sick, but he hadn't looked anything like this when I saw him yesterday.

"Aidyn," he said, a soft expression crossing his face as he stood up from his office chair.

He approached me but halted before passing his desk, the expression dropping from his face. My Omega let out another involuntary whine, Luke's head snapping up to look at me when the sound reached him. I stifled the purr that threatened to vibrate through my chest, knowing that my Omega was reacting to the Alpha's distress and wanted to soothe his anguish. Without thinking, I wrapped a protective hand around my middle and winced when Luke followed the movement. His scent increased with a burst of citrus, indicating he was happy about the idea, and a low purr rumbled from his chest, causing me to close my eyes against its pull. I could feel my body responding, slick gathering at my entrance.

"You're pregnant?"

I had hoped I had a little longer before my scent change was more noticeable, but it appears I couldn't deny it anymore, and he could detect the light floral scent like I had when I first woke up after my heat.

"I'm not keeping it," I said, defiantly raising my head.

Luke looked like he wanted to say something, his scent changing again, but he swayed slightly where he stood, grabbing the desk to support himself, the tone of his skin growing ever paler. Unable to resist any longer, I moved toward him as he swayed, reaching out to hold him upright and move him to one of the chairs in front of his desk. I pulled out my water bottle from my backpack and offered it to him, which he accepted slowly. He seemed lethargic, and I became genuinely concerned about his present state.

"You should've stayed home. You don't look well," I said, kneeling beside him to look at him better.

"I hoped you would come see me. I had to come."

My stomach knotted at his words. I wasn't here with the best intentions. I wanted answers and to return his keys until we could sort out whatever this was. My Omega whimpered in distress, and he turned to look at me, a sad expression on his face as he tapped the bandaged mark on my shoulder.

"I'm being punished, as I should be. It'll pass."

It took a second for my brain to realize what he was telling me, but it clicked once I analyzed the symptoms I was seeing. Bonding sickness was a serious matter, and there was zero reason why Luke should be at work right now. Although rare, people have been hospitalized and even died due to the illness. Bonding sickness typically occurs when an Alpha bites an Omega and initiates the bonding process, but the Omega doesn't reciprocate, the first symptom showing up within twelve hours of the incomplete bonding. While the bite on an Omega fades after three days if it is not tended to by the Alpha, bonding sickness lasts about a week, as if they were being punished, which is clearly how Luke saw it.

"Why?"

He looked at me, his gaze searching my face, but I could see the pain and regret in his expression.

"I have nothing but excuses. The night of your heat, my parents invited an Omega and her parents for Thanksgiving. The second I arrived, they had me take a shower, washing all traces of you from my body. I was annoyed, but I wanted to keep the peace, foolishly thinking it was because they didn't want to scent you, until I saw her. I realized that they were just torturing this poor woman with false hopes. I had already chosen my mate, and my parents wouldn't hear differently, so we argued. I left when I saw your message, and I found you in your nest. You were so perfect, waiting for me, and I became weak. Through the haze of rut, I realized that our bites and marks would heal and no one would know that we were together, and I lost it. I have no other excuse besides the fact that I gave in to my Alpha before I even realized what I had done. It's not how I would've done things, I swear to God. It's not where I would've placed my mark, and I wouldn't have done it in the thralls of your heat."

"The condom?" My voice cracked at the question, and Luke groaned, putting his face in his hands and threading his fingers into his hair.

"My mind was elsewhere, consumed by rut and the need to show the world that you were mine and I was yours. It wasn't intentional by any means. I know I fucked up, and I swear to God, I will spend the rest of my life trying to make it up to you."

I sat back on my heels and watched the Alpha before me. I could tell by his scent that he genuinely felt guilty about the situation we now found ourselves in, and my brain was a jumbled mess trying to make sense of what he told me. I needed time to think about what he said, the future, and us, to process everything.

Luke's alarm cut through the silence, reminding us where we were and that the world had moved on despite our turmoil. I watched in mild fascination as Luke mustered up all his strength to slowly move out of the chair, his face blank as he reached for his phone.

"I brought something for you, in case you came. I thought...I thought you might need it."

I cocked my head to the side, curious about what it could possibly be. He moved around his desk, picked up his bag from the floor, and pulled out the stuffed otter from my nest. I couldn't help the squeal of excitement that left me as I dashed toward him to grab the otter, clutching it close to my body. I buried my nose in its fur, inhaling the mixed scent of us. Some of the tension in my body left as I had a part of my nest with me, and I couldn't help the overwhelming desire to cry. I had a piece of my nest with me, and I instantly became calmer than when I walked through his office door.

"Thank you," I whispered, glancing at him through damp lashes.

Aidyn

Pheromones are a tricky thing. While I can scent the pheromones of Alphas and other Omegas, I cannot scent my own. My pheromones smell different to each person as well. While I may smell like a forest to Luke, I also have the potential to smell like rotting pumpkins to someone else. When the pheromones of another person smell pleasant to us, we know that they have the potential to be our mates as long as we click outside of our pheromones. Just because our scents are agreeable doesn't mean we would work out as a couple; it just helps attract attraction. But because I couldn't smell my own scent, it took me a moment to realize why some of the students already in Luke's classroom were staring at me as I headed toward the back of the class. I realized that, despite the de-scenter spraying on my body when I left Luke's office, it didn't cover up the scent of my pregnancy. I clutched my backpack against my chest, feeling the otter that I had placed inside as my bag rested on my lap. Closing my eyes, I took a deep breath, trying to drown out the whispering and the eyes that seemed to be fixated on me.

"Aidyn?"

I sighed heavily before opening my eyes, my gaze falling on Erik before me. He looked apprehensive, as if he didn't know if it was okay to approach me— it wasn't. I did not have the energy to continue our argument, least of all in public.

"Go sit down," I responded, eyes narrowing.

"I want to apologize for this morning,"

"You've been apologizing a lot today, and it's not even lunch. Go sit down."

"Don't be a dick—"

Oh my fucking god! Me? Be a dick? Are you fucking kidding me right now?

"Then fucking go sit down," I growled, an edge to my voice that had a few of the students looking in our direction again.

Erik glared at me before resuming his seat on the other side of the classroom, which was fine by me. I wanted him nowhere near me right now. Before the rumors and questions could begin, the eyes of every Alpha and Omega turned to the door, with some whimpers coming from the Omegas, mine included. Despite the suppressant use regulation the university had in place, the distressed pheromones of a Dominant Alpha still reached us before Luke had entered the classroom, and it hadn't registered until this moment that he was having difficulty controlling his pheromones. God, I was slow today. When he entered, Luke looked no better than when I left him, and my Omega whined again, desperate to soothe our Alpha. When he spoke, his voice was cracked as if his throat was parched, resulting in him clearing his throat before trying again.

"I'm sorry, but class is canceled for the week. Please review Chapters 22 and 23 of your textbooks, and we'll have a quiz next week. Sorry for the inconvenience."

His words took a moment to take root, with students looking at each other before gathering their things and slowly exiting from the classroom. Luke didn't leave, however, his eyes dancing from student to student, giving an apologetic smile, but his gaze flicked toward me as I left. The desire to scent Luke was strong, and I gripped my backpack tight against my body, my gaze downward as I entered the hallway. I made it to the stairs when a voice stopped me, and I groaned in frustration. How many assholes did I have to deal with today?

"Not so superior now, are you? Typical Omega behavior, spreading their legs for any Alpha and getting knocked up."

"What's your problem?" I asked, turning around to see the Alpha I had fought with months ago.

"You think I don't notice how the teacher looks at you? He sure was aggressive after our debate," he said, ignoring my question and moving toward me. The emphasis on the last word told me that he didn't see it as a simple debate. In his eyes, it was an offense to challenge the Alpha way of thinking.

"Couldn't pass his class without sleeping with him? Now look at you. Pathetic."

"What's pathetic is you accosting me in the hallway for some one-sided vendetta. You'll have to help me understand; I am a dumb Omega, after all. Are you pissed that I might've slept with the teacher? Or because I busted your little Alpha bubble when I challenged your way of thinking? Or is it because I have the second-highest score in the class? Or is it because, despite you trying to paint me as a whore, I still wouldn't spread my legs for a lowly Alpha like yourself?"

The Alpha growled at me, and he released his pheromones, causing me to involuntarily gag. It was a mixture of ketchup and spoiled milk, and the combination had my eyes watering as I met his pheromones on my own, putting more of my energy into it as a dominant Omega. I watched his eyes flash in anger as he realized that I technically outranked him as a dominant. I foolishly expected him to back down and try to have a final say before walking away. I hadn't expected him to shove me. Whether he shoved me out of his way or shoved me in anger as he realized where he ranked with me, I wasn't sure. I was, however, fully aware of Luke screaming my name as my body fell backwards down the stairs.

Luke

I couldn't breathe. The scent of a burning forest reached me from inside the classroom, and I instantly knew Aidyn was in distress and angry at something. I exited my classroom just in time to watch Forester push him. I watched as Aidyn lost his balance on the flight of stairs behind him and fell backwards before landing on the small landing, his arm around his stomach, pain etched into his face. My tunnel vision narrowed on Forester, a deep, angry growl emitting from my chest, and the next thing I knew, I was across the hall, Forester pinned against the wall by my arm across his neck.

I had clearly punched him, not that I remember doing so, but his eyes were bloodshot, with a bruise forming on his cheek, blood spurting down his face from a broken nose. I released a pool of pheromones, my anger evident at the Alpha who dared to hurt my mate. I growled at him as the color drained from his face, his fingernails clawing at my arm in a desperate attempt to release himself from my grasp, scratching until he drew blood. My face twisted in a snarl as I let out an inhumane sound.

"LUKE! Stop!"

I turned to my left and found Aidyn struggling to get off the floor. Reaching for the handrails to pull himself up, he limped up the stairs, his eyes wide. But there was fear in his expression. He clutched one wrist close against his body, the other around his stomach. Instantly, my Alpha took over, desperate to check on our mate. His scent was drenched in fear and distress. I moved to his side, my face nuzzling into his hair as I scented him, ignoring the students in the hall. I could still smell the scent of burning forest, but the light floral scent of our pup was there. I couldn't tell anything more than that, and the way Aidyn clutched at his stomach, I could tell he was concerned the fall hurt the pup.

"I think...I think I hurt my wrist. Can you drive me to the clinic?" he asked softly. He moved his arm away from his belly to wrap the fingers of his good hand around my wrist.

I nodded, my arm around Aidyn's lower back, cautiously watching him as we descended the stairs. I stopped for a brief moment to grab his backpack that lay on the landing before I guided him into the parking lot. I opened the car door for him and eased him into the passenger seat, my Alpha growling at the hiss of pain that Aidyn exuded. I wasn't mad at him; I was pissed at Forester, who decided to push Aidyn, and I would bring this before the board for harassment, but for now, my focus was on Aidyn.

I handed him his backpack, and he struggled to take the otter out, clutching it close against him as I made my way to the driver's side, starting the car. I drove past the clinic, and Aidyn watched it go with a curious expression on his face. His scent spiked in mild fear, but it didn't last long. He trusted me to know what to do and where to take him. Ryan didn't work at the clinic on Tuesdays unless he had something scheduled, so taking Aidyn to the hospital was the better option. I needed the best to help my mate.

Pulling into the hospital parking structure, I stuffed the parking ticket into my pocket before exiting the car and helped Aidyn remove his seat belt. He left the otter on the floorboards of the passenger seat, but I grabbed it before locking the car, and I could see the relief on Aidyn's face when he saw it. It pained me that he felt so insecure to leave the stuffie behind, but I knew he needed it at that moment. We checked in at the front desk, and after providing my name and requesting Ryan, we were immediately put into a private room to wait for my best friend.

"I thought you didn't want Dr. Easton to know about us," Aidyn mumbled, trying to get onto the exam chair but struggling without using his injured wrist.

Without seeking permission, I moved over to him, effortlessly lifting him up and placing him on the table, the sanitary tissue paper crinkling under him. I offered him the otter, and he placed it on his lap as I moved awkwardly to stand beside him.

"You're injured, and I'm taking you to the best of the best. I just didn't want him to know who I was seeing, he knows far too much about my life as it is."

A knock interrupted us, and Ryan walked in, his eyes wide in surprise as he looked at both of us. He looked down at the chart in his hand, then up at us both before sighing.

"The Omega you've been seeing is my patient?" He turned his gaze toward Aidyn. "And your Alpha is my best friend? This is a huge conflict of interest, you know that, right?"

"So is being best friends with the family that has been our primary care physician for years," I observed, eyebrow raised.

"Touché. Why do you reek of pheromones? Even I can scent you."

I glanced at Aidyn, catching his eye. The scent of burning forest spiked briefly before it lowered back down to a simmer. "We'll discuss it later. Right now, I need you to look at Aidyn."

Ryan looked between the two of us and nodded, setting the file down on the counter. "Hello again, Mr. Keller. And what brings you to the hospital and not the clinic?"

Aidyn's gaze turned from me to the floor, and silence enveloped the room. I fought not to take control of the situation. I wanted to make it easier for him and less uncomfortable, but I could do nothing.

"Alpha," he whispered softly, reaching out to grab me with his good hand. I took his hand and interlaced our fingers together.

I could finally breathe again. Simply touching Aidyn in an intimate way allowed the blockage in my lungs to pass, and I could take a full gulp of air. I still felt like shit, but less so. Aidyn took a deep breath and raised his head to look at Ryan.

"I fell down some stairs and landed on my wrist. It hurts like hell. I don't know if it's broken. And…" He was silent again, glancing at me as if seeking my approval or my reassurance. I nodded slowly, squeezing his hand. "And I need to make sure that the pup didn't get hurt in the fall."

Ryan's head snapped to me at the news, eyes almost comically large. It took a moment before he regained cognitive function. He dug out a gown from the bottom drawer and handed it to Aidyn.

"I know the wrist hurts like hell, but hang on a little while longer. We need to ensure the pup is okay first. I need you to undress completely and put the gown on; I need access to your abdomen and, unfortunately, your womb, so there is a sheet there to cover your front with. Is it okay if Luke and I talk in the hallway while you get undressed?"

Aidyn hesitated, clutching the otter closer to his body before he nodded. I wrapped my arm around his shoulders, pulling him against me as I kissed his temple, informing him that I would return in a moment, and stepped out with Ryan. The door had barely closed behind him before he began laying into me.

"What the actual fucking fuck! Not only is he your fucking student, but he's also fucking pregnant?! How do you fuck up this badly?! Is that why I can scent you? Some Alpha macho 'must protect my delicate mate' bullshit?"

"No," I responded sadly, rubbing the back of my neck before looking at him. "I went into rut during his heat and accidentally started the bonding process."

"Oh, this just gets better and better! When did this fucking happen?"

"His heat ended yesterday." I winced at the groan that Ryan emanated, his palm slapping into his face as he glared at me. "I just found out a few hours ago he was pregnant. I had gone out to get more protein bars because we were running low and I didn't know how much longer his heat was going to be, and when I returned, he was gone. I tried to talk to him and ended up fighting with his roommate."

"Explains the bruise."

"Indeed. The bond is incomplete. I'm going through the stages of bonding sickness. After everything, I don't think Aidyn will want to bond with me. I've fucked it all up. He already told me that he's not keeping the pup. I can't force him to; it's not my decision; he's the one that will have to carry the pup for the next nine months."

"Nine months is for Beta parents, not Omegas and Alphas." Ryan corrected. "You're looking at about a seven-month pregnancy since your bodies develop faster than Betas. However, Aidyn is male, and there isn't a whole lot of room for pups to grow, so you're looking at around six to six and a half months, and it's not going to be an easy pregnancy if he goes through with it. His stomach can only expand so far, and you'll actually start to see a difference in his abdomen after the first month. Even if he doesn't want to keep it, it's best to make sure he's okay so that we don't have to worry about a miscarriage and potentially bleeding out."

"That's possible?" I asked, suddenly alarmed, and I swayed slightly where I stood.

Ryan's face softened, and he reached out to squeeze my arm in an attempt to reassure me. "Hey, he seems to be okay, just a little shaken, but we'll know more after an examination. Bleeding out is very rare, but we have to prepare for everything. Do your parents know?"

I shook my head. "They know about him; they're not happy. Remind me to tell you about Thanksgiving later."

"Oh boy! Can't wait for that drama!"

I smiled sadly, and he turned to knock on the exam room door before opening it. Aidyn sat on the exam table, his clothes lying on the spare chair in a heap, with the otter sitting on top of it. He reached for me the second he saw me, and I instantly moved toward him, taking his hand in mine. Ryan instructed Aidyn to lay down on the table before drawing some blood from Aidyn's arm to run a few tests, asking Aidyn if he felt any pain anywhere besides his wrist. Aidyn shook his head, and Ryan moved the gown, exposing his chest and abdomen. I couldn't help the growl that came from my chest.

"Chill, Alpha," Ryan chuckled, smirking at me. "It's so fun to see you actually act like an Alpha."

"Fuck you," I growled.

Ryan chuckled again before using two fingers to push around Aidyn's abdomen, watching the Omega's face for any sign of discomfort or pain. He asked a few questions, inquiring if certain locations hurt or were tender. Again, Aidyn responded no. With a loud clunk, Ryan pulled out a set of stirrups from the side of the exam table, instructing Aidyn to scooch down until his ass was toward the end of the table. Aidyn's cheeks were flushed a scarlet red as he did as he was instructed, wiggling his body down and putting his feet into the stirrups provided. A low rattle started in my chest again while Aidyn squeezed my hand, looking directly at me and not at Ryan. Ryan gave me an apologetic smile as he pulled out a set of sanitation gloves, pulling them on and applying lubrication to his forefinger and middle finger.

"Sorry, Luke, it needs to be done. This isn't fun for me either," Ryan said, before instructing Aidyn to take a deep breath.

Aidyn buried his face into the side of my hand as Ryan inserted his fingers into him. It was awkward and uncomfortable for everyone, and Ryan did his best to move things along as quickly and as medically possible. After a moment, Ryan nodded, removing his fingers and instructing Aidyn that he could sit up before tearing off the gloves

"Unfortunately, because the pregnancy is so new, we can't do an ultrasound. There seems to be no internal bleeding, which is good, and your womb seems to be fine, but I'll run the blood tests. There have been developments in medicine that if the child is in distress, it'll show up in your blood, so I should get the results in a day or so since I'm going to order a rush to the tests. There doesn't seem to be any discomfort or pain as I was poking around, which is good. If you start to feel pain or notice any bleeding, go to the ER and call me. Luke has my personal number. Now, let's take a look at your wrist. Can you wiggle your fingers for me? Good, you can move them, which is a good sign. What about moving your wrist up and down? Okay, let's go do a few X-rays. We have a machine down the hall, but I'm pretty sure we're looking at a severe sprain rather than a broken wrist. Why don't you get dressed and meet me outside. Luke, I want you to stay here while I care for Aidyn."

My Alpha growled at the idea of being separated from my wounded mate, and the look of amusement crossing Ryan's face only pissed me off more. I knew Ryan would tease me about finding a mate, but I wasn't in the mood right now. Not when my mate was not only angry at me and probably hated my guts but also injured and being taken away from me.

"Yes, yes. Rawr, big, big scary Alpha. I'll be waiting just outside the door, Aidyn. Come out when you're ready."

Fortunately, the X-rays confirmed that Aidyn had nothing more than a sprained wrist, and Ryan advised him to ice the wrist when he got home and wear a brace when he wasn't icing it. He asked me if I wanted any medication to help with the worst of the bonding sickness, but I declined, insisting on going through the illness without assistance to atone for what I had done. After validating our parking ticket, we left the hospital and returned to the car, sitting in silence for a moment.

"I'll take you to get a brace, and then I'll take you home," I said softly.

"I don't want to go home."

"I'll take you wherever you want to go."

Silence deafened the space between us. I glanced at Aidyn, who stared straight ahead, clutching the otter tightly, but I could see tears sliding down his cheeks. Part of me worried the otter's head would pop off with how tightly he held the plush.

"E-even if you cleaned it up, can I return to my nest?"

"Yea, little fawn. I'll take you to your nest."

Luke

Returning to my apartment to find that Aidyn had left me the day his heat broke was one of the worst moments of my life. The feeling of dread and panic that consumed my being is a feeling I will never forget. It never even occurred to me that he was pregnant. I merely thought it was the bonding mark that had caused him to run. I never cleaned up the nest that lay at the foot of my bed, it was the last place I saw Aidyn. It was the last place we spent a moment together, and I couldn't bring myself to clean it up, so I left a note for housekeeping not to enter the bedroom. I also couldn't bring myself to sleep in the bedroom, choosing the couch in the living room instead of sleeping in the room that still held our scent.

When I returned to the apartment after the altercation at Aidyn's apartment, I had opened the windows mainly to air out the scent of heat and slick, but his forest scent still clung to the fabric of his nest. However, without him here, I still didn't permit myself to step foot inside the nest.

Aidyn dropped his backpack by the front door when we entered the apartment. He removed his jacket and struggled to get undressed, letting out a sound of distress and frustration at being unable to remove his clothing quickly. Without saying anything, I stepped in beside him and helped him, pulling off his shirt and jeans. He leaned down to pull off his socks, and my eyes zeroed in on the band-aid covering my mark at his neck. In just his boxers, he opened the bedroom door, and the sound of distress turned into an audible sound of happiness. Climbing into his nest, he began rolling in the blankets and curling up like a cat, purring in happiness. He opened his eyes and caught me watching him, his purr stopping instantly, shattering my heart.

My mistake had created a wedge between us, and his Omega didn't trust me enough to purr for my Alpha anymore. I put him in a situation I never intended to, and he kept his distance. I couldn't imagine how awkward this moment must have been for him, having a nest in the shared space by someone who hurt you. I smiled at him sadly, ensuring he was comfy before turning to leave when his voice called out to me.

"Where are you going?"

"The living room. Let me know if you need anything."

Aidyn watched me, saying nothing as I moved into the other room. I began to collect Aidyn's clothing, folding them and setting them on the back of the couch before I folded up the blanket I had used overnight and sat on the couch with a sigh.

I was so fucking exhausted. Bonding sickness was zapping my energy, and it was as if I was running off fumes while battling the worst flu of my life. I had woken up feeling nauseous with a severe headache and chills, and neither had gone away, which is why I still sat in my jacket despite the heater running in my apartment.

I didn't know how to handle being this sick. Typically, whenever I had a cold or the flu, I would order hot and sour soup from the local Chinese place and drink enough green tea to drown a human being, but those would do nothing for a metaphysical illness. This was simply something I had to wait out. It was a good thing I had canceled classes for the week. Everything I had read on bonding sickness told me that this would get worse long before it got better. Some Alphas reported being unable to get out of bed and others reported vomiting and diarrhea. I prayed to the Gods above that I didn't get that last one. Vomiting I could handle, but honestly I'd rather not be shitting my pants, thank you very much.

I leaned my head against the back of the couch and closed my eyes. The apartment was quiet, and I could tell Aidyn was content by his scent wafting from the bedroom. Not happy, but calm and content. My phone vibrated, and I dug into my pocket before pulling out the device and seeing a text from Ryan.

> *If Mr. Keller keeps the pup, his due date would be at the end of April or early May, assuming he can go full term, which is rare. An April pup would be likely.*

An April pup. My birthday is in April, and I loved the idea of having a pup to share the month with, but I couldn't let myself dream about such an idea. I wanted this pup without question. I also loved the idea of Aidyn's stomach growing round with the life we created together, and it made my chest ache in a way that I couldn't explain.

"What are you thinking about?"

I jolted in surprise, turning to see Aidyn standing by the bedroom door still in his underwear, but his glasses were gone, curiosity on his face. I hadn't heard him move, so naturally, he had scared the crap out of me. He tilted his head and watched me; I couldn't lie to him, not ever and especially not now.

"Ryan texted me a projected due date if you kept the pup. How did you know I was thinking about something?"

"Your scent is really, really strong right now, and the change in the scent let me know that something was making you happy. This pup makes you happy?"

"Of course it does," I said honestly, getting up from the couch and moving toward him but keeping space between us as I looked down at him. "It's a part of you, a part of us. I know you're not happy about it, and I know you don't want to keep it, so I'm not entertaining any particular notion."

"Dr. Easton said that not many doctors would terminate an Omega's pregnancy, but if it's the choice I want, he would do it."

"Ryan is a good guy. I know he will care for you. Let me know if you want me there."

Aidyn stared at me then, his eyes large in surprise, his face an expression of disbelief and shock.

"You would be there for the termination of your pup? You'd support that decision?"

"The idea hurts," I responded, shrugging. I couldn't stop myself from reaching out and placing my hand on his abdomen, running my thumb across his belly. My gaze tilted toward the place where our pup was growing inside him. "But it's not my choice. I fucked up enough. I'll support you in any way you want me to, however much you want. If you don't want me there, then I won't be there. If you want to terminate this pregnancy, I'll support that. If you want to keep it, I'll support that."

Aidyn lowered his gaze to where my hand rested, staring at it before he placed his hand on mine. "I can't keep it, Luke. Even if I wanted to."

Even if he wanted to? "Do you want to?"

Silence.

"Little fawn. Do you think you can't keep it?"

"I'm only twenty, and I don't know if I'm ready to be a parent yet. But aside from that, I'm still in school, have no job, and have a whole career and life planned out. I can't have this pup."

"Baby," I pulled him against my body, nuzzling my face into his hair and breathing in his scent. The floral undertones only drew me to him more, and while different, it was certainly a scent I could get used to. "You're looking at this as if you'll be the sole provider for this pup. You'll still finish college, get your degree, and start your career. We'll work around that. I can hire a nanny if needed. I won't lie and say nothing will have to change because a pup will change our lives, but you'll still be on track for everything. Remember, I have an income, too. I will provide everything you need. We'll figure it out. No one is ever ready for a pup. We have these ideas of what it'll be like, but we never factor in that every pup is different and comes with their own personalities. It's never going to be perfect, and we will doubt our decisions and choices every step of the way. We'll always wonder if we are doing the right thing or doing enough to help them grow. But I think you'd be an amazing parent."

Aidyn was quiet for a moment, mulling over my words. "When did Ryan say I'm due?"

"According to Ryan, it's very rare for male Omegas to carry to term, so the pup will be early. We'd be looking at mid to late April."

"April. Only a month after graduation. God, I'm going to be huge."

"You'll look beautiful."

Silence filled the void between us again before Aidyn turned around, making his way back into the bedroom. He pulled me along with him, dragging me into his nest as he sat down. Once I was lying down, he curled against me, his leg over my thigh, his hand resting on his abdomen, and his scent tinged with happiness.

"You'll provide for me?"

"Always. Anything you ask."

"So, if I asked you to help me look for an apartment that caters to students, would you help me?"

I pulled my upper body back a little, my neck at an odd angle so that I could look down at my mate, forcing him to look at me when I tipped his chin upward with a finger guiding my movement.

"Why do you need an apartment?"

"I heard what Erik said to you yesterday. The walls are thin, and the bathroom is just on the other side of the front door. We got into a big fight this morning, and I realized that our friendship is over. It's partially my fault, and I acknowledge that. I made mistakes, too. But I don't think rooming together is such a good idea anymore, and I told him after I visit my family during Christmas, I'll move out over winter break, so I'll have a little under a month to find a new apartment."

"Move in here; the apartment is big enough. I'll sleep on the couch, but you're welcome to stay here as long as you need to."

"Why the fuck would you sleep on the couch in your own home? This is your space, and I won't intrude upon that."

"You wouldn't be intruding, I'm offering. I can even sell this condo, and we'll get an actual home if that's what you want. I'm not under any illusion that we're okay and that I'm forgiven for what I've done. I won't make you uncomfortable and force you to share a space with me. I don't know where our relationship stands right now, and that scares me, but I'm willing to do whatever you need me to do. If it's just to provide financial support, I'm okay with that."

"Why on earth would you be okay with that? Why would I keep you around for financial reasons? That's shallow and fucked up. Besides, if I keep this pup, it'll need a father. Like you said, you're not magically forgiven, I'm still pissed. But I can't imagine my life without you, and I certainly can't imagine having this pup without you."

"You'll keep it?" I asked, hope latching on to my words.

"I'll think about it," Aidyn replied honestly.

I woke yesterday feeling like I had been hit by a truck, and this morning, like I was drowning in nausea. I had barely rolled over before bile crept up my throat, and I dashed to the bathroom, emptying the contents of my stomach into the porcelain. By the time my body had nothing left to offer, sweat ran down my back and forehead, and I groaned, leaning my head against my arm that was draped across the toilet seat.

"Hey, only one of us gets to throw up in the morning."

I turned to see Aidyn standing in the doorway in a pair of my black boxer briefs, his face worried.

"I didn't mean to wake you," I said groggily.

"You didn't completely. Your phone started vibrating after you dashed off."

I made a small sound of acknowledgment and leaned against the wall. Aidyn moved to sit beside me, and I glanced at him, worry still etched on his face. I reached over and took his hand, kissing the back of it and smiling weakly.

"Morning sickness kicking in yet?"

"No," Aidyn said, shaking his head and looking down at his stomach. "I have about a week or two to decide if I'm keeping this baby. If I do, then that's also about the time frame in which morning sickness kicks in. Apparently, it's common with male Omegas, so I'm totally looking forward to that."

I chuckled softly at his touch of sarcasm, rubbing the back of his hand with my thumb.

"Luke. Let me return the mark. You'll feel better —-"

"No."

Aidyn looked surprised then, even a little wounded at my outright refusal. I struggled to get up and reached for the mouthwash on the counter, rinsing my mouth out quickly before reaching down for Aidyn. When he stood up, I picked him up and set him down on the counter so that we were eye-to-eye, and I could lightly nuzzle his neck, breathing him in.

"I've wanted to mark you the moment I met you. I know where I want my mark to be, and this"—my thumb brushed over the mark I had placed at the junction of his collarbone. "Isn't where I wanted. I forced my bite on you, and this is punishment for doing so. I won't force you to bite me to make me feel better."

"It wouldn't be forced," Aidyn mumbled, avoiding my gaze.

My Alpha preened, knowing that Aidyn would willingly return my mark despite everything that had happened between us, but now wasn't the time.

"I want to do it right. I want you to be coherent and consent to my mark fully. And after we recover from me marking you again, you'll give me yours, and I know exactly where I want it too."

I ran my fingers on the inside of his thigh, his breath catching at my touch. "I'll mark you here, on your inner thigh. Every day, you'll have to spread your legs for me, and only me, so that I may tend to the mark, licking and sucking it each morning, making you want me."

"I already want you," Aidyn said, but his voice was breathless. I raised my gaze to look at him, and his cheeks were flushed beneath hooded eyes, his pheromones spiking with his arousal, and I knew if I touched his entrance, he'd be wet for me. I growled quietly at the thought, brushing against him so that he could feel what the thought had done to me, and he moaned softly.

"A-and where would my mark go?" he struggled to ask, his voice laced with arousal.

I picked up his hand and placed it at the base of my skull on the back of my neck. "I want your mark here after you've topped me."

"What?!" Aidyn's eyes grew large. Gone was the scent of arousal, replaced with surprise and unease. "Alphas don't bottom or submit to Omegas, Luke."

"And I'm not a normal Alpha, and you're not a normal Omega. I want the world to know that I submitted to my Omega. That I will always submit to my Omega, my mate, whenever he asks it of me."

Aidyn stared at me with wide eyes, but I could see the unshed tears that filled them. He leaned forward, pressing a kiss to my lips. I tried to pull off, aware that mouthwash wasn't sufficient enough to erase the emptying of my stomach, but Aidyn pulled me closer, kissing me again.

"I love you," he said finally. "I know I haven't told you that yet, but I want you to know I do. I can be mad at you all I want, pissed off at the situation you put us in, but I know that that doesn't change how I feel about you. You're my Alpha, my Mate, and we'll deal with this together."

Luke

"Should you be drinking coffee while pregnant?" I asked curiously, looking at Aidyn as I entered the kitchen. I saw him purring around a travel mug of coffee, taking a small sip of the liquid bliss.

The purring stopped, and Aidyn glared at me as he sat the mug on the counter, screwing the lid of the mug in place. Even though the bonding sickness had forced me to take the week off, I still offered to take Aidyn to school—after I had assured him several times that I was well enough to do so.

"If we don't want me arrested for homicide, yes. This pup will come out with a caffeine addiction like it's papa."

I couldn't help the large grin that spread across my face as we exited the door. My phone beeped, and I realized I had forgotten to see who had called me so early this morning. I found three missed calls from my mother and another from the dean of the university. Curious, I played the voice message as we took the elevator to the parking garage and listened as the dean requested a meeting with me around two this afternoon and requested a video conference. I knew my scent changed as I could feel my stomach drop based on the look Aidyn was giving me, but I gave him a fake smile and shook my head, rearranging my emotions and trying to rein in what little control over my pheromones I had so that I didn't worry Aidyn. It was clear this wouldn't be good, but it could be dealt with later. However, this did mean that I might not be able to pick him up after classes, depending on how long the meeting took.

"Can I take a rideshare here after class?" Aidyn asked, getting in the car. "I still don't want to go home. Unless you want your space, I don't want to impose."

I could tell by his tone that he was curious, but he never pushed, fully trusting me to tell him when I was ready. Of course, this made me feel worse because we were in this situation because he trusted me at one point.

"Please, I want you here with me." I reached into my pocket and pulled out one of my credit cards and handed it to him. He blinked at it before looking at me, head tilted. "Let me pay for the trip. It'll make me feel better since I can't pick you up."

"Fine," he grumbled adorably, putting my card in his wallet before shoving it into his backpack. "But I will take the long way around and really rack up those pennies. Would it be okay if I took you up on the offer to move in?"

"We could go get your things this evening or this weekend. Whichever works better for you. Or we can abandon everything and buy new stuff."

"How dare you!" Aidyn mocked in anger. "I cannot abandon my books. Besides, there is a hoodie or two of yours at my apartment, and they need me."

"I can always get more hoodies, Aidyn."

"You should definitely get more hoodies. I need a new one every day of the week."

I chuckled as I pulled into the parking lot and into my faculty parking spot out of habit. Aidyn sat in his seat, staring at the doors we usually walked through together, his scent taking on a slight smoky scent.

"I hate that you won't be here. I hate that I can't carry your scent with me in your absence."

"I know," I said, taking his hand and bringing it to my lips, kissing the back of his hand. "Only for a few hours, then I will drown you in my scent when you come home."

"Mmm, promise?"

I leaned over the center console, grabbing him by the back of the neck to meet me as I crushed my lips against him, swallowing the sound of his surprised grunt. He opened his mouth to me, and I explored his taste, deepening the kiss and threading my fingers into his hair to hold him in place. When I pulled back, his pupils were blown, his breathing heavy as he eyed me, and his cheeks flushed pink. I smirked at him and settled back into my seat, straightening my shirt as if nothing had happened.

"Have a good day in class, little fawn."

Aidyn

I slammed the condo door harder than intended, stripping off my jacket and tossing my backpack by the front door. I was livid. Angrier than I have ever been in my damn life, and I needed fucking answers. The apartment was dark and silent; a thick layer of spiced tea hung in the air, letting me know that Luke was still here and he was just as unhappy as I was. I followed the scent of his pheromones until I found him in his office, the curtain drawn to darken the room as he lay on the couch in his office.

He looked even paler than this morning, dampening my rage to a smolder. I approached him slowly, placing the skin of my wrist against his forehead and groaning when I realized he had a fever. I knew bonding sickness was terrible, but I didn't realize it was this bad, and I couldn't help but feel a pang of guilt as he continued to suffer through the phenomenon.

He was stubborn, refusing to let me return the mark to make him feel better, but I understood his reasoning.

He slowly opened his eyes and took a moment to focus on me before he gave a weak smile, removing my wrist from his forehead and kissing it.

"I can tell from your scent that you're upset. What's wrong?"

I shook my head; we could discuss what fucking James Forester told me later. In the hallway bathroom, I ran a washcloth under cold water. I dug through the drawers, looking for a fever reducer and growling when I couldn't find anything. I moved to the bathroom in the bedroom and still couldn't find anything. I'll have to go out later to pick some up.

I brought the cloth to Luke's forehead and dipped it around his temples and down his face, neck, and chest. Luke sighed softly, closing his eyes again before wrapping his hot fingers around my forearm.

"You're upset too, Alpha," I said softly. "And you're burning up. You don't have any medication."

"I'm fine, just a headache."

"No, it's a fever. Your pheromones are out of control, and you're upset. What happened while I was at school?"

Luke groaned, shaking his head and stopping immediately. He sighed and opened his eyes to look at me. "I have been reported for violating several of the university's codes of conduct, and my employment with the university ends in June. They kindly gave me another semester so current students can enroll in my class as they begin looking for my replacement."

"What the actual fuck! They can't do that! You did nothing wrong!"

"But I did." He lifted my wrist and kissed it again. "I slept with a student, impregnated him, marked him, and attacked another student. Not to mention, my pheromones are out of whack until this illness is over. We're lucky they're allowing me to stay on until the end of spring."

"So that asshole was right." Anger surged through me, and I looked at Luke, who looked at me confused. "I ran into our good friend, James Forester, while waiting for my ride. He was so proud of himself, stating he got you fired and that it was my fault for sleeping with you in the first place. Called me another Omega, ruining the lives of Alphas. You only attacked him to protect your mate, who is in a delicate condition."

"There is nothing delicate about you, Aidyn. But that kid needs some serious help. The way he talks is borderline designationist. He thinks so lowly of Omegas and that they live merely to serve him simply because he got lucky and was born an Alpha."

"Most Alphas think that way, Luke, it's nothing new."

"Forester doesn't know it yet, but he will be placed on academic probation for pushing a pregnant Omega, regardless of my part in it. It's not your fault; you know that, right?"

I took a deep breath and closed my eyes. Some metaphysical craziness was at play when we met. We were destined to be together, but we couldn't fight that. Luke tried to fight that until I came onto him in his office, and that's why my insecurities latched onto the idea that maybe this was all my fault. If I hadn't made the first move, he would still have a job, but we would be strangers, and I wouldn't be carrying his pup. I couldn't help but pull my arm from his hold, wrapping them around my middle.

It didn't hit me until this moment that I wanted it. I want *our* pup. I want a life where we were tired from the pup screaming at all hours of the night. A life of Luke holding our little one, whispering to it softly as I slept on the couch, exhausted after a chest feed while he lulls our pup to sleep. I want to chase a naked child through the hallways of our apartment, trying to dress them after a bath. The scent of a new pup that is a slight mixture of us and the floral scent all pups had until they reached puberty. The universe worked hard so we could be together. I was different for Luke. I made him feel like a natural Alpha, not an imposter among his kind, and maybe the condom was forgotten that night for a reason. I hate that things played out this way so soon, but I wouldn't change it.

"I want it."

Luke turned his gaze toward me, schooling his features to hide any emotion from me as he sat up slowly, the cloth falling from his forehead onto his lap. "What?"

I couldn't stop the tears that fell down my cheeks at that moment, my arms tightening around my middle. I couldn't stop the inhuman sob that escaped from my throat as anxiety washed over me, mixing with fear and worry. It was like my body was finally coming to terms with everything that had happened since my heat, and my life was changing far faster than I could keep up. I had lost my best friend. I have a mate who is protective over me and the life we have created. He wants me, he wants us, and I am moving in to be with him. He wants to bond with me, and despite the fact that I want all of these things with him, it was a lot very quickly. But I want this. I want all of this.

Luke fell to his knees beside me on the floor, taking my face in his hands as he forced me to look into his concerned gaze.

"What do you want, little fawn?"

The sobs wouldn't stop, and he pulled me against his chest as I released all the pain, fear, betrayal, and confusion over the past few days, my body shaking in his arms.

"I want this. I want us," I practically cried out through my tears. "We have to rebuild, and I know we'll be stronger for it, but this is the worst fucking time for this. I want our pup, but we can't."

"Why can't we, baby?"

Luke's voice rumbled through his chest, mingling with the purr that started low within him, working to soothe the anxiety that clung to me with the same ferocity as he did.

"I'm a student, and you're about to be unemployed. How will we afford a pup?"

"Aidyn, my sweet darling boy."

He shifted his body so that he sat on his ass, making more space for me to climb onto his lap as he reached over and grabbed his phone off the coffee table beside us. As my sobs teetered off, he began tapping away at the screen, rocking me back and forth. He tapped me lightly, showing me the screen.

It took my eyes a bit to adjust to the bright screen in such a dark room, but I was floored by what was on the screen. It was his bank app displaying his checking and savings accounts. It was cliche as fuck, but Luke was rich, and stupidly so.

"Did you forget that I have investment properties all over? This apartment tower being one of them. We'll be fine. Our pup, and any that may come after it, will want for nothing. You will want for nothing. I taught at the university because I wanted to. I lost a job I enjoyed. But at the same time, if I'm not teaching, I can watch over our pup while you start your career. It'll be okay. If you want this pup, then I'll make sure you get what you want."

A fresh wave of tears flowed down my cheeks, but this time, it was for a different reason. But before we could be truly happy, Luke steadily got worse as his bonding sickness progressed, despite his mark fading from my throat. By the next day, he was bedridden, and his body was covered in sweat; the medication I had picked up from the pharmacy did little except curb the migraines he was having. He struggled to keep food down, and the only thing I could get him to eat was soup. He claimed it was easier on his stomach if it came back up. He tried to sleep in the living room, refusing to sleep in our nest for fear of soiling it.

"Things can be washed, Luke, you need to stay here. I need you to stay here."

He was too weak to fight me. I chose to call out of classes, emailing the professors that there was illness in the house. They kindly sent me the homework that I needed to do to remain caught up with my missed classes. One teacher even sent me the notes, which I was grateful for; it saved me from reaching out to the rest of the class. I sat by Luke's side, dipping a cool cloth in a bucket of water to wipe away the sweat from his body.

The fever eventually gave way to chills, and he struggled to remain warm while my heart hurt to see him in such distress. I tried to coat him in our pheromones as he struggled through sleep, but it did little to help him. But by the weekend, he seemed to be doing better, finally exiting the nest to shower. I swear he stood under the spray for a solid hour while I loaded the nesting material into the washing machine. He found me standing in the bedroom, staring at the bed, a thoughtful expression on my face.

"What's wrong?"

I glanced at him and forced my eyes away from his towel-clad hips to greet his eyes.

"I'm thinking about my — our nest. I want to build a nest, one that is perfect for us and the pup we bring into it. The floor was perfect for space, but it's going to be a pain trying to get down to the floor and back up again with a belly."

I watched as a glint of darkness crossed Luke's eyes, and I couldn't help but smirk at the bulge now forming under the towel. He was picturing me with a pregnant belly. Perv.

"So move it to the bed."

"That's the issue. I don't know if the bed is big enough, and things will fall out as we move around."

Luke made a noise that let me know he understood as he wrapped his arms around me, pulling me against him. I could feel his hard-on against my ass, and I fought not to wiggle my hips against it.

"We could get a bigger bed. They make these bumper things you can install along the edge of the bed for parents who co-sleep with their pups. It prevents the pup from falling out, but we could install them early to keep your nest intact on the bed."

Holy shit, why hadn't I thought of those before! "Luke! You're a genius! That's perfect. I want to get some stuff for the pup, if that's okay after you're 100%, of course."

"Of course it's okay," He nuzzled my neck, kissing it lightly. "We're going to have a pup."

"We are. And I need to tell my parents. I can't decide if they will freak out or be happy for us. They didn't even know I was seeing someone."

Luke sighed heavily before pulling off me, taking his fresh scent and body heat with him. I turned to watch him get dressed, looking a little too long at his ass as he pulled on sweats. His words returned to me then on how he wanted me to top him, and suddenly I became nervous. I've never topped anyone. What if I hurt him? I obviously know what it's like from the bottom; after all, male Omegas are always the bottom, or so society tells us. I produce a lubricant, but Luke does not. My body was designed to take him, his body will fight me. But maybe with my experience, I can help him, and he can help me.

"I don't know what you're thinking about, but I can scent your slick from here and don't have the energy to respond to it. Have mercy, little fawn."

I realized I had spaced out, and Luke was dressed in sweatpants, watching me with a smirk. I couldn't help but blush and shake my head, moving toward him and wrapping my arms around him.

"I'll tell you later."

"Probably for the best. Like you, I need to tell my parents, and I need all the energy I have left for that conversation."

As we had expected, the conversation didn't go well. It resulted in a yelling match over the phone, with Luke taking offense at his father's suggestion that he should have the pup terminated and 'do the right thing' by breaking up with me and marrying someone more respectable. He lied and told them that we were already bonded and he would never give me or our pup up. The conversation ended with him hanging up on his parents, his scent laced with burnt spices. This did not help my nerves as I waited for my mom to answer the video call. I didn't have to wait long before her smiling face filled my screen.

I honestly really loved my parents. My parents did everything they could for me, often researching and engaging in uncomfortable conversations with strangers to meet the needs of raising an Omega child. It wasn't easy; mistakes were made, but we learned from them, and it allowed us to grow as a family. It didn't mean I wasn't nervous to tell them our news. Luke asked if I wanted him to be on the call with them, but I told him that as much as I appreciated it, I wanted to do this alone. So I lay in our nest, looking at my mother. I honestly looked more like my mother than my father, and my mind briefly wondered who our pup was going to take after the most. I couldn't help but grin as my mother greeted me.

"Hello, stranger! I see you finally remembered you have parents."

"I'm sorry, I meant to call earlier, but a lot is going on." I chuckled at her. "Dad there?"

"Mmm, I think so. Unless I lost him to the garden again. You know, we were supposed to see more of each other after he retired, but I swear we see less of each other now. It's one hobby after another."

As my mom stood up to get my father, the rapid movement of the camera created a wave of motion sickness, and I suppressed a groan, closing my eyes until I heard my mother's voice again.

"What's wrong?"

I opened my eyes to find my father seated by my mother on our living room couch, and a feeling of nostalgia and longing replaced the nausea. I missed them both in ways I couldn't put into words, and now I was about to tell them one of the biggest news of my life.

"I'm pregnant." Okay, so not the best way I could've said it. My brain told me to rip the band-aid off instead of easing them into it, but that wasn't the best course of action. Neither was the word vomit that just erupted after what I said. "I-I know it's not the future you envisioned for me. A-and I know I'm young and this is sudden, but I met this Alpha, and we've been dating for a bit. It-it was an accident, and neither of us planned this, but it's happened and —"

"Aidyn." My father's stern voice cut me off, and suddenly, I was five again, unable to meet his gaze through the screen. "Does the Alpha treat you well?"

I tilted my head slightly and smiled. "Yeah, he does."

"Are you happy?"

"Yeah, Dad, I am. A lot is going on in my life with classes, school, and life in general, but Luke has been patient and is not trying to sway me in any direction. I was scared when I found out, and he's been by my side even when I tried to push him away. I'm not worried about what's going to come next."

"Ha!" my mom barked out. "Just wait until the baby is here. You'll never stop worrying after that, even when your baby is about to start a family of his own."

I couldn't help but laugh at that.

"I won't lie and say that I'm not surprised, shocked even." Dad started, his voice lighter. "But ultimately, we want you happy, and if he takes care of you, that's all we could want. Our vision for your future was that you were happy, nothing more than that."

"I am. I really love him. Would it be okay if we could visit at Christmas?"

"We'll come to you; you just worry about finishing your semester and growing my grandbaby!" Mom said with a grin and Dad nodded beside her.

The vast difference between my parents and Luke's hit me then. My parents were more concerned about my happiness and well-being than the pregnancy itself. I knew my parents loved me— they never hid that fact—but to love me this deeply and have such unwavering support was something I didn't expect. I thought for sure they were going to at least be disappointed. I couldn't stop the tears filling my eyes as I gave them a watery smile.

"Thanks, guys, I'll let Luke know. The condo might be too small for you to stay with us, but we'll figure it out."

"I'm sure there is a hotel around the corner. Don't worry about us."

The call ended after we exchanged our love and plans to discuss more soon. I settled in the silence of the aftermath of the phone call, shooting Luke a text to let him know I was done with my call. It didn't take him long before he entered the bedroom, stepping into the nest and pulling me against him. I nuzzled against his side, nose buried into his neck as I inhaled his scent. The exchange and rush of emotions exhausted me, but I was happy. At least one set of grandparents was delighted for us.

"They want to meet you." I breathed against him, his body shuddering as my words puffed out against his neck. "They didn't outright say they were excited, but they're happy for us. They just wanted to make sure you treat me well, and that you'll take care of us."

"Until my dying breath," Luke said, tilting his head to rest on mine. "Think they'll adopt me?"

I chuckled, pulling him tightly against me as my eyes closed slowly. "Probably. They'll love you so much, they'll forget all about me."

"No one can forget about you,"

I let out a sound in response before drifting into sleep.

Aidyn

It didn't take long to put my belongings in the rental truck we borrowed for the weekend. Luke had insisted I not lift a damn thing and told me just to put the things I was taking into boxes for him. This was also the compromise to him just hiring a team of movers, which I told him wasn't needed.

I texted Erik to let him know the plans and told him I would toss my key over the patio wall once I had locked up. He hadn't blocked me yet, so he read my messages but refused to respond. Eventually, I would have to inform my parents of our friendship, but that conversation could wait until I figured out what to tell them. Stating that the boy they welcomed into their home didn't want to be my friend anymore because I didn't want to date him wasn't something I wanted to handle lightly.

Luke had already begun renovating his home to accommodate me. A larger bed and bumpers had been ordered and should arrive in about a week. Bookshelves had been placed in the living room for my books, and a second dresser had been purchased for my clothing, matching the other one in the room, thank God. A third dresser had also been purchased to accommodate his hoodies and other things I may need for nesting, but he told me to keep two drawers empty for now. When I asked him about it, he told me I'll find out soon.

The answer to that question came in a small delivery package. Luke grinned from ear to ear as he brought it to me one evening, shaking me awake as I dozed on the couch. Much to my irritation, Luke's bonding sickness disappeared just in time for me to experience morning sickness, which refused to stay confined to just the mornings, like I could vomit at any given time. As humiliating as it was, I had begun to carry a stack of disposable bags with me at all times. They were also stashed all over the house in case I couldn't get to the bathroom in time, which has happened a few times. My embarrassment was immeasurable as Luke had to clean up the aftermath while I sobbed through my apologies. I also struggled to keep food down, yet strawberry milkshakes and lightly salted fries were cravings I couldn't ignore. Oddly, it was one of the few things I could keep in my system.

"Open it," he said excitedly, as if he were a child on Christmas.

I pushed myself up into a seated position and tore into the box, peering inside. I was confused.

"Hoodies?"

Luke, equally confused, peered into the box. He reached his hand into the box, digging under the hoodies before his smile returned, withdrawing his hand. Okay, so something was under the hoodies. As he had, I slid my hand under the weighted fabrics and touched cold plastic, but it was squishy. Tilting my head, I pulled it from the box and looked at it. Tears sprang to my eyes as I ripped apart the vacuum-sealed bag, freeing the plush baby blanket from its packaging as it expanded. The background was a sea of ombré blues with otters all over the fabric. Some of the otters even had a little otter on their bellies. I laid the blanket across my lap, my hand petting the soft material, and I looked up at Luke, who had the biggest grin on his face.

"When did you buy this? Where did you buy it?"

"The night you returned home. You joked that I should order more hoodies, so I did, but while I was ordering, I saw the blanket."

"But I didn't even know if I was keeping the pup then. What if I had decided to get rid of it?"

Luke's eyes softened, and he reached over and grabbed my hand. "Then I would've hidden it until you were ready for a pup. You are my future. I knew that even if you chose not to keep this pup, there may be more in the future, and we could have used it then. It's why I told you to keep the two drawers empty, so that we could have some place to put baby stuff. I didn't want to get any clothing in case the pup was too big or too small, or you didn't want to keep it, but I thought a blanket would be okay."

"It's perfect. You know this is going in our nest, right?"

"How else will the pup get used to our scents?"

God, he was perfect.

The following two weeks passed in a whirlwind, with more morning sickness and doctor appointments. We needed to get an accurate time frame of when the baby will be born, as well as a birth plan going forward. Luke was a little weirded out by the fact that Dr. Easton would continue to be my provider throughout the pregnancy, but he assured Luke that he would not be in the delivery room, just the birthing specialists. My mother was constantly texting me tips she learned during her pregnancy with me while also checking in to make sure I was eating and doing okay.

Luke was permitted to return to teaching once his bonding sickness was over, but it was with the understanding that we would not have any contact while we were both on campus. This made getting to school awkward, and it was decided that he would drop me off less than a block away, and I could walk onto campus without him by my side. We also found that this stressed out my Omega, and the stress created horrid heartburn. To help alleviate this, I began wearing his hoodies to class, board of directors be damned.

Erik continued to pretend that I didn't exist, and I treated him like a stranger. I did catch him glancing down at my midriff from time to time, but he didn't say anything to me. James Forester continued to give me and Luke the stink eye despite being slightly smug about this being Luke's final months, but he didn't openly approach me again. Of course, I threatened him with a restraining order if he did, and that would go on his record.

We had a sonogram appointment with Dr. Easton the evening before my final exams, and I found myself bouncing in anticipation. I had already noticed a slight swell in my abdomen, which I couldn't stop caressing each morning as I got dressed for the day. Luke wasn't paying too close attention to me as it took him a bit to notice, but once he did, he loved to lay his head in my lap, facing my slight bulge.

"I can hear it," he said softly, caressing it one evening as we lay in bed.

"You cannot!" I chuckled, running my hands through his hair.

"Can too! It's a girl."

"A girl, huh?"

"Uh-huh. And her name is Autumn."

"Decided that all on your own without discussing it with me?"

"I didn't decide anything, the pup told me."

"Okay, pup whisperer, why 'Autumn'?"

"Because her parents met in the fall, of course."

I froze momentarily, my fingers still tangled in Luke's hair as he rambled to my stomach. I hadn't even started thinking about names yet, but it was clear that Luke had. Autumn felt like the perfect name if it was a girl, though I couldn't help but laugh at the idea that a spring pup would be called Autumn.

However, the sonogram appointment confirmed that Luke might be a pup whisperer. A little girl is expected in mid-April, her strong heartbeat echoing loudly in the exam room. Luke couldn't take his eyes off the monitor, and I saw them glisten with unshed tears for the first time. I squeezed his hand slightly until he looked down at me with a big smile.

"You have a daughter," I grinned back.

"*We* have a daughter."

Our happiness, however, was short-lived as I made my way down the block to wait for Luke to finish with the last of his exam students. I often waited for Luke at the small seating area beside the cafe on the corner, but today, a man dressed in a three-piece suit sat at the table, watching the road. His cold blue eyes zeroed in on me as I approached cautiously. He had a sharp jaw peppered with a tight, dark beard laced with gray, matching his close-cut hair. His suit was equally as dark, a dark, inky blue that looked tailored to his body. He wasn't unattractive, but he certainly gave the air that he wasn't to be approached without reason. The scent of his pheromones reached me, bitter like burnt diner coffee, and I stalled in my steps. He was an Alpha, but not a dominant.

"Aidyn Keller?"

"Do I know you?"

His eyes narrowed at my response as he stood up, buttoning his suit jacket at his waist and extending his hand towards me while he introduced him. "I am Jason Ellis, Luke's father. I assume I am in the presence of his.....lover?"

I fought not to smirk at how he struggled to say that last word. I pulled my shoulders back, straightening my spine and lifting my head. "His *mate*. Yes, you are. How can I assist you?"

I ignored his hand while I fished out my phone, dialing Luke before slipping it back into my pocket. Even if Luke didn't pick up, the answering service would record part of our conversation. I didn't think Luke's father would hurt me in any way; after all, it was considered bad manners to hurt a pregnant Omega, but I didn't want to take my chances. Mr. Ellis lowered his hand, a look of disgust and offense etched onto his face, but his gaze darted to my neck, no doubt looking for a mark.

"I wish to discuss a business proposition with you."

"I'm not interested."

"With all due respect, Mr. Keller —"

"No, you've come here without any respect at all," I interrupted, staring him in the eye. "Not once have you shown me or your son an ounce of respect. Luke told you he was having a baby, and you told him the best thing for him to do was to have it terminated and leave me to marry someone you decided was worthy. You act like he doesn't talk to me about such things, that we're not partners. I know everything."

"Then you know —"

"I know that you don't understand your son in the slightest. You honestly don't care about his happiness or what he wants for his life. You couldn't care less. You thought that by coming here, I would what? Take some money, terminate this pregnancy, and walk away from him so you can continue to use him as a pawn? Not happening. I won't abandon my mate."

"You're not his mate," Mr. Ellis practically growled. "He is broken and will never be able to bond with you completely. You're wasting your potential. I could help you find a suitable match, like I have for him."

"*I* am his suitable match. You don't get to dictate who we should love based on archaic views that you refuse to let go of for the sake of your family. Luke isn't broken, and I'm sorry you can't see past that. Even if he couldn't bond with me, he is still who I want."

"That pup inside you will be just as defective —"

"Even if this pup has whatever Luke does, this pup will have a loving and understanding father, something Luke clearly never had. I'd be so proud if they grew up to be even half the person Luke is. He is not defective. It's hilarious that you keep referring to him as broken and defective, yet you still want to marry him off to make pups with someone else, knowing his condition could be hereditary. You just don't want him to have a pup with someone you didn't authorize."

The scent of burnt coffee grew stronger, choking me as Mr. Ellis crowded my space. I stood my ground, refusing to let him intimidate me, but I couldn't help placing a protective arm around my bump. I will protect her, and I'll defend Luke.

"You need to learn your place, Omega."

I have had enough. I was tired of his family trying to interfere and take Luke away from me. While I hated what Luke had done during my heat, I understood it, especially now after meeting his family. They would stop at nothing to separate us. I closed my eyes and took a deep breath, letting the anger be the core of my pheromones, releasing them in force, pushing back against the tidal wave of burnt coffee. When I opened my eyes, Mr. Ellis stared at me with wide eyes, struggling against my assault as I revealed that I was far more worthy of his son than anyone he had imagined. I found it interesting that, technically, Luke outranked his father by being a dominant Alpha, but family hierarchy kept him subservient to him—a limitation I did not have. My scent surrounded him, and I prayed to whatever higher being existed that my pheromones were some of the most rancid things on the planet and that I was suffocating him while he struggled for air.

"Aidyn."

My gaze left Mr. Ellis's pale face as I glanced at Luke, his face emotionless as he watched the scene before him. I reined in my pheromones, my body shaking with the overexertion, and I momentarily panicked that the power behind my pheromones could harm the pup, but nothing felt wrong. Looking at Luke, who only had eyes for me, I began to calm down. I wasn't aware my feet had moved until Luke wrapped me in his embrace, his citrus honey scent drowning out the burnt coffee. He didn't look at his father; he just herded me toward the car.

"Let's go home."

AIDYN

I lay in the lukewarm bath, absentmindedly running my hands over my little bump. The interaction between Mr. Ellis and myself was still very fresh in my mind. The apartment was quiet since Luke had left, though not without protest, to pick up this fantastic eggplant rollatini that was served at a little mom-and-pop Italian restaurant near my old apartment. Luke was hesitant to leave me alone long enough to drive across town, but I assured him several times that I would be fine. I used the tracking app on my phone to monitor his location, which notified me that he was stuck in traffic on his way back to the apartment. The silence bred unsavory thoughts about the recent encounter, but simultaneously, a choice had been made.

I had looked into bonding and inquired if it was safe to do so while pregnant. I had even asked the nurse as I got dressed during my last ultrasound to ensure that knotting wouldn't result in a miscarriage. As long as we weren't rough in our sex, we would be fine. My body was designed to take a knot, regardless of pregnancy. She also confirmed that for some, bonding and having my mate perform a pheromone shower could ease the stress of the pregnancy and make the side effects less aggressive.

By the time the front door beeped open, the bath had cooled and I dried off, curling up on the couch to wait while I scrolled through my phone. I was instantly hit with the scent of herbs, tomato sauce, and vegetables. My stomach rumbled, and I scampered out of the tub, rushing to dry myself off. I pulled on a clean pair of Luke's underwear and a t-shirt, surrounding myself and our pup in his scent as he pulled down the dishes from the cupboard.

"Doing okay?" he asked hesitantly, his face concerned.

It was as if Luke wanted me to be more traumatized by the encounter with his father than I actually was. I was shaken up when it happened, but hours had passed, and right now, my concern was not impacting stress upon our pup and instead on how many garlic breadsticks I could steal. His phone vibrated on the table, and the screen lit up, revealing at least a hundred missed calls from his mother, thirty from his father, about five from his sister, and a mixture of text messages he was ignoring. Now that he was home, he reached for his phone and pressed the two buttons on the sides of his phone to turn it off completely. He said nothing as he sat down and began to tear apart the paper bags that housed our food.

"I'm fine, just starving," I responded, stealing a breadstick and nibbling on it.

"That's good news then," Luke grinned, putting my meal on a plate first and handing it to me.

Usually, I was a meat eater, but sometimes I enjoy a good vegetable lasagna or veggie burger. That's how I discovered this rollatini, and my mouth watered as the scents of seasonings and vegetables reached my nose. I eagerly picked up my fork, cut into the baked vegetable smothered in cheese, and popped it into my mouth. The flavor exploded against my tongue, and I moaned, unable to stop the little happy dance I did in my chair while chewing. I reached for another bite when my current one reached my stomach, and instantly, nausea hit me. Bile threatened to bring forth the bite I had just swallowed as I dropped my fork, letting it clatter against the plate. I dashed off to the hallway bathroom, Luke close behind, and emptied the contents of my stomach into the bowl.

Tears filled my eyes before I could stop them, unable to stop the sob that accompanied them. Kneeling in front of me, Luke tried to rub my shoulders, then down my arms before settling on holding my hands, his pheromones surrounding us to calm my distress.

"We're going to starve!" I sobbed out, voicing the fear I had held in since the first bout of morning sickness.

"You're not going to starve, little fawn," Luke said softly, his Alpha's purr vibrating in his chest. "We'll just find things you can keep down. We know the pup likes those strawberry milkshakes and fries. We'll figure it out."

"We can't survive on strawberry milkshakes and french fries."

"Certainly not with that attitude."

I glared at him, brushing the tears from my face. I really wanted that eggplant rollatini.

"What can I do to help?" Luke asked.

"Bond me."

His hands, which had returned to running up and down my arms to soothe me, froze on my biceps. Even his purr died in his chest. I glanced at him, amusement gone from his expression as he looked back at me.

"I know today has been a lot, but —"

"No," I said flatly. "Don't give me that bullshit. I won't lie and say this isn't about your family because part of it is, but you would do it anyway, right? You said you would! Having a bond with my mate will help ease the morning sickness. I looked into it, and a lot of research supports this theory! Maybe I could keep food down better. Maybe the pup knows we're not bonded, and it's anxious, and that's why I'm so sick! Worst case, nothing changes, but if it does...do you not want to be bonded anymore?"

"Of course I do, baby!" Luke cried, his voice loud against the tile. "But the last time I attempted, it didn't go well, and negative emotions fueled it. I want this to be different."

"Would it be so bad even if it was fueled by negativity? Once we're bonded, your family will have to accept me, or they can not be a part of their grandbaby's life. Once we're bonded, you can't bond with someone else unless I'm dead."

"Don't talk about your death so casually, Aidyn."

A dark cloud crossed the features of his face, his eyes hardening as if in anger. He rarely used my name, preferring to use nicknames instead, so I knew he didn't appreciate my comment.

"I'm not. I'm simply stating a fact. Pregnancy and birth are hard on male Omegas; it's why our pups come early. I'm simply stating a potential reality."

"A reality I don't want to entertain, thank you very much. You won't starve, and you and the pup will be fine. Ryan isn't even concerned."

"Your parents have the next five to six months to push and push. They'll stop when I'm bonded because nothing can be done then. You can't bond with another Omega. I won't have them take you away from me, from us, and I refuse to go through this pregnancy with that threat looming above our heads."

Reaching out, I took his hand in mine, and I fought to put my emotions into words. "Those that are bonded have said that it feels like a mental connection, a presence in your mind that you know is your partner. I need to feel you there. I need to feel that you're mine and by my side. I refuse to go through this pregnancy with the threat of your parents trying to ambush me any chance they get."

"Fine," Luke sighed, pinching the bridge of his nose. "When?"

"Now?" I suggested, trying to pull a playful grin.

Luke turned his hardened gaze toward me again, but this time, it was also different. I saw the heat behind the glare.

"Why don't you pack away dinner? Call Dr. Easton if you have to. I'll brush my teeth and get ready for you."

Luke still looked unconvinced, but he helped me to my feet, pulling out his phone as I brushed my teeth. I could hear his low conversation, no doubt harassing Dr. Easton with questions. This would take some time, allowing me to implement my idea.

I silently slipped into the bedroom, shutting the door quietly, and moved toward my half of the dresser, setting my glasses on the nightstand. Kneeling, I opened the drawer and pushed aside the clothing that hid the lingerie that I had purchased on a whim a few weeks ago. While it came in a set, I opted to pull out the panties. Lately, my nipples have been hurting to the point that wearing my piercing was becoming painful as it rubbed against my shirts, so I ended up removing it a few days ago. The idea of lace against them made my skin crawl. Nothing chafe-worthy, please.

The panties were designed more like a jockstrap with lace straps that would cup my ass and present it nicely for my Alpha. It had a sheer front, but the indigo coloring made it harder to see my cock behind the fabric. But my favorite part, and why I had bought it, was a little frilled skirt at the waist. It was made of the same lace and wasn't lengthy at all. It may have stuck out half an inch, but it looked adorable. A mating bond was the perfect time to wear it. Or so I told myself.

I contemplated pulling out the thigh-high stockings as well, but I remembered Luke's comment about wanting his mark on my thigh and felt they would only get in the way. My face warmed at what we were about to do as I quickly got undressed, slipping the lace on, and admired myself in the mirror. The blue looked stunning against my pale skin, and the skirt tucked itself under my little bump, making it more notable than before.

"Okay, I called Ryan, and holy fuck—"

Luke stalled in his steps as he entered the bedroom, his eyes falling on me, mouth agape. I grinned and spun slowly so he could get a good look at the lingerie. A low growl rumbled from his chest as he tossed his phone onto the floor, quickly removing his shirt and pants, his boxers tenting obscenely at the groin.

"You like?" I mused, knowing the answer.

"When did you order this?"

"Weeks ago, I just never wore it."

Luke approached me, capturing my lips with his as he pressed his body against me, his fingers tracing the lace over my hips and down the straps that framed my ass cheeks. I moaned into him as his fingers slipped into the seam of my ass, dancing over my entrance before he pulled back to trace the hem that sat below my bump.

"Good God, I'm not going to last at all if you wear this, yet I want to take you in it and ruin the fabric."

He cupped my tight balls before moving his hand up the length of my cock, its tip leaking into the mesh fabric.

"I could always buy more," I suggested, my voice coming out in a groan.

"You *should* buy more,"

I couldn't help but grin as I pulled him toward our new, larger bed and into the nest we had created together. Once it had been put together, I began to sleep better, which was good because I was always exhausted. I laid on my back with Luke above me, kissing his way up my body, starting from the fabric, up my side, over my tender nipples, and across my neck.

"I want to take you like this, but knotting will be tight in this position because there isn't enough room. It's the only way I can mark here," Luke said. He sat on his knees and lifted my right leg, placing a kiss on my inner thigh. "Do you think you'll be okay?"

"Yes, Alpha." I breathed, slick already gathering at my entrance. "Are we marking you tonight as well or in the morning?"

"I don't want to waste another second not being bonded to you."

He lowered my leg and enveloped my body with his, nuzzling into my throat. He kissed me again, his tongue slipping between my lips as his hand slid beneath the fabric of my panties, encasing my hard cock in his warm hand. Unable to help myself, I thrust upwards into his grip, moaning at the touch.

"I want to fuck you in these, may I?"

Unable to answer properly, I only nodded frantically. I hadn't realized I had closed my eyes until I had opened them again, glancing down the length of my body to watch his hand move beneath the fabric of my lace panties. He withdrew his hand slowly, bringing it to his lips as his tongue cleaned his fingers of my precum, his eyes bleeding from lust to hunger. He slid between my legs, finally kicking off his boxers to reveal his thick cock, the tip wet with precum and flushed a dark red, knot already starting to swell slightly. I would never get over watching him reveal his body as he undressed. It didn't matter if he was in a state of arousal or not; I enjoyed watching him. He was so attractive, pride swelling in my chest, reminding me that he was mine and I would be able to look at him for the rest of our lives.

He licked the shaft of my cock through the lace of my panties before taking each of my balls into his mouth. He sucked on each one gently, rolling and caressing his tongue over the sensitive sac. He released my ball gently, running his nose down my perineum as his tongue flicked at my entrance. My breath caught in my throat, and I made a mental note to return the favor when it was my turn. Luke said he had never taken anything into his ass before, which had me believing receiving anal foreplay of any kind was foreign to him. I groaned, my back lifting slightly off the bed as I dug my hands into his hair, pulling at the strands. He reached with a hand to cup my chest, stopping instantly when I hissed in discomfort.

"Sorry," he mumbled, his breath puffing out against my exposed hole.

"Not your fault," I smiled down at him.

"I mean," Luke chuckled, moving a hand down to settle on my bump. "It kind of is."

I couldn't help but chuckle at the truth behind that statement but stopped when he inserted a finger into me, quickly followed by a second.

"You're so wet for me, little fawn, and you're not even in heat."

"I'm just so excited to bond you to me," I purred. "Forever."

His fingers hit my center at that moment, and I squirmed in pleasure, my cry echoing through the room and releasing a gush of slick from my body, coating his fist. Precum continued to leak from my cock as it throbbed heavily against the lace, causing the fabric to stick against it. It seeped between the design, and as if he couldn't help himself, Luke leaned forward to lavish his tongue against it, tasting me. I was so wound tight that I exploded against his tongue, cum soaking into the panties as I panted, my eyes struggling to regain focus.

"Mmm, pregnancy has made you more sensitive, and I can't wait to use that to my advantage. But another day, you got another one or two in you?"

I only nodded as Luke removed his fingers. He settled between my legs on his knees, pulling my thighs onto his, and I realized the position gave him the perfect angle to fuck me while also avoiding any pressure on my stomach. It was awkward, but it would work. He lined his cock up with my entrance, watching me for any hint of discomfort as he slowly pressed inside, my body clinging to him instantly. This was the first time we had sex since my heat, and I didn't realize how much I missed him until that moment, my Omega letting out a soft purr in contentment that was sporadic through my moans and hitched breaths. Luke looked at me then, and I realized he had tears in his eyes as he leaned over me gently, cupping my face and kissing me wetly.

"You haven't purred for me since I fucked up," He rubbed his nose against mine, and I couldn't help the tears that filled my eyes, my purr stronger than before.

He was right, I hadn't. I was so caught up in everything, from the betrayal of being marked without my consent to finding out I was pregnant and Luke was sick to him losing his job. My Omega didn't purr to ease his sickness, nor did it calm him down after the fight with his parents. Guilt gripped me tightly in that moment, as if I had been a bad Omega, and the tears fell silently down my cheeks.

"I'm sorry," I whispered.

"Don't be. I understood. I'm just happy to hear it once more."

He angled his hips upwards, his cock hitting my prostate and sending electric shocks of pleasure through my body. He gripped my hips firmly, pulling me onto his cock over and over while he straightened his back. Luke's knot began to thicken at the base of his cock, catching on my rim, willing my body to open up to him and accommodate him. I dug my nails into his thighs, unable to do anything more than drown in the pleasure he provided. A soft whine escaped my throat, my Omega calling out to him—for his knot—as our pheromones filled the room, smelling strongly of warm tea in a damp forest.

"Aidyn—"

"Mark me!"

At my words, a sharp pain shot up from my thigh, my eyes landing on Luke, who watched me with wild eyes. Blood dripped down his chin and my thigh, splattering onto the bed sheet before his knot pushed into my body. The angle made it a tight fit, tighter than if I had been on my knees. My body protested the stretch, but I enjoyed every moment of it, my cock spurting into my panties once more. His cock twitched inside me, and I couldn't help but squeeze my muscles, clutching around his knot and milking him as he groaned, licking his mark on my thigh. Warmth flooded through my body, a purr rumbling from his chest in contentment as he lapped at the mark. I couldn't stop staring at it. I would feel it over the next few days, even my jeans would remind me we were bonded, and I couldn't be happier. I put my emotion into my pheromones, my purr meeting his as we waited for his knot to deflate. He finished cleaning his mark and shifted us so that he lay beside me, nuzzling his face into the crook of my neck and wrapping his arms around me.

"How are you feeling?" Luke asked cautiously.

"Content. Happy. You'll find out soon enough after we're bonded."

"I've been following a Beta diet. One that is supposed to be good for those that bottom. Lots of vegetables, greens, nuts, and things with plenty of fiber. I've also been trying to prepare myself in the shower occasionally."

The idea of Luke prepping his virgin hole for me had my cock twitching, and Luke groaned while my body clenched around him in excitement.

"You've really thought this through," I said, raising my eyebrow at him.

It was true that Beta males who enjoyed bottoming could benefit from a high-fiber diet to ensure embarrassing moments didn't happen when they were with their partners, but Omegas didn't have to follow such diets. Our bodies were designed to bottom, and slick acted as an almost cleanser to our systems. Betas didn't have that benefit. Bottom diets weren't mandatory, but they helped.

"Of course," Luke said matter-of-factly, moving us into a more comfortable position. I groaned at the feeling of his cock shifting inside me. "I want to do this right."

We pulled apart when his knot deflated enough, and Luke started the shower. I couldn't help but wonder if he was prepping himself, and curiosity got the better of me. I rolled over and climbed out of the bed, peeling off the panties as I went. I found Luke in the shower, bracing against the wall opposite the shower, the showerhead spray cascading down his body. His ass was jutted out a bit, with his middle finger slowly opening his body in preparation for me.

"Fuck, that's hot," I breathed.

I tossed the panties into the sink and stepped in, blocking the spray of the water. Luke's cheeks flushed, his eyes refusing to look at me, but I refused to let him be embarrassed. The world will look at him with questioning eyes once they see an Omega's bite on the back of his neck to seal the bond. After all, marking was only done through sex, so they would know what position he was in for a mark to be placed there. This was his moment of weakness, ashamed to be caught fingering himself despite his earlier bravado, but I was the last person he should be embarrassed with.

I nudged Luke to move, and we shuffled awkwardly in the shower before he faced away from the shower's spray. I reached up and adjusted it slightly so that it wasn't hitting him at all.

"Water makes for shitty lubricant. Soap is better, but also not the best."

I reached behind me, sliding my own fingers into my back entrance. I was wet enough for the both of us due to slick and his cum, and I was confident I could use it as lubricant to open him up. I wrapped my arm around his waist and pushed on his abdomen to angle his ass toward me, and I marveled at the fact that not only had Luke been trying to prepare for me, but he had also removed any hair around his entrance. I could tell by the slight razor burn, and I honestly adored that he was going to such lengths. I had never thought about it, even though I kept myself waxed for hygiene purposes.

I had never prepped someone else. I had never topped anyone else or experimented, and I was comfortable in my assumed role as an Omega to always be the receiver. To say I was nervous and excited was an understatement, but I worried about hurting Luke. It was like I was a virgin all over again, wanting to make sure my partner was enjoying himself. I moved my slicked fingers over Luke's entrance, and he tensed slightly before relaxing, which was a normal reaction to what we were about to do.

"Take a deep breath in, and exhale slowly."

On his exhale, I inserted a finger slowly into him, and he groaned, his body tensing again, but he relaxed against me once more. He did it again without my prompting, and I slid further into him, marveling at the way his hole swallowed my finger. It was tight, and his body resisted me, but it was surreal to experience what I had from the other end. I knew what it was like to be entered; Luke had fingered me only moments before, but this was different.

"Good, Alpha," I purred, slowly working my finger in and out of him.

Slowly, his body began to relax more and more, and soft sounds came from him as he began to open up to me. I removed my finger, gathered more cum and slick, and instructed him to breathe again, this time inserting two fingers. He hissed at the slight burn but didn't tell me to stop. I worked him slowly, spreading my fingers to open him more to accommodate me. My fingers finally found his prostate, and his breath hitched with a high moan, shuddering at my touch, and I couldn't help but grin.

"And that's the spot I enjoy the most."

He chuckled softly, shyly turning to look at me over his shoulder. His pupils were blown with lust, his skin was flushed with a slight tinge of pink as he panted, watching me. A feeling of lust and adoration washed over me. I kissed his back, pulling my fingers from his body, and stepped back.

"Come to the bed when you're ready. I'll make sure no one comes between us again."

He seemed a little unsteady on his feet as he turned around to kiss me, giving me space to wash my cock of the dried cum and my ass of our fluids, hissing slightly as the hot water hit his bite mark. I kissed him again before stepping out of the shower, filling the sink with lukewarm water to let the panties soak before giving him his privacy.

I pulled the lubricant from his bedside table and set it on the bed. I didn't know if we needed it. I wanted to use my slick, but for the sake of my anxiety, I also wanted to over-prepare. The bathroom door opened, and Luke stepped back into the bedroom. I had never seen him so shy, not even during our first time, but his cheeks were flushed, and he avoided eye contact.

"Come here, Alpha," I said gently, offering him my hand.

He looked up with a shy smile as he reached out to me, taking my hand. I pulled him onto the bed once more, rising on my knees to meet him as I asked him.

"You sure about this?"

"Yeah," he nodded, avoiding my eyes again. I didn't like that one bit. It was starting to make me insecure, and I couldn't handle my Alpha not looking at me.

"Luke," I said, forcing his gaze back to me. "I need you not to avoid me. We must communicate, especially since this is our first time doing this, okay?"

Luke nodded again, taking a deep breath and smiling at me sheepishly. "Sorry, I don't know why I'm so nervous and shy. It's not like this is our first time having sex."

"It's not, but our roles are reversed for the first time. It's normal to be nervous. It's a new experience. I'm nervous."

"You are?"

Jesus fuck, he was cute. "Yes. But also excited. Do you have a safe word to use if you want me to stop?"

"Forest."

I couldn't help but laugh. My safe word was based on his scent, and he chose the same, basing it off of mine. I respected it and kissed him, using the scent of my pheromones and the sound of my purr to ease the tension in his body. I pushed against him, forcing him to lie on his back. I nipped at his neck, my hand cupping his warm balls and rolling them gently before wrapping around his soft cock. It didn't take long before it thickened in my hand, and I stroked it lazily, my tongue lapping at his nipples. He moaned softly, his fingers digging into my soft hair as he cradled my head in his palm. I moved down his body, nipping and kissing at his flesh as I did. I couldn't resist nuzzling his balls with my face, inhaling the clean scent of soap, citrus honey, and something that was purely him. His body was still warm from the shower, and I loved how soft and warm he was against me. I nipped at his inner thigh, making him squirm while I tightened my grip on his cock, watching a bead of precum crest the tip. I let out a sound of glee as I flicked my tongue across it, refusing to give him a break before I enveloped his cock with my mouth, taking him as far as my throat would allow.

"Fuck!"

His exclamation only encouraged me to ministrations, and I opened my throat, allowing him further down my throat. His hips began to move with me, his dick thrusting into my mouth before I pulled off him, refusing to let him get lost in his pleasure. I pushed at his hips, motioning for him to get into position. It took a moment for him to catch his breath, his gaze unfocused as he slowly moved, kneeling before me, his ass exposed to my gaze. Giving him no time to think, I wrapped my hand around his cock once more to stroke him as I buried my face in his crease. The taste of soap and something innately him greeted me with a surprise cry from Luke. I couldn't help but chuckle as he jolted in surprise, but eventually, he pressed back against me, encouraging me to continue. With my tongue, I began to work on opening him up to me once more, spearing into him as I licked and sucked, softening him to my touch. Curses flowed freely from Luke as he struggled beneath me. The feeling of dominance took over, knowing that Luke had to submit to what I was doing to him, and I couldn't help the pathetic growl that erupted from my throat. It was nothing close to the Alpha one he gave, but it was my form of possessiveness that only made Luke moan more.

I inserted fingers from my free hand into his hole along with my tongue, stretching him as my hand refused to stop stroking his hard cock. By now, my cock was angry and eager, despite having already come twice.

"Ready, big guy?" I asked, biting into the meat of his ass as I rose up, tapping my cock at his entrance.

"Fuck yes," he moaned.

"From experience, despite me trying to prepare you, it might hurt at first. Just bear with it, it'll get better. I promise."

By now, slick ran down my thighs, and I noticed it caused a light sting to the mark he had left, but I honestly loved it. It reminded me of what we were doing and how it was up to me to solidify our bond. I reached behind me, gathering slick onto my finger and penetrating him once more, lubricating his entrance before reaching behind me once more. I used my fingers to fuck myself, pushing against them to produce as much slick as I could to coat my hand. Once I was satisfied, I slid my hand over my aching cock, a groan escaping me as I coated it in my slick, followed by running my fingers over Luke once more.

"Deep breath, and exhale."

Luke did as I instructed, and just like in the shower, upon his exhale, I pushed the tip of my cock into him. Together, we groaned, my head falling forward, and I slowly entered him. His body fought my intrusion, and I reached under him once more to stroke his cock, which had deflated a little as I entered him. He moaned, pushing against me, trying to rush me, but I soothed him, my Omega purring loudly.

"Easy, I don't want to hurt you. Fuck, you're taking me so well, Alpha. So good for your Omega."

Luke whimpered at my praise, and it hit me that Alphas rarely got praised like Omegas do. It's almost natural to shower praise upon an Omega, but no one thinks that maybe Alphas wanted to hear the same thing.

"Almost there, you're doing so good for me. Fuck, it's like nothing I've ever felt before." I breathed, pulling back slightly before pushing back in, this time bottoming out with a groan.

"So big," Luck sighed.

"Only because you've never had anything here before," I chuckled, kissing his upper back. "But you're so tight, Luke, strangling my Omega cock with your pretty Alpha hole. Feel that?"

I pulled back slightly, moving my abdomen against the top of his ass, my tiny baby bump tapping him lightly as I wiggled my hips. "Topped by your Omega while your pup grows within him. Such a perverted Alpha."

"Fuuuuck."

I was addicted, and I had no right to be. I had never inserted my cock into anything besides the toy that Luke had used once. I didn't know what to expect, but the heat of his body called to me in ways that left me practically feral. But I had no reason to believe this would happen again, so I committed everything to memory. The scent of his pheromones as I began to move, the way his body shook at the pleasure I provided, hitting his prostate the way he did for me. The feeling of his larger body under me was euphoric, and I could see why Alphas loved being in control. To command his body to feel something it usually didn't. I hit something within him that made him cry out, not in pain, but in pleasure, and his body shook more. His pleasured state became almost frantic as he pushed back against me, trying to get as much of me into him as he could to hit that spot over and over.

"I'm close!" he cried out. "Don't even think of pulling out. I want you to fill your Alpha."

Oh, sweet fucking Jesus! His words almost had me slipping in control over my orgasm, and I couldn't help it anymore, leaning over him as I pounded my Omega cock into his ass. My balls began to tighten as my orgasm rushed through my body. My teeth sunk into the back of his neck while pushing my pheromones into my bite. The taste of copper pennies exploded across my tongue as my smaller Omega canines slid into his flesh, sealing our bond and connecting our tether. Immediately, I was flooded with a mixture of emotions: pain, happiness, sorrow, love, and an indescribable feeling of a puzzle piece falling into place.

Luke's hole gripped my sensitive cock as he orgasmed beneath me, pulling a groan from my lips. My tongue moved flatly over the mark, cleaning it as our bond strengthened under whatever metaphysical power was in play. We fell onto our sides, our chests heaving as we fought to catch our breaths. Moving slightly to pull out of him, to make him more comfortable, he stopped me by reaching backward, stilling my efforts. He pushed his ass back against me, forcing my softening cock back into him.

"No," Luke grumbled quietly. "Stay as if you've knotted me."

"They make toys for that, you know," I grinned, wrapping an arm around his waist and pulling his larger body closer to my smaller one, pressing a kiss to his shoulder before lapping at my mark again.

"So you've told the whole class, remember?"

I chuckled, and Luke groaned at the vibration, my exhausted cock twitching at the sound. But there would not be another round; my aching balls would make sure of that. Outside of a heat cycle, I had never come so many times in my adult life.

"How are you feeling?"

"Sore. But I'm happy. Can't you tell?"

I focused on our bond at his words. It was still developing and would continue to do so over the next few days. When it was solid, I would be able to feel him in my head the way I could sense my Omega. Not his thoughts, per se, but the emotions he felt on a daily basis, and it would be effortless. I would be able to tell if he was happy, scared, angry, or aroused all through our bond. I buried my face against his back and smiled.

"Would you ever consider doing this again?"

"God, yes!" Luke exclaimed a little too excitedly. "But no one tells you how exhausting bottoming is. So give me a few hours."

I couldn't help but chuckle at his enthusiasm, and I rose slightly to kiss him. "You feel things with your whole body. It's such an emotional thing, and your body's senses are in overdrive, but it's worth it. You did so well, Alpha."

Luke made a slight noise in response to my praise, but shortly a soft snore filled the room. Through our bond, I could sense his contentment and pleasure. The sorrow he experienced earlier, I realized, was regret. Regret that things hadn't gone right the first time, but relief that our puzzle was now complete. As I drifted off to follow Luke in sleep, I felt a little tug at the bond, my eyes flying open immediately. Luke was still sleeping, my cock had softened enough to pull out of him, but nothing seemed different. That's when I felt it again, and I couldn't help the grin and tears that filled my eyes. I smoothed my hand over my bump and looked down at it, a wet smile on my face.

"Hello, Autumn."

Luke

Three years later....

"Odie!"

I chased after the little toddler, her dark pigtails bobbing as she teetered over to Aidyn, who bent to scoop her up. 'Odie' was a term meaning 'other dad' that Aidyn and I had agreed upon as a way for our pup to address him to differentiate between her parents. Autumn was very much her Odie's girl despite being home with me the majority of the time. He nuzzled her, blowing raspberries against her cheeks, her giggle echoing through the room before being distracted by the multitude of colorful fish that swam around us in the underwater tunnel.

"Did you know there are no changing rooms in Alpha bathrooms?" I quipped, setting the diaper bag on top of the stroller.

"Why didn't you use the family bathroom?"

"Someone was already using it, and I wasn't about to drag her to the other side of the aquarium to find one."

"You should've grabbed me to take her to the Omega bathroom."

I shrugged, wheeling the stroller out of the tunnel. I had never noticed the lack of pup care facilities in Alpha-only spaces until after Autumn was born. It was as if society had dictated that Omegas were the only ones who could raise a pup, and therefore, there was no need for things like a changing table in an Alpha-only bathroom. Because of this, I upgraded all my properties to include an area for pup care, regardless of the designation of the parent.

I had been true to my word, ensuring Aidyn graduated with as little disruption as possible. However, Autumn had other plans, arriving earlier than her projected early due date for a male Omega offspring. I still have nightmares about the amount of blood that soaked our bed, both of us terrified that Aidyn was losing the baby. We rushed him to the hospital, where he was immediately processed for an emergency C-section. I wasn't even allowed in the room, making the wait for information the most agonizing two hours of my life. Aidyn's parents had flown in for his graduation and the birth of Autumn, staying in the guest bedroom of the new house we had purchased outside the city. They sat with me, often in silence, his mother trying her best to soothe my fears. In my weakest moment, I prayed to whatever powerful being was out there to save Aidyn. Maybe we could try for another child later, but please, *please* don't take my little fawn from me.

The sudden wave of guilt and sorrow at the thought was devastating. That I was willing to pick my mate over the life we had created together so fucking quickly. It was made worse by the fact that I couldn't feel him. He had passed out during the trip to the hospital, shutting off our bond, but I still slightly felt the one for our pup. She was in distress, and I could do nothing about it. Aidyn said he felt her constantly, almost as strongly as he felt me, but she was a flutter on my end, yet at that moment, she was my only connection to him. It was as though I had failed my mate and child.

It wasn't until a wave of happiness flooded through our bond that I realized he was awake. He was worried, fear tightening around me to the point that I felt violently sick, but he was okay. When I finally held our pup, I broke down, apologizing to her for my thoughts that she didn't understand. Despite his exhaustion, Aidyn's purr rumbled through the hospital room, soothing me and the crying pup in my arms. His parents took her from me, and Aidyn pulled me into the hospital bed with him, wincing as I jostled him slightly. I felt like a fucking child, curling around my mate, my head on his chest. Staff and my in-laws left us alone as Aidyn purred to soothe my anxiety, whispering that he was okay and so was our little girl. He had an incision on his lower abdomen that rested right above his pubic hair, which had been shaved for the surgery, but it was the third most precious thing to me. A reminder that I had almost lost him. Of the daughter, he gave me and the life we had created together.

He had graduated college from the maternity ward, something he hadn't wanted and gripped about, but was unavoidable. Autumn was far too small to go home right away, and she was forced to stay in the hospital for the first two months of her life before we could finally take her home. Several tests were conducted to ensure she was healthy, but a designation test had also been done. The nurse explained that they no longer had to wait until Autumn had reached puberty like Aidyn, and I had to find out her designation. The test confirmed that Autumn was an Omega, the first one born in my family in centuries. I didn't care what she was, just as long as she was healthy. However, I began to realize the true panic of raising an Omega in an Alpha-dominated society, and I was making myself sick with trying to figure out how best to protect her. Aidyn assured me, time and time again, that if she were anything like him, she wouldn't take shit from anyone.

After discussing it with his parents and seeking their permission, I legally changed my last name, choosing to take the surname of my Omega. My parents cut ties with me after I sent them pictures of our bonding marks and a sonogram of Autumn, and changing my name severed that connection completely. That suited me just fine, I didn't want them around either.

Aidyn put himself on the trial suppressants that had been discussed the second he was permitted by Ryan, and they seemed to be doing well for him. He still had heats, but they weren't nearly as long or as difficult—minor inconveniences that Aidyn said he was willing to live with while something was still being worked on. He got a job a year after Autumn was born and was doing really well in his field of Omega Specialty Care. He thrived at his job, quickly moving up the ranks to the point that his employer had put him in charge of his own facility three months ago. We had celebrated with a quiet night at home, and Aidyn assured me he preferred it that way. When we had purchased the new house, I immediately set up an office in one of the bedrooms so that I could look after our daughter while also tending to the investment properties I currently possessed. I took a more intimate approach, and each property was flourishing enough that I was looking to create a clinic for Aidyn for his own facility. Not that he knew that yet; I was still looking into locations.

We paused at the otters like we did every time we visited the aquarium. Aidyn lifted Autumn to the lookout glass, and she squealed excitedly at the pile of otters sleeping right at eye level. She mumbled in toddler speech, and I could only assume she was giving them each a name as he held her. I watched the color slowly drain from Aidyn's face as he held her up, pushing her against the wall to support her better. I abandoned the stroller by the opposite wall, away from everyone so it wasn't in the way, and moved behind them.

"You okay, little fawn?" I whispered against his ear.

Aidyn melted against me, using me to support the two of them, and he only nodded, his emotions damped. He had insisted on coming to the aquarium, even though his heat had ended two days ago, against my concerns that he wouldn't be up to the task. Now, I was beginning to think I was right. Once Autumn was done with the otters, we left, stopping at the sensory tanks to touch rays, sea cucumbers, and other ocean life. This was Autumn's favorite part after the otters, so we often spent more time here than at the other exhibits. By the time we were done, Autumn was asleep in her stroller, and Aidyn looked paler by the second.

"Let's get you home," I said, mentally making a note to call Ryan once I was alone.

Aidyn only shook his head, smiling at me as he moved through the gift shop. No matter how many times we came to the aquarium, at least several times a year, he always had to get something. I had difficulty telling him no, especially if it was just another otter plush he didn't already have that he wanted to add to the collection outside our nest. However, he went to the children's clothing, picking out a sundress with sharks on it and a two-piece outfit with my head tilted.

"I think you grabbed the wrong size, babe. Autumn is too big for that; that's for a newborn pup —"

My words halted in my throat, my gaze flickering between the outfit he held in his hand and the look on his face.

"You're terrible at this," he joked.

The actual fuck?! The aquarium had scent neutralizers, and everything smelled of fish, water, and seaweed that I hadn't even noticed. Autumn was still a child, so it was natural that her scent was still lightly floral, and I thought I had been scenting her. Aidyn had been talking about having a second child and I told him whenever he was ready. I hadn't anticipated him to mean this soon. Excitement built in my chest but was immediately swallowed by panic and fear.

"Hey, hey!" Aidyn immediately moved to my side, pulling me into the corner with dishes and Christmas ornaments that no one looked at this time of year. "I thought you would be happy."

"I am, I want to be. But Aidyn. I almost lost you last time!"

"I know," A low purr rumbled through him as he pushed calm through our bond. "I know. What happened with Autumn is rare, and there is no guarantee it'll happen again. I'm healthy, and I'll be okay. I called Ryan yesterday and booked an appointment, but he said there is no reason to believe we'll repeat what happened last time, and he's agreed to monitor my final months more carefully. Hell, I told him he could stay in our guest house the final months of my pregnancy."

"Did you really?" I asked, unable to stop my smile.

"I did. He said, and I quote, 'If that's what it takes to ease your big, scary, and protective Alpha's fears, I'll be the biggest pain in your side until this pup is born.'"

I couldn't help but laugh, pulling Aidyn closer to me. I pressed our foreheads together, his purr rumbling over me as I took in the news.

"A pup."

"A pup." Aidyn echoed.

The End.

Acknowledgements

I cannot believe this book is out in the wild. Imposter Syndrome is one of the worst things any creative person can experience, and it can dampen the creativity and motivation one has. I never expected anyone to be able to meet Luke and Aidyn, no matter how badly I wanted them to. It is important to surround yourself with those who will push, support, and guide you with their kindness, knowledge, and friendship. Without them, Broken Alpha would not be in your hands right now, and I wanted to take a moment to thank them so very much for helping my little characters see the world.

To the person I will only call 'H.' I know this started off as a joke late one night as my hyperfixation with the Omegaverse took off. I jokingly said you looked like an Omega and fabricated a story for your counterpart that grew and grew the more we joked about it. I didn't realize our jokes would turn into a novel that I obsessed over for two years. Your excitement helped push me to keep going, and your enthusiasm and responses kept me company when I thought I couldn't do this. Thank you for allowing me to tease you and torment you, and impregnate you hahaha.

ACKNOWLEDGEMENTS

To author Abby Hunter. You let me prattle on about my boys and helped me get my foot in the door with groups, authors, and events. Your guidance has been so valuable in this weird journey and I'm so grateful for you every day. Thank you for taking a newbie under your wing and teaching her the ropes.

To authors N. Slater and Avanne Michaels. You are my guardian angels, my therapists, my muses, and my rocks. Thank you for walking me through the complicated world of creativity, edits, publication, and beyond (you know what you did. For that I will be so fucking grateful). You always had a direct line available if I needed to soundboard, vent, or ask questions. You created a space where I never felt stupid or like a failure and helped me so much when my brain was against me. You guys are amazing. I love you so much.

To Nova and Spyder. While my pairing wasn't one you usually read, you supported me effortlessly and without a second thought. You hyped me up constantly, allowed me to ramble, and never made me feel like I was too much. You never judged and allowed me to explore safely. You're my sisters, and I am grateful to have you in my life every day.

To my Alpha/Beta Readers, this book would not be possible without any of you. You accepted a flawed manuscript to help it improve and grow into the best it could, knowing it would be rough since you're not in my head. Your assistance mattered, and I appreciate every one of you.

And to you, Current Reader. Thank you for picking up Broken Alpha. Publishing a book has been a dream of mine since I was a child. While the genres and subject matter I write about have changed since I was seven, the dream of my book being out there never did. I'm so happy you chose to pick up my book. I'm so happy I could share Luke and Aidyn with you, and I hope you enjoyed our company. From the bottom of my heart, thank you.

If you wish you stay up to date about future books, you can find me on instagram at https://www.instagram.com/everleighfoxauthor

Printed in Dunstable, United Kingdom